D1045116

Wheels in the Dust

**Center Point
Large Print**

**This Large Print Book carries the
Seal of Approval of N.A.V.H.**

Wheels in the Dust

WILLIAM COLT MACDONALD

CENTER POINT PUBLISHING
THORNDIKE, MAINE

This Center Point Large Print edition
is published in the year 2005 by arrangement with
Golden West Literary Agency.

The text of this Large Print edition is unabridged. In other
aspects, this book may vary from the original edition. Printed in
Thailand. Set in 16-point Times New Roman type.

ISBN 1-58547-571-8

Library of Congress Cataloging-in-Publication Data

MacDonald, William Colt, 1891-1968.
    Wheels in the dust / William Colt MacDonald.--Center Point large print ed.
        p. cm.
    ISBN 1-58547-571-8 (lib. bdg. : alk. paper)
        1. Large type books. I. Title.

PS3525.A2122W48 2005
813'.52--dc22

                                                                    2004020927

1
Mistaken Identity?

The two passengers who had alighted from the Limited to stretch their legs, when the train halted, were still discussing ways and means of settling the wilder sections of the West, when Murragh, valise in hand, pushed through the scattering of people on the station platform and started out in the direction of Millman City's main thoroughfare. The voice of one of the pair came to Murragh through a shower of cinders and swirling clouds of steam and black smoke from the panting locomotive, the tones carrying a distinct penetrating quality in the early morning air:

". . . this town right here, Millman City, is a case in point . . . so quiet and peaceful you'd scarcely know it . . . but ten, twelve months back it was a regular ripsnorter. It only takes one good gun fighter to put the quietus on a tough town, and Wyatt Holliday was that man. This is Wyatt Holliday's town, all right. He's got Millman City eating right out of his hand. . . ."

Wyatt Holliday's town! The words struck with considerable impact against Hoyt Murragh's hearing. A frown creased his face. Never figured to find him here, Murragh mused. I'll have to arrange to keep out of his way, or . . .

The thought went uncompleted as he strode along, a well-built rangy man with good, though somewhat bony, features and an expression that verged on the sar-

5

donic, an expression that was relieved not at all by the black triangle of hair that slashed down across his forehead and the humorous lines about his gray eyes. The cheekbones were a trifle higher than average, the skin stretched tautly to sinewy jaws, and the closely cropped black mustache beneath the aquiline nose seemed but a few shades darker than the heavily tanned skin.

A flat-topped black sombrero sat at a somewhat jaunty angle on Murragh's head. His single-breasted coat was of some deep gray material, as were the trousers tucked into knee-length, spurless boots. A light colored soft-collared shirt, black four-in-hand necktie and vest completed his visible attire.

The sun's rays were commencing to creep across building roofs when Murragh found the hotel and stage station on a corner of the town's main street. There were a few men collected about the hotel corner, though it was still a bit early for many people to be astir. Murragh entered the hotel and found the stage "office," presided over by a clerk at a chest-high desk, situated in one corner of the hotel lobby. Three men and a Mexican woman with parcels and grips were buying seats on the next stage out of town. Murragh set down his valise and awaited his turn.

Just ahead of him a bulky-shouldered man with brown hair, slightly gray at the temples, was securing transportation for Lanyard, the terminus of the stage line. The thought ran through Murragh's mind, "Looks like I'll have company all the way through." While he waited, he studied a faded, fly-specked placard tacked to the wall:

GORDON STAGE & FREIGHTING COMPANY

Regular Trips Made Between MILLMAN CITY
And LANYARD
With Speed And The Utmost Safety In Modern
Concord Coaches Designed With Latest Improvements
For Comfort and Swift Travel.
Southbound: Monday, Wednesday, Friday.
Northbound: Tuesday, Thursday, Saturday.

No Trips Made On Sunday.
Coaches Leave Promptly at 7 o'clock, A.M.

PRICES FOR PASSAGE

MILLMAN CITY	‒‒‒‒
FLAPJACK	$2.25
DUST CREEK	4.80
FISHHOOK	6.75
SULPHUR TANKS	9.15
COTTONWOOD SPRINGS	11.40
DRY BONE RANCH	13.05
PEYOTE FLAT	14.85
LANYARD	17.40

Stops made at intermediate points when requested.
Passengers are allowed 25 pounds of baggage, exclu-
sive of arms and blankets. Weight in excess of 25
pounds charged for at the rate of 10 cents the pound.

Dinner served Without Charge, at Sulphur Springs, to
all passengers riding the entire route.

The clerk's sharp "Where to, mister?" interrupted Murragh's perusal of the yellowed placard.

"Lanyard," Murragh gave his destination.

The clerk dropped Murragh's valise on the nearby weighing machine and studied the result a moment, then returned it. "No excess there. You travel light, friend. Seventeen-forty to Lanyard."

He scribbled some words on a slip of paper. Murragh gave him a twenty-dollar gold piece and received the scribbled slip and some change in silver, with the suggestion, "Leave that grip here until departure time if you like."

"Thanks, I'll keep it with me."

The hotel dining room appeared to be full of break-fasters, so Murragh again made his way to the street. A restaurant a few doors down the block furnished him with bacon, eggs, and coffee. By the time he returned to the hotel the stagecoach with its six horses had been brought up. There were more people abroad now. A small crowd had collected to see the stage off. Murragh glanced at his watch. Quarter to seven. He looked within the coach. The seats inside were already taken. That meant riding on top. Two men already sat up there, one of them the bulky-shouldered man with the grayish-brown hair whom he had seen securing transportation to Lanyard just ahead of him.

Fifteen minutes yet before starting time. Murragh decided it was best not to draw attention to himself by climbing to the top of the stage, until the last minute. He stood with his back against the front wall of the hotel, the valise at his feet. Pedestrians passed continually.

The shadows along the street were growing shorter by this time.

A man called suddenly from a knot of people near the coach: "Hi-yuh, Miss Lindy! Y'all ridin' shotgun, today?"

"Needs must when we're short-handed, Sam. You heading for Lanyard, this morning?"

"Only as far as Flapjack, Miss Lindy . . ."

Murragh saw she was young, and pretty as well, with a heavy knob of maize-colored hair beneath the rear of her brown sombrero, tanned features and dark eyes with long black lashes. He took in the whole picture as she emerged from the hotel—the easy stride in the divided riding skirt and boots, mannish flannel shirt, short leather jacket that surely must have been cut originally for some man; it wasn't customary woman's attire. The shotgun alone seemed to be missing, so far. Murragh's gray eyes held a wealth of amusement. What was the West coming to? A lady guard on a stagecoach!

So intent was he on the girl's appearance that he had failed at first to notice the man who accompanied her from the hotel. When he did, a terse bit of profanity escaped Murragh's lips and he flattened himself as inconspicuously as possible against the building wall. But the maneuver came too late. Already the girl's companion had spied him and was approaching with wide steps, a broad smile on his hawklike features, one greeting hand outstretched.

"Hoyt Murragh! You cantankerous old horned toad! What you doing in Millman City? If I'd had a hint you were coming—"

He broke off short at the lack of recognition in Murragh's cold eyes. Murragh had swiftly taken in the six-shooter at either hip, the marshal's badge on the unbuttoned vest, and was ignoring the outstretched hand.

"I reckon you've somebody else in mind, Mister Marshal," Murragh was saying in courteous, albeit frigidly formal, tones. "You've the wrong name this time."

The eyes of the two men locked for a brief instant; the smile faded from Wyatt Holliday's chiseled features. Abruptly, he nodded. "My mistake," Holliday acknowledged. "Thought at first you were an old friend. I see now you're not. A matter of mistaken identity, you might say." Murragh conceded that and relaxed a trifle. Holliday went on, "My apologies, sir. No harm done, I hope."

"I think not, Mister Marshal," Murragh replied quietly.

Holliday bowed and turned away, taking with him the attention of the crowd. At that moment one of the men on top of the coach suddenly descended and quickly lost himself among the pedestrians moving along the sidewalk. The crowd, its eyes on Holliday, failed to note the man's abrupt departure.

A few minutes later the driver of the stagecoach rounded the hotel corner, carrying his long whip and a sawed-off, double-barreled shotgun. These objects he handed up to the girl in the divided riding skirt, who was already seated on the left side of the driver's seat.

"All right," the driver called, "who's for Lanyard and way stations? Get a move on! We can't wait all day. It's nigh seven o'clock now." He stuck his head within the coach and collected tickets. Murragh stepped up and surrendered his slip of paper, and the driver said, "Let me chuck your valise in the forward boot, out of your way, mister. Climb atop pronto! We've got to get rolling!"

Murragh and another man hauled themselves to the top deck of the coach and seated themselves at the rear, facing backward, their legs dangling over the edge. A third man was sitting just behind the driver's seat where the girl—Miss Lindy, was it?—was waiting. Below, on the ground, the driver busied himself with baggage and mail sacks, packing them methodically in the rear boot. Coming near the front of the coach once more, he paused to consult a heavy silver watch. "Half minute to seven," he announced. He was a thick-middled man with long, tobacco-stained mustaches and a battered sombrero.

A not unusual argument had broken out within the coach. Some of the passengers wanted the windows closed, some open. ". . . but it will be too hot with 'em closed," a man objected. "That sun's risin' up fast and—"

"We cert'ly don't intend our dresses to get full of dust," a woman said plaintively.

The driver listened gravely to the arguments a moment. "You'd better arbitrate," he suggested finally.

"Arbitrate how?" one of the men demanded.

"Open 'em on one side, close 'em on t'other," the driver guffawed. Turning away, he hoisted himself lightly to the driver's seat. Here he lighted a stub of cigar and puffed out rank clouds of smoke.

11

Murragh heard the girl seated next to him say, "Let's get going, Zach. It's past seven."

Zach Decker gathered the reins in his hand, but beyond that made no move to start the horses. "I was sort of procrastinatin', waiting for 'Lonzo Vaiden, Miss Lindy. He had a ticket. He was here once. Don't know where-at he went."

"See if he's in the hotel bar," the girl said impatiently.

Decker sighed and climbed down from the coach. He reappeared within the minute and regained his seat. " 'Lonzo ain't been in there," he announced.

"Get out your watch, Zach," the girl said tersely, a small spot of angry color appearing in her cheeks. "We'll give him exactly one minute more."

The man seated beside Murragh on the rear of the coach top was leaning over, conversing with a friend on the ground beside the vehicle. Murragh took out a small notebook and stub of lead pencil, wrote a few swift words, then tore the sheet of note paper from the book. He glanced up. Several yards away, Marshal Wyatt Holliday lounged carelessly against the front wall of the hotel building. A quick, brief look flashed between the two men. Murragh allowed the slip of paper to drop from his fingers to the road below, where it landed in the dust near a rear wheel. Except Holliday, no one saw the maneuver.

From the front seat the girl spoke again, quick and impatient, "The minute's run out, Zach, and more, too. Alonzo Vaiden has made this trip often enough to know we start on time—generally. He's not big enough to delay a Gordon stage any longer. Get rolling."

12

Reluctantly Decker kicked off the brake and gathered the reins. "I sure hate to leave a passenger, but it's correct like you say, Miss Lindy. Here we go!" He spoke to the horses, his long whip sailed out and curled into a sudden snapping report. The coach commenced to move, lurching a trifle as it got rolling. Those on top grasped more tightly the metal railing that bordered the roof of the stage.

Once a turn had been made into a street leading to open country, Decker's whiplash cracked again and the six horses threw their galloping weight against the harness. Through the dust that rolled up at the rear of the coach, Murragh saw Wyatt Holliday move nonchalantly out to the road, stoop down and pluck a bit of paper from the earth. All other eyes were, apparently, on the departing stagecoach.

Murragh calmly considered the situation. "I sure hope nobody caught the name when Wyatt hailed me. If they did—well, the harm is done, if any, and I'll just have to make the best of it."

2

Linda Gordon

The stagecoach rolled on, rocking easily on its thorough braces, through an unvarying, seemingly endless sea of alkali, low hills, and sagebrush clumps. The sun was well up now. Heat waves quivered and danced along the horizon's dividing line of undulating plain and turquoise sky. Dust boiled up from beneath the rear of the swiftly moving stage. Murragh knotted a bandanna about his neck and drew it up across his mouth and nostrils. The man seated next to him sat huddled down, drawing on a dead cigar butt, while a layer of whitish-yellow dust settled thickly on his hatbrim and shoulders.

There was little cracking of the driver's whip now; that wasn't necessary. The horses knew their job and gave their best. Now and then the coach slowed a trifle while Zach Decker deftly guided his spans around a chuckhole that lay in their path. Then Zach would resume the conversation he'd been holding with the passenger seated behind the girl on the driver's seat. Murragh twisted about and surveyed the girl. Her slim form, now dust-covered, swayed easily with the motion of the coach. Far ahead, Murragh saw the road, curving like a narrow, ever diminishing yellow ribbon between wide oceans of sage and mesquite. The hills to the right were growing higher now, and beyond the hills, peaks of considerable height drew saw-toothed edges along the expanse of cloudless blue sky. Murragh asked a question of the man seated beside him.

The man straightened up, glanced around. "Part of the Sierra Crista Range," he replied, sucking on the dead cigar. "Something better than a hundred miles north of here, the Sierra Cristas split up into two ranges, the San Xavier Mountains and the Medicine Wind Mountains. Them's the Medicine Winds you see. If you're going through to Lanyard you'll pass through the Medicine Winds right after you leave Dry Bone Station. Must be you're a stranger hereabouts."

"Must be," Murragh admitted.

His companion nodded, tried to light his dead cigar, failed, and again slumped down, muttering, "Damn this wind!"

The coach reached Flapjack almost before Murragh realized it. Flapjack was typical of the small stations on stage roads of that day: there were a few adobe huts, a barn, a couple of corrals. Six fresh horses were already waiting when the stage rolled to a stop. Here the man seated up near the driver also descended, and with a "S'long, Zach, Miss Lindy," disappeared into one of the nearest huts.

Zach leaped down from the coach and helped with the harnessing of the fresh horses the attendant had had ready. A couple of passengers got out to get a drink and quickly returned. There was little time lost between drives. Within a few minutes the coach was again lurching into forward motion and once more the vast spread of semidesert growth and sand went flowing past. It wasn't yet a quarter to nine when Murragh studied his watch and a fifteen-mile drive lay behind; stages made swift time these days.

Seventeen miles farther on, the sweat- and dust-streaked horses rattled across a plank bridge over a dry wash lined with cottonwoods and came to a stop at Dust Creek Station. Dust Creek was but little larger than Flapjack had been, but it boasted a saloon of sorts, and Murragh's companion climbed down to grab a "snort," as he phrased it. A man passenger and a Mexican woman, burdened with parcels she'd refused to entrust to the coach boot, also left the stage at this point.

"Two seats inside," Decker bawled, and jerked out orders to a stable attendant to "bring up them fresh hawsses pronto."

Murragh dropped lightly to the earth beside the coach. His erstwhile companion of the top deck came scurrying from the saloon, wiping his mouth with the back of a hairy hand, and darted within the coach. Murragh followed and settled to a worn cushioned seat on the outside, facing forward, beside the man. "We'll eat just as much dust down here as up above," the fellow commented dryly, "only it won't be so hot to the taste."

The coach jerked into action once more. Wind, alkali dust, and heat flowed through the open windows. Murragh studied the other four passengers he and his companion of the upper deck had joined. Two of them, tobacco or liquor drummers, probably, had a suitcase between them and were playing a desultory game of seven-up such time as they weren't "joshing" two girls on the front seat, facing toward Murragh.

The girls—one was a thin blonde of what is known as the "peroxide" type; the other a flashy brunette—were bedecked in considerable finery for stage travel. Their skirts rustled when the lurching of the coach brought on sudden movement; artificial roses nodded on their wide picture hats. Their cheeks were carmine; their lips rouged; even through the dust, traces of rice powder were visible. The brunette fanned herself continually with a fine lace handkerchief.

Further conversation between the girls and the drummers brought out the fact they were all heading for Sulphur Tanks. "We heard it was a real lively town," the blonde said with a giggle.

"Business is good if that's what you mean," one of the drummers replied. "Chauncey, here, and me, we make the trip regular. Never yet failed to sell a bill of goods, did we, Chaunce?"

Chaunce studied his seven-up hand a moment, then winked. "We not only sell; we've been known to spend a right smart bit of change when business is done with."

"Now there's a man after my own heart," the brunette said in a husky contralto. "Good spenders seem harder to find every day."

The first drummer laid down a card on the suitcase. "You girls figuring to go to work in the mine at Sulphur Tanks?" he inquired with a leer. The blonde giggled some more; the brunette emitted a sort of hiccuppy laugh.

Chauncey grinned widely. "Bet you they do some tall digging, anyway." That brought on another fit of giggling.

The man at Murragh's left shoulder had fallen asleep. After a time the brunette, too, let her head drop back and snored with open-mouthed abandon. Chauncey said to the blonde, "Your friend must have had a tough night."

"Oh, *you!*" the blonde simpered. "Viola's just about wore out from this long ride. At home we had our own carriage and pair, and this rough travel just . . ." The words died away in a gust of sand and wind that came sweeping into the coach. The vehicle swayed to one side, righted itself, and sped on.

Murragh drew a long thin cigar from his vest pocket

and after asking the blonde's permission touched flame to the end of the weed. The girl seemed willing to give him more of her attention, but he shunted aside her questions and before long she too had fallen asleep, with her head on the other girl's shoulder. The drummers put aside their cards after a time and studied order books, talking "shop" meanwhile. The man at Murragh's shoulder awakened when one of the drummers passed cigars of the brand he was peddling. The other drummer produced a flask that went around, even Viola rousing long enough to accept a healthy swig before resuming her open-mouthed snoring. Both drummers dwelt at considerable length on the merits of the liquors and cigars they sold.

Fishhook Station was reached a short time later. Undoubtedly it took its name from the large quantity of *Ferocactus wislizenii,* or fishhook cactus, which dotted the slopes on all sides. Fishhook Station differed but little from the others—the usual stable and corrals and a handful of shabby huts looking as though they had been dropped there by a passing sandstorm and were just waiting for another storm to sweep them away again.

An hour and a half later the stage pulled into Sulphur Tanks, an ugly, sprawling town that owed its existence to the Silver Belle Mine located a mile back in the hills. Nearer at hand was the smelting plant whose stacks continually vomited clouds of smoke that enveloped Sulphur Tanks in a brassy, fuliginous haze. The buildings were of frame or adobe.

A wizened individual with whiskers, a torn-brim

sombrero, and patched overalls greeted Zach Decker when the coach rolled to a stop. "Got here at last, did ye?" a cackling voice emerged from the bewhiskered face. "Where ye been keepin' yourself, Zach? Y'realize it's nigh onto one o'clock?" He shook a long driver's whip in one gnarled hand. "Hi, Lindy! Zach musta druv his teams through a mess of flypaper, didn't he?" He laughed derisively. "It takes a man to tool a Conkerd these days."

"Hello there, Uncle Jimmy," the girl laughed from the top of the coach. "I thought we made right good time."

"Don't you pay Jimmy no attention, Miss Lindy," Zach Decker growled. "He's been cheatin' the undertaker so long, time don't mean nothing to him, even when it's stuck right under his nose."

"Is that so!" Uncle Jimmy commenced indignantly, but Decker was paying him no further attention as he climbed stiffly down from the driver's seat and commenced to unload baggage and a mail sack. He lifted his voice, "All out for Sulphur Tanks! Half-hour layover for chow!" But the passengers had already dismounted and were engaged in finding their grips or slapping dust from their clothing. A thick haze of alkali enveloped the vicinity of the stage. Decker seized his whip and turned back to Uncle Jimmy: "There she is, Methuselah. If you can snake that coach along the last half of the trip as fast as I druv the first half, I'll eat my Stet hat—and your'n is the shortest half, too."

"Ye'd best prepare to spill some catsup on that bonnet so she'll taste like somethin' then," Uncle Jimmy cackled. "Once I get my mitts on them ribbons, them hawsses will sure think they've been took with jackrabbit tendencies. If I don't tool that stage so fast the hawsses will be runnin' in its own wheel ruts, I'll help you eat that Stet hat."

"By Gawd! If you ain't the boastin'est man I ever see," Decker growled, at loss for a more stinging retort. He stalked off, leaving the responsibilities of the remainder of the trip to his relief driver. For Zach Decker the workday was concluded.

Contrary to expectations and in contrast to the rest of Sulphur Tanks, Murragh found the dining room of the stage station clean and neat, with whitewashed 'dobe walls and an oak dining table covered with spotless oil-cloth. Instead of the customary chili beans, mutton, and watery coffee, there were beefsteak, boiled potatoes, and pie, not to mention the coffee, which was excellent. Miss Linda and Zach Decker were the only other two at the table served by a neat Mexican girl. Murragh ate in silence, while the other two talked stage business. He judged the passengers who had accompanied him thus far had found another place to eat; perhaps they'd reached their destinations. Regarding Viola and the giggling blonde, he knew this to be the case.

Abruptly, from outside, came Uncle Jimmy's urgent voice, "Time's aburnin', Lindy! We ain't got all day to get rollin'."

"Drat him anyway," the girl said, then looked directly at Murragh: "Take your time, mister. We're not in that much of a rush."

"I'm just about finished, anyway," Murragh replied.

He pushed back his chair and started to roll a brown-paper cigarette. The girl nodded and turned back to Decker. "I'll see you again, Zach. If the new guard doesn't pan out, let me know. But I think anybody Holliday gets will be all right."

"I reckon so, Miss Lindy." Zach loosened his belt and called to the Mexican girl for a second helping. Miss Linda departed for the outside.

By the time Murragh emerged from the dining room, Uncle Jimmy Cochrane was sitting impatiently on the driver's seat of the coach. On the ground, below, Miss Linda stood talking to him. Murragh got into the coach and took the rear seat, facing forward. The other seat was also unoccupied, except for the sawed-off double-barreled shotgun that lay on the cushion. Murragh heard the girl say, "Shove along, Uncle Jimmy," just before she stepped into the coach and sat down opposite him, slamming the coach door behind her. She shoved the shotgun to one side and relaxed on the cushions. The stage wheels commenced to turn and the next "drive" was under way.

Murragh said quietly, "Looks as though I'm your sole passenger from here on."

"Unless we pick up someone at Cottonwood Springs, Dry Bone, or Peyote—which isn't likely." The girl smothered a yawn and turned a tired gaze toward the swiftly retreating vista of country that flowed unevenly past the rocking coach. Every line of her slim form spoke of intense weariness. Murragh was wondering if she was disinclined toward conversation, when she suddenly turned her gaze on him.

"It's over fifty miles yet to Lanyard. We might as well get acquainted. I'm Linda Gordon."

Murragh bowed. "Related to the Gordon Stage Company?"

"Gordon Stage & Freighting Company," the girl corrected with a slight smile. "I am the company—my father and I, that is."

"And this riding shotgun," Murragh commented, to cover his surprise, "is some sort of hobby, I presume."

"Not on your life," the girl laughed, her even teeth showing whitely against her tanned face. "It's a job I wouldn't want as a regular thing. I'm short-handed for a day or so."

"And I'm to have the pleasure of your company for the remainder of the trip? I always thought the shotgun rider rode atop with the driver."

"I ride the cushions when there's a seat, especially with Uncle Jimmy driving. He's thoroughly reliable, best driver we have. Anyway, there's nothing to guard today—no strongbox or pay roll. Besides, I never did agree with the idea that the guard should ride up above. Why should he place himself in full view of any road agent who gets a sudden desire to shoot somebody? A guard inside the coach has an even break against any holdup man, don't you think?"

"Perhaps you're right." Murragh found himself wanting to agree with this girl's opinions. "Do all your guards ride inside when there's room?"

Linda Gordon shook her head. "I haven't insisted on it. If a man's vanity tells him to sit up where everybody can see him, why—" A smile finished the sentence. "To me it's just plain common sense for a shotgun rider to stay out of sight until he's needed."

"Have you had much trouble with holdup men?"

The girl's dark eyes clouded momentarily. "More than I like to think of. Never when *I've* been riding shotgun, though." She added with sudden honesty, "Probably that's because it happens I've never had anything to guard when I'm riding."

"Or perhaps your bandits are too chivalrous to hold up a woman."

"Chivalrous? Fiddlesticks! I've just been lucky."

They fell silent a moment. The coach was ascending a grade now. Glancing from the window, Murragh saw that the mountains had come closer. At spots, on the lower slopes, were heavy stands of oak, cedar, and piñon, with now and then a clump of prickly pear. Huge granite boulders were to be seen from time to time. The crest of the grade was negotiated, and the coach dipped down.

Linda Gordon said suddenly, "You're Hoyt Murragh." It was a statement of fact, not a question.

Murragh considered the girl a moment. "Am I?"

"I heard Wyatt Holliday speak your name."

"He could have made a mistake. A lot of other people heard him admit he was mistaken."

"Naturally. A lawman with the reputation Mr. Holliday has earned draws attention to anyone he speaks to—especially a Hoyt Murragh who, unless rumor is wrong, carries a distinction on a par, at least, with Mr. Holliday's. Let's see . . . if I remember correctly it was down around San Antonio . . . something to do with the

Texas Rangers . . . about three years back . . ." The girl cocked an inquisitive eye at Murragh.

The man smiled. "I was always taught, when a youngster," he said easily, "never to put any faith in rumors."

Linda Gordon's cool laughter sounded skeptical. "At any rate, you can't deny you're a Texan. All you Texans sound alike when you talk."

"There's a heap of people come from Texas. *Quién sabe?* I might even be related to this Murragh you mentioned. I'll even admit being in the Texas Rangers at one time."

"But not to being *the* Hoyt Murragh?"

Murragh shrugged careless shoulders. "Even that, if you insist."

"I don't insist. So far as I'm concerned your business in Lanyard is nothing to me—so far as I know. I'll forget the name, as well, if you'll feel more comfortable. Only, I'll keep remembering that Wyatt Holliday doesn't make mistakes in his friends."

Murragh started to reply, changed his mind, drew out his papers and sack of tobacco and with the girl's permission rolled and lighted a cigarette. No further talk passed between them for some time.

Cottonwood Springs was reached and a quick change of horses effected to the accompaniment of considerable profanity on Uncle Jimmy's part directed at a stable attendant who was as slow as a "gall-sored, spavined, broken-down tortoise." The stableman grinned tolerantly at the abuse, and the coach started off again.

24

The sun had swung to the west by this time, and the mountains were closing in on either side. Much of the time the coach was clothed in shadow, either from steep bluffs bordering the road or thick growths of pine and juniper. Once the coach dipped into a narrow canyon and the hoofbeats of the horses resounded from the canyon walls. Coming out, there was a stretch of sand that made hard going, but with Uncle Jimmy's profanity and skillful use of the reins the horses finally made it. When the coach had climbed to good going again, Uncle Jimmy's cantankerous tones floated down to the occupants of the coach: "A few tons of crushed granite wouldn't harm that stretch none, Lindy." The remark was punctuated with the sharp crack of Uncle Jimmy's whip.

The girl laughed softly, "He makes that same remark every time he drives over that sandy stretch. I've never known it to fail."

"He's right, though, isn't he?"

"Of course he is. We've hauled ton after ton after ton of rock to that point, but the sand always seems to work to the surface within a short time. That's just one of the problems of operating a stage line."

It wasn't until they reached Dry Bone Ranch Station that Uncle Jimmy had real cause to become angry.

3

Coyotero Pass

If Murragh had expected to find ranch buildings at Dry Bone Ranch Station, he was mistaken. Here there was nothing except an adobe building for the use of the station agent, a large hay barn, and a couple of pole corrals. A sort of lean-to stood at one side of the hay barn and stable. If Uncle Jimmy Cochrane had expected to find six fresh horses awaiting his arrival, as was customary and as he had every right to expect, he was sadly disappointed, and his disappointment voiced itself in a lurid flow of purple language.

There wasn't anyone in sight when he pulled to a halt. A clump of tall cottonwood trees made rustling sounds in the breeze. Except for the indignant expletives spat by Uncle Jimmy, no other sound was to be heard. His booted feet struck the earth with a solid, enraged thump. An instant later his face appeared in a window opening on one side, every whisker bristling and—almost—emitting sparks. "Now what in the tarnation hell do ye think of this, Lindy? D'ye reckon Zwing has took to hittin' the jug again?"

Linda sighed. "He promised me he wouldn't. You'd better go see what's what."

From where they sat, Linda and Murragh couldn't see the door of the building without stretching their necks through the window. They settled back on the cushions; then, hearing a door slammed, looked out again. An unshaven man in dirty overalls and a collarless shirt had appeared around one corner of the house. "Where the tarnation hell is Zwing?" Uncle Jimmy demanded.

The two men held a conversation for a few minutes. Uncle Jimmy returned to the coach. "Of all things," he sputtered, "to happen at a time like this. Jist when it looked like I'd set me a new record for drivin' time, too—"

"What is wrong?" Linda demanded sharply. "Is Zwing—?"

"Nope. 'Tain't Zwing. That feller there"—jerking one calloused thumb over his shoulder—"is Zwing's wife's brother from Sulphur Tanks. Zwing has been gone since this mawnin' early. This feller brung the word—"

"Word of what?" Linda interrupted. "Gracious sakes! What are you trying to say?"

"Now hold your hawsses, I'm gettin' to it. A body'd think it was your troubles, 'stead of mine. Zwing's mother was took bad sick—ain't expected to live. This feller, here"—again the thumb jerked over shoulder—"brung the news and took over the station till Zwing comes back. Zwing hitched up that light stage wagon and druv to Sulphur Tanks with his wife. Whut gripes my innards, Zwing took my best pair of leaders, leavin' me that span of half-broke hammerheads to drive. Says the feller here, he'd have had the horses ready, only he didn't know whut time we was due to arrive."

"What are you crabbing about?" Linda snapped. "Are the hammerheads beyond your handling?"

A grieved expression crept over the whiskered face. "Now, Lindy, ye know better than to make a remark like that. Have y'ever knowed any hawss I couldn't handle?"

Linda started to rise. "I'd better go see what's what."

"Don't ye think of it, Lindy. Thet man's filthy trash and not fitten for your association. Let me handle this."

"Well, handle it, then. Go tell him to bring out those horses."

"Already told him."

"You'd better go see what's keeping him, then."

Lindy leaned back in her seat, while Uncle Jimmy disappeared with short, angry steps. Eventually the pair in the coach heard Uncle Jimmy's voice again, and the sounds of moving horses. Harness rattled. The minutes passed. Then a violent explosion from Uncle Jimmy: "Great jumpin' Jehoshaphat! Put *them* in the swings. You put that pair of jugheads in the leaders and there'll be hell to pay and no pitch hot! Once we start rollin' down Coyotero, I don't aim to have my stage tumblin' stern over appetite ahead of my animals—no, dammity hell, *that* span is the wheelers! Ain't you never buckled up stage hawsses before?"

Harness slapped the earth, chains and buckles rattled, poles thumped the dust. A horse snorted nervously, and there came quick scrabbling hoof thuds. Through it all, Uncle Jimmy's vitriolic remarks rasped out a savage symphony against the other man's sullen, resentful undertones. Listening, Linda Gordon smiled amusedly at Murragh. The man said, "Could I get out and lend a hand, do you suppose?"

Linda's eyes widened. "My grief, no! It would be the final humiliation if a passenger had to help Uncle

Jimmy harness up. That *would* bring on an explosion. Just leave him be. These things happen right along, you know. I've found it best always to let my drivers handle their own problems—as is their right, of course."

The profanity outside the coach died away after a time. Murragh judged the fresh horses were finally harnessed, though a continual grumbling still emanated from Uncle Jimmy, to which the other man, apparently, had no answer. The coach body dipped, momentarily, to the right side as Uncle Jimmy climbed to his seat. An instant later he swore and got down again. Linda inclined her head toward the window. "Gracious me! *Now* what's wrong?"

"Left my billy-be-damned whip back in that 'ere stable," Uncle Jimmy growled defensively. "And ye needn't to be so sharp, nuther, Lindy. Ain't a body been tried enough, 'thout you . . ." The words died away, and Uncle Jimmy raised his voice again, as though to vindicate his own forgetfulness, venting further wrath on the substitute stable attendant, "And mind what I tell ye, feller, you see that them hawsses I brung in is rubbed down good and blankets thrun on 'em, pronto," he ordered. The tired horses of their own accord had already headed for the stable. "And go easy on the water, don't let 'em drink much ontil they've cooled a mite . . ."

His voice died away with the retreating footsteps of the two. Murragh and the girl had leaned back on their cushions again. Murragh said, "Why do they call this Dry Bone Ranch Station? I expected to find a ranch here."

Linda shook her head. "Never was a ranch here. Years ago an easterner came out and allowed how he was going to run cattle here, but nothing came of it after he'd put up a 'dobe shack. There's little grass, and no water at all for miles—not enough for a herd, that is. It got to be a joke, and people commenced calling it Dry-as-a-Bone Ranch. The name stuck."

"I see. You know, in spite of Uncle Jimmy's crabbing about loss of time, I think we've traveled right swift. Of course, your line hasn't any real steep grades to speak of. I remember one trip I took through the San Diego Mountains, the road ran up and down along the edge of a steep cliff. It was right scary at times."

Linda Gordon smiled. "We'll give you a taste of that farther on, when we go through Coyotero Pass—"

She paused. Footsteps were heard outside the coach, then the body of the vehicle shifted momentarily under the ascending driver's weight. Linda called, "Get your whip all right, Uncle Jimmy?"

A sound somewhere between a grunt and a growled profanity came back. The brake was released, the whip cracked and the coach rolled forward. Linda chuckled, "Uncle Jimmy's still feeling right wrathful, I reckon."

"Sounded that way," Murragh agreed.

Wind and dust were again flowing through the windows. The thorough braces creaked under the strain of the moving coach. A glance at his watch told Murragh it was nearing four-thirty. High rock bluffs crowded in at either side, and only occasionally did a patch of sunlight enter the stage. Where there weren't any bluffs, clumps of oak or cottonwood, close to the road, were passed. Linda glanced through the windows. "Coyotero Pass isn't much farther ahead. Once we've made that, it's not long to Peyote Flat. Then, seventeen miles more and we're home—downgrade every inch of the way."

They rode in silence for a time. For the past five minutes the coach had been rapidly losing speed. Murragh observed, "This stretch must be a heap steeper than it appears."

"Steep, all right," Linda agreed, "but there's no need to slow down to this extent." Five more minutes drifted away. Impatient lights showed in Linda's eyes; she called suddenly, "Uncle Jimmy! Are you taking a nap, up there?"

That got results!

Crack! Crack! Crack! The whiplash, in the driver's hand, produced sounds closely akin to the vicious reports of a high-powered rifle. And *Crack! Crack! Crack!* again. The horses were being lashed in real earnest now. The coach lifted, hurtled through the air, with an abrupt violence that threw Linda to the opposite seat. The shotgun clattered to the floor of the bouncing stage. Murragh steadied the girl, while she settled, breathless, beside him. She drew a long breath, gazed astounded at the man, and laughed suddenly. "My golly! I certainly made Uncle Jimmy mad when I criticized his driving that way."

Rocks, trees, brush rushed past in an unbroken panorama; wind and sand whipped against their faces. The coach lunged from side to side, struck an imbedded rock in the road, pitched into the air, righted itself, and resumed its mad rush through space.

"This," Linda jerked out, holding tightly to the side of the lurching coach, "should teach me to keep my mouth shut from now on." "Uncle Jimm-ee-ee!" she raised her voice in an urgent plea. "It's—it's all right with—me—if you—want to take—a nap."

The words were interrupted by a sudden swerving of the coach across a stretch of loose gravel, hurling the girl against the window frame. Murragh managed to say, "Does Uncle Jimmy often act this way?"

"Nev—never knew it to—hap—happen before," the girl gasped. A sudden jolt threw her across Murragh's lap. Pushing her back to the seat, Murragh flung off his sombrero and thrust his head through the right door window, leaning so far beyond the frame that Linda feared he'd fall out. Next she heard something that sounded like, "Great God on the Mountains!" and the girl saw that Murragh was actually climbing through, forcing his shoulders diagonally past the opening.

It proved a tight squeeze, but eventually his hips were drawn clear and his body twisted that he might secure a foothold on the window ledge. The next instant both booted feet were withdrawn from view and Linda realized the man had hoisted himself to the top of the madly careening stagecoach.

Until he had actually reached the top of the vehicle and crouched there, balanced on one knee, hand tightly gripping the metal railing, Murragh couldn't really believe the driver had definitely disappeared. But of Uncle Jimmy Cochrane there wasn't a trace to be seen. The six horses, unguided, driverless, apparently demon-inspired, were whipping the coach along at an insane, terrific pace that threatened but one inevitable, devastating conclusion. Murragh risked a quick look to the rear, half expecting to see Uncle Jimmy's prone form stretched somewhere along the road, but boiling clouds of yellow dust obscured his vision.

He glanced ahead, making precarious progress toward the driver's seat, meanwhile, seeing beyond the tossing manes and heaving brown backs, wet with sweat, the road where it ran between two precipitous, granite bluffs. That narrow passageway seemed to be rushing toward him at a fearful rate. By this time Murragh was in the driver's seat. Momentarily, he considered the brake and disregarded the thought immediately. A sudden braking might pile up the coach and horses against those granite walls, from the wreckage of which there'd be small chance of emerging alive. The reins were not immediately visible; a slight braking would have no effect at all on the maddened animals before Coyotero Pass could be reached.

Beyond the pass, the man could see only blue sky, indicating an abrupt curve, or a sudden drop—perhaps both. His eyes, still searching for the reins, saw them whipping in tangled confusion across the horses' backs below; one rein was already dragging along the swiftly moving yellowish-gray ribbon that flowed ceaselessly beneath the galloping hoofs of the six frenzied animals.

Almost before he realized what he was doing, Murragh had lowered himself from the footboard to the tongue of the coach. The footing was dangerously uncertain. He felt himself flung against one heaving back; somehow he maintained a sort of balance and moved farther along where the tossing manes and wild eyes were very close. The fingers of one hand closed on a leather collar, he swung down and secured a grip on the dangling rein. An instant later he had gathered two more reins. Sparks darted from the flying hoofs; particles of gravel stung his cheeks; dust blinded his eyes. Somehow he managed to retrieve all of the reins and found himself scrambling back to the driver's seat, catching a quick glimpse of the girl now on top, just as the coach flashed into the entrance of Coyotero Pass.

Choked, half blinded with dust, he endeavored to exert some guidance, check, to the frantic animals, but the unaccustomed tangle of reins was too much for instant comprehension. He swore bitterly, "Damn' if I ever saw such a mess of ribbons!" Frustration, fear, rage brought to his arms a hitherto unrealized strength as he fought to, at the least, hold the coach upright in its headlong rush through the pass. One foot tentatively felt for the brake, but until the reins were straightened out, he'd have to move carefully. He heard Linda voicing some sort of advice, but the words were unintelligible in the rush of wind and sound.

Granite walls flashed past in a blurred pattern of dust and pounding hoofs and wicked body jolts as the coach lurched crazily about, at times seeming to leave the earth altogether to fly drunkenly through space, only to alight again with a jarring thud and a wild scattering of gravel and loose rock. The horses had slacked their terrific pace not at all, the insane behavior of the "half-broke" pair having infected the remaining four with a sort of contagious frenzy. Murragh was finding it a man-sized job just to stay aboard, let alone manipulate the reins and brake.

Abruptly the steep bluffs on either side dropped away and a curve showed ahead, a long snaky curve that wound sharply down along one shoulder of a mountainside. To Murragh's right rose a sheer wall of granite; to the left was open space; though far below, the man had a brief flashing glimpse of pine treetops and a vast piñon forest.

The first sharp turn in the road rushed up with express-train velocity. Murragh braced his body as the leaders whipped frenziedly around the bend. The coach skidded crazily as he touched the brake, one rear wheel spinning madly in space as it slipped over the edge of the roadway. Then, miraculously, all four wheels were once more back on the road—though not simultaneously—and the horses had again straightened out. Whether this marvel was due to some remaining innate fragment of horse sense, or to his driving, which couldn't really be termed driving, Murragh wasn't certain; nor had he the inclination, right then, to give the problem full consideration. Behind him there was the scrape of a booted foot and Linda's voice: "What became of Uncle Jimmy—?" The tones changed, sharp and urgent: "Don't bunch those reins! You can't drive that way!"

Murragh snapped back, "What do you think I'm doing now?"

Her reply reached him but faintly, "I'm sorry. But

you've got to spread them out—each rein between two fingers." Her voice was swept away on the wind. Another curve lay ahead. Murragh swore under his breath. He'd *never* make this one! Linda spoke again, "Easy on that brake! You'll skid us over the edge of the—"

The wheels screeched wildly. The coach swerved violently to the outer rim of the road, colliding against a big rock which, knocked from its ancient bed, went crashing down the precipice until it eventually came to rest amid a splintered, thrashing tumult of broken tree limbs. The stagecoach rocked insanely; again settled down as the horses straightened out. That second curve had been negotiated! Murragh felt cold perspiration trickling down into his eyes.

"Give me those reins! Now get over to that other seat!"

Even in the stress of that mad, reeling pitching ride, Murragh found time to marvel at his confidence in Linda Gordon. With no word of protest, he handed back the reins, slid to the adjoining seat, and steadied the girl while she slipped down on the driver's cushion, where she deftly sorted and distributed the reins between her fingers.

The following curve was negotiated with a wider margin of safety; the horses commenced to slacken speed slightly. Occasionally, all four coach wheels touched the road at the same time. There was still a job ahead, but Linda Gordon was equal to it. No further word passed between the two. Murragh was admiring now the expert handling of reins, the sure, delicate touch on the brake when needed. The coach rolled down and down the mountain shoulder, entered a deep canyon with high granite walls, clattered over chunks of loose rock, and bumped finally to a halt, with a steep upgrade just ahead. For a second neither the man nor the girl spoke. Murragh drew a long breath and relaxed. Linda closed her eyes and leaned back. Suddenly she opened them and spoke wrathfully to the horses: "You fools, oh, you fools!"

Instantly, with that out of her system, the girl's mood changed, sobered. "What ever became of Uncle Jimmy? I don't understand—"

"When I reached the top of the coach"—Murragh shook his head—"all I saw of him was his whip." He turned around. "Even that seems to be gone now."

"I saw it fly off that time we nearly went over the edge. I was right on your heels, you know. Didn't dare speak to you any sooner. You had your hands full, and I was only hanging on by the skin of my teeth." Her lips curved faintly. "I'll bet that's the first time you ever handled six horses."

"And the last, I hope. Never drove more than two before."

The girl said seriously, "You did a darn' good job, Mr. Murragh. It isn't everybody can handle six horses."

"I'm not yet convinced I did. You showed me how, though."

"I've been driving three spans, off and on, for quite a few years."

Murragh spoke impulsively, "A woman driver?"

Linda smiled scornfully. "Why not a woman driver?

37

Ever hear of Charlie Pankhurst? She masqueraded as a man and drove stage nearly all her life. They didn't discover she was a woman until she died." The girl frowned suddenly. "You know, I still can't understand how you got down among those horses and returned alive. . . ."

They climbed down from the coach. Linda said something about her knees still being shaky. They examined the droop-headed horses, exhausted and without movement except for an occasional quivering muscle. Steam rose from their sweat-and-foam-drenched hides. The coach next underwent an inspection. All parts had held together, apparently. Linda continued to speak of Uncle Jimmy. "I can't understand it," she insisted. "What could have happened to him?"

"Could he have fallen asleep and dropped over the side?"

"Not Uncle Jimmy. I'm wondering if he had a heart attack or something."

"Is he subject to such attacks?"

Linda shook her head. "Doc Bradley predicted he'd live to a hundred. . . . I don't like it, Mr. Murragh."

"No more do I," Murragh returned. "What's the answer, do we turn and go back?" He added, "My hat must have blown off somewhere along the road. I didn't miss it until now."

"It's inside the coach. Don't you remember throwing it off, just before you climbed out? Well, you did." Her frown deepened. "Turn back?" She considered the narrow passage where the coach had stopped, and the high steep walls. "It would be a job turning this coach here. We'd have to unharness and—No, we won't turn back."

"I could ride one of the horses back," Murragh proposed.

Linda considered that too, then vetoed the idea. "Suppose you found Uncle Jimmy injured, broken leg, or something of the sort. How could you bring him in?" Murragh had no answer for that one. The girl continued, "We'd best continue on to Peyote Flat. I can send the man there to backtrack our trail. Peyote's only about four miles farther on."

They climbed back to the driver's seat. The sun was dropping fast now, only the top of one canyon wall being bathed in light. Linda took off the brake and manipulated the reins. However, the weary horses showed little desire to get moving again. "If I only had a whip . . ." Linda speculated grimly. "You, Buck, quit that stalling! Blue Eye, lay into it. Come on, boys—up, up!"

The reluctant animals finally made the grade, and the coach started the long down drive, the horses moving sedately enough to suit anyone now. Far ahead there was still sunlight, and Murragh saw the country had changed rapidly, taking on a semidesert appearance. It wasn't yet six o'clock when they rolled into Peyote Flat Station.

4
Murder!

A stableman and assistant awaited the coach at Peyote, with fresh horses. There wasn't any town there; just the usual stables, corrals, and a handful of adobe buildings. As the stage rolled to a stop, a tall man with a long nose spoke, "Cripes, Miss Linda, you driving? Where's Uncle Jimmy?"

"That's what we're wondering, Bert. Get those horses changed quick as you can." The other man had already started unharnessing. Bert Echardt jumped to help, while Linda explained briefly what had happened. Neither the girl nor Murragh had descended from the coach.

Echardt uncoupled a trace, frowning. "Darned if I can understand it."

"No more do I." Linda spoke soberly. "If it hadn't been for Mr.—er—for our passenger's quick thinking, this coach would never have reached here."

Echardt and the other man glanced with a certain respect toward Murragh, one of them commenting, "The time schedule wa'n't changed much, anyway. First, delay and then the horses running like that—" He broke off. "I wonder who that strange jasper was at Dry Bone? I never knew Zwing's wife had ary brother . . . knew her family from quite a spell back, too." He slapped the leaders on the flanks, and they moved leisurely toward the stables.

Linda continued, "What you'll have to do, Bert, is hitch up that stage wagon, fast as you can, and go look for Uncle Jimmy. I'm afraid you'll find him with broken bones or something."

"I dunno," Bert surmised. "He's a pretty tough old root—"

"Tough old roots don't fall off a driver's seat unless something is radically wrong," Linda interrupted. "Particularly if they're strong enough to hand out the horse-lashing Uncle Jimmy did, just before he spilled off." She listened a moment to the other man, then shook her head. "No, he hadn't been drinking. . . . Bert, here's another thing: if anything seriously wrong has happened to Jimmy, and I'm afraid it has, you'll have to take over his drive to Sulphur Tanks tomorrow morning. Is all this going to be too much of a chore for you—going after Uncle Jimmy, and all?"

"I can make out, Miss Linda. You say Jimmy fell off just t'other side of Coyotero, eh? I'll get going just the minute you leave."

The men had worked fast while they talked; the fresh spans were ready to go. Linda tightened her grip on the reins, calling back over her shoulder as the coach lurched into motion, "And please bring me word as soon as possible, Bert. I'll be waiting up—anxious."

The stage swept on its way, moving through a broad expanse of greasewood, yucca, creosote bush, and opuntia. Occasionally a giant cactus raised rigid arms to the sky as though in mute appeal to Deity to delay the swift lowering of the sun which, by now, had touched

41

the distant westward peaks of the lofty San Xavier Mountains.

Murragh and the girl had been riding in silence for some time when Murragh asked, "That Bert you spoke to back there—"

"Relief driver," the girl forestalled the question. "We have one at either end of the line. Why, were you thinking of asking for the job?" she finished, smiling.

"God forbid," Murragh said fervently. "No, it's just that I had a strong hunch to go back with him to look for Uncle Jimmy. Only that I want to get to Lanyard without delay—"

"You'll get there." The girl urged the horses to better effort. "Step into it, boys! You, Jack, quit your fooling!" The reins snapped. "Darn it! Why didn't I borrow Bert's whip?"

The coach rolled smoothly along, all downgrade going now. It grew darker. Far, far ahead, a jewel-like twinkling of lights appeared. "There's Lanyard," the girl observed.

Lights shone along Lanyard's main street when the coach halted an hour later before the Lanyard Hotel. Stablemen were ready to take horses and vehicle around to the stables. A few loiterers lounged in front of the hotel building. There were immediate questions concerning the whereabouts of Uncle Jimmy Cochrane, but the girl put off the questioners for the moment. She and Murragh descended from the coach, and the man secured his valise from the boot. He hesitated a moment. "Thanks for the ride," he said dryly.

The girl gave him a worried smile. "Glad to have you.

That burst of speed through Coyotero is something we save for customers we particularly like. . . . Will I see you again?"

Murragh nodded. "I want to look up—a man, then get a bite of supper. I'll be back later to find out about Uncle Jimmy."

"I'm as anxious about him as you are. Well, *hasta la vista.*"

"Adios, señorita."

Murragh doffed his hat and made his way into the hotel lobby. A clerk greeted him at the desk and spun the register around. "A room, mister?"

"Probably. First, have you a man named Kennard—Russ Kennard—staying here?"

The clerk hesitated. "We-ell, yes and no. You see . . ."

Murragh caught the idea. "You mean he's registered here, but you don't see much of him."

"That's about the size of it."

Murragh scowled and said, half to himself, "I was afraid of something like this."

"If you're looking for Mr. Kennard, I don't think you'll have any trouble. I see him on the street occasionally."

"I'll find him." Murragh picked up the pen, dipped it into the ink bottle, then paused, frowning. After a moment he wrote in a bold hand, Hoyt Murragh, San Antonio, Texas. The cleric whirled back the book, glanced at the signature, then consulted a rack of keys at his back. "Number 9's a good room," he observed, and tossed a key on the desk. "Upstairs, turn to your right."

Murragh picked up the key. "What's the law on wearing a gun in Lanyard?" he asked.

"There's an ordinance against it. However, nobody pays it any mind. The law just acts when somebody gets to throwing lead around promiscuous."

"Not much crime, here, I take it."

"Lanyard's law officers don't stand for any fooling."

Murragh picked up his valise and ascended the stairs. In the dimly lit hall above he located Number 9, inserted the key and entered, closing the door behind him. Through a window opposite, a certain amount of light was reflected from Main Street, below. Murragh found an oil lamp, scratched a match, and touched flame to the wick. He replaced the chimney and glanced about the sparsely furnished room. A double bed, two straight-backed chairs, a dresser holding the lamp, a basin, and a pitcher of water. One of a row of hooks on the front wall held a towel; otherwise the walls were bare as was the plank floor.

Murragh removed his shirt and shaved, after opening the valise, the razor giving off ringing sounds as it scraped through the day's accumulation of beard, sand, and alkali dust. He donned a clean shirt of wool and replaced the four-in-hand necktie with a knotted blue bandanna. The dark trousers were changed for a pair of worn brown corduroys, tucked into boot tops. Next he took from the open valise on the bed a pair of holstered .44 six-shooters and cartridge belts. One belt and gun he strapped about his hips; the other was returned to the bag. He slapped at his coat with his flat-topped black sombrero, raising considerable dust, then put on the coat, adjusted the crease in the hat, and donned that also, before blowing out the flame in the oil lamp.

When he descended to the lower floor the hotel dining room was closed. The clerk told him, "Joe Low across the street can fix you with some supper." Murragh left the hotel and crossed the unpaved thoroughfare, walking in the direction of a lighted window with the words JOE LOW painted on its surface. The restaurant, which contained a long counter running along one side and a few bare-topped board tables, was operated by a fat-bodied Chinese of indeterminate age. About half the stools at the counter were occupied, so Murragh, craving a period of unbroken thought for the time being, settled at one of the tables, where he ordered steak, fried potatoes, pie, and coffee. The food, when the Chinese brought it, proved to be as good as he'd hoped.

He was just draining his coffee cup when he heard one of the men at the counter say, "Evenin', Cass," and looked up to see a skinny-framed individual in rather sloppy clothing closing the door behind him. The man's overalls were cuffed at the ankles of his run-over riding boots; his sombrero was a rather shapeless, well-weathered thing; bony wrists protruded from his coat sleeves, and from one of the coat pockets peeked the top edge of a red-bound book. He had an elongated horse face, the shaven beard showing blue along the jaws, and shrewd eyes which ran quickly along the counter stools, then shifted to the table at which Murragh sat.

As he turned, Murragh caught the quick glint of metal on the flimsy vest beneath the coat. The man crossed

45

the floor to Murragh's table, pulled out a chair and sat down. "Figured I might find you here."

Murragh studied the shrewd eyes a moment. "I didn't expect," he said quietly, "that I'd been in Lanyard long enough to figure in anybody's plans."

"Expect?" The other smiled whimsically, " 'Oft expectation fails—' "

" 'And most oft,' " Murragh finished the quotation, " 'there where most it promises.' But what can I—?"

The shrewd eyes beamed with delight. "You know Shakespeare?"

Murragh shook his head. "No, he died before I was born," he said dryly and added, "A good deal of him was crammed into my head when I went to school, and some of it has stayed with me."

"He's all the schooling I ever had," the other said. "My old dad heired me a set of his works." He fished the red-bound book out of his coat pocket. "Now, this here *Merchant of Venice* is—"

"Just what," Murragh interrupted, "did you come in here to see me about?"

"Well, she sort of avoided giving me your name, said I'd have to ask you—"

"You're talking about Miss Gordon?"

"Who else? So I took a look at the hotel register and it said 'Hoyt Murragh,' and the clerk described you, and you're the only man in here with a black forelock who don't let his mustache range all over his face and—"

"All right. I'm Hoyt Murragh. What's on your mind?"

"I'm Cass Henley, deputy sheriff of Lanyard County—" He broke off as the Chinese appeared, silent-footed, at the table to ascertain if further service was required.

"Yes, another wedge of that apricot pie and more Java," Murragh said. "Better bring him the same"— indicating the deputy. "'Yon Cassius has a lean and hungry look.'"

The Chinese padded away, while Cass Henley pounded the table ecstatically. "Cripes A'mighty!" he said admiringly. "You and me are going to get along like two brothers. That's from *Julius Caesar*—"

"My mistake in bringing it up. I'm waiting to hear your business with me."

Henley nodded. "I got the story from Linda, of course, but being what happened took place in this county, I'd like to get your idea of what happened to Uncle Jimmy Cochrane."

"I don't think I can give you anything Miss Gordon hasn't already told you. Why come to me?"

"I didn't come to just you, like you was an ordinary man. I come to Hoyt Murragh. Even 'way back in here in the Territory, like we are, we get news now and then. We know Hoyt Murragh made a certain rep with the Texas Rangers a few years back. Yeah, we read newspapers now and then. Suddenly Hoyt Murragh shows up here. Now wait, I'm not asking what you're here for, and I know the Texas Rangers haven't any authority in this neck of the country. So maybe you're not with the Rangers and I don't figure it's any of my business. But you were on that stage, and I want to know what you think of it?"

The Chinese returned with coffee. Murragh produced

47

two long slim cigars and gave his version of the affair. Henley listened intently, finally saying, "Yeah, that's just about the way Linda gave it. It could have been an accident. Uncle Jimmy had a temper when he was riled. He was never given to lashing his spans, but he might have been aggravated and then lost his balance when the coach started up sudden. Maybe I'm all wrong giving this so much attention until we know exact what happened, when we talk to him. With any other driver I wouldn't—but you see Uncle Jimmy's always been solid, dependable. How's the whole thing look to you?"

"I'll tell you more later, when we learn more," Murragh evaded. "Meanwhile, what can you tell me about a man named Russ Kennard?"

A contemptuous look came into the deputy's eyes. "Oh, him. He's just building himself a flock of trouble."

"Drinking?"

"Too much—but never enough so I get an excuse to take him in. He's orderly enough, so far as the law goes."

"Female trouble?"

"How'd you know?"

"I knew it would be one or the other."

Henley nodded. "And that's something else that isn't strictly any of my business—leastwise, until the explosion comes. Then I'll have to pick up the pieces and maybe see to burying them."

"Who is she?"

"Girl named Isabel Fanchon—she's a looker. Runs a woman's hat shop here. Vaiden's got to take notice of it someday."

48

"Vaiden?" Murragh asked. "Alonzo Vaiden? Well-built hombre, hair commencing to gray at the sides?"

"That's him. But he doesn't take underestimatin'. That gray is premature. Every ounce of his body is in trim. He's a heller in a fight."

"Gun or fists?"

"Both—though I just know the former from hearsay."

"Keep talking."

Cass Henley frowned. "Isabel Fanchon has always been considered Vaiden's woman. Then this Kennard came along. I reckon Isabel liked the way he played his hands, because Kennard is getting away with it. Weeks ago, I expected that Vaiden would interfere, but he's not saying anything, and that's not like 'Lonzo Vaiden. There's an explosion overdue, and I wouldn't want to be in Kennard's boots."

"What's Vaiden do?"

"Runs the Rafter-AV outfit—him and Senator Welch, who is part owner of the ranch. No, Max Welch isn't a regular senator. He's a lawyer by trade, but he's always fooling with politics. Ran for office a couple of times, but was defeated. Folks don't like him much as lawyer or politician. Mostly he hangs around the capital, though, trying to horn in on some political proposition or other, while he leaves the running of the ranch to Vaiden. They're equal partners in the Rafter-AV, however. . . . Where did you ever meet Vaiden?"

"I didn't. He was on the stage this morning, but got off just before we started—either accidentally or by design."

Henley said meaningly, "He picked a good trip to get off."

"You hinting," Murragh asked, "that Vaiden knew there'd be an attempt to wreck the stage?"

"I didn't say that. That's something that would have to be arranged with Uncle Jimmy, and he wouldn't go against Linda Gordon." He added, "It's just something that looks funny, that's all, just as it looks funny that this Russ Kennard came here giving out that he was a cattle buyer and hasn't yet made a move to go out to any of the ranches."

Murragh considered that, but didn't offer any explanation, even if he had one. He rose and tossed a bill on the table and reached for his hat. "Let's take a *pasear* around a bit. I need some air, and I'd like to take a look at your town."

They moved out to the street. Most of the buildings were dark now, but as they strolled along the plank sidewalks, neither talking to any extent, Murragh noticed a bank, two or three saloons, a couple of general stores, and various other places of commercial enterprise. On the corner of Tombstone Street and Main, Henley took him into the sheriff's office and introduced him to Sheriff Jake Farley, a solid-bodied, middle-aged man who was engaged in worrying an account sheet on the desk in front of him, and so immediately returned to his task as soon as he had shaken hands. On the street again, a minute later, Henley said, "Jake always gets that fretted look this time of month. Tomorrow he'll remember to ask me what your name is and what you're doing here, but right now he's so busy doping out cash received and cash paid out that he's plumb absent-minded."

And, thought Murragh, probably leaves most of his duties to his loyal deputy. . . . The town seemed orderly. There weren't many people abroad, though it wasn't yet ten o'clock. Beyond the sheriff's office and jail the town seemed to be devoted to a sort of Mexican section, and here, where the houses were more scattered, Murragh could see a row of cattle pens near the railroad tracks, the white fence boards showing ghostly white through the night gloom.

They crossed the street and returned on the opposite side. A matter of a block and a half farther on, Cass Henley gestured toward a small frame building with a darkened shop window. "Isabel Fanchon's place," he said. "We could go around to the back, where she lives, and if there's a light there you'd have a good chance of seeing that Kennard hombre."

Murragh shook his head. "I'll see him soon enough."

Eventually they were back at the hotel corner. Next to the hotel a lighted window enabled Murragh to read the words, GORDON STAGE & FREIGHTING COMPANY. He said, "I wonder if Miss Gordon has had any sort of word yet."

But the girl wasn't there when they entered and stopped before a short counter that ran halfway across the room. A tall elderly man in spotless broadcloth and a white shirt, immaculately neat, and with a thick thatch of silvery hair, rose from a desk in one corner, where he'd been partially penned in by a weighing machine and a heavy iron safe. Henley said, "Where's Linda,

Silvertop?" And to Murragh, "This is Linda's dad."

"Linda decided to go home and catch a mite of shut-eye. I'm going to let her know if we learn anything." He extended one hand as Henley completed the introduction. "Excuse the left, Mr. Murragh," Gordon smiled.

His right arm was held in a sling, close to his body. "My daughter mentioned that her passenger did a bang-up job of holding the horses today."

"Holding onto the stage, is a better way to put it," Murragh laughed.

Henley explained about the arm. "Holdup man, about a month back, when Silvertop was riding shotgun. The feller didn't like it when Silvertop gave him an argument."

"Did you save the cashbox?" Murragh asked.

Silvertop nodded. "I missed my shot and he didn't, but we got away. It was like drawing to a bobtail flush and filling it." Further conversation brought out the fact that Silvertop had done his shooting after being wounded. They talked for a while, then Henley suggested it was drink time. "You two run along," Silvertop said. "I promised Linda I'd wait here."

Four hours later Henley came pounding up the hotel stairs to knock loudly on the door of Number 9. Murragh sat up in bed. "Yes, who is it?"

"Cass Henley. Let me in."

Murragh smiled in the darkness. "Look, Cass, didn't we finish Shakespeare with that last bottle of beer?"

"I'm talking about Uncle Jimmy, not Shakespeare, now."

Murragh got out of bed and opened the door. "Well, what about him?"

"Bert Echardt just brought him in."

"Was he hurt bad?"

"His body's down to the undertaker's. He'd been shot—"

"Th' hell you say!"

"—through the heart. Probably with a forty-five or a forty-four—leastwise a heavy-caliber gun. Uncle Jimmy's gun was still in its holster. It hadn't been fired. Echardt found the body layin' in the road a few miles this side of Dry Bone."

"That sounds like murder, Cass," Murragh said soberly. "Wait until I get into my clothes. I want to look at that body."

5

Challenge

The stars overhead were frosty-clear when Murragh and Cass Henley stepped down to the quiet street, dark except for the feeble lights cast from one saloon and an all-night restaurant. Murragh glanced toward the afterglow of the waning moon palely outlined against the peaks of the Medicine Wind Mountains and judged it was around three o'clock. A chill breeze lifted across the surrounding semidesert country and, finding a corridor along Main Street, sent an old newspaper flapping and tumbling into the path of the two men as their booted feet clumped hollowly on the plank sidewalks.

Halfway to the undertaker's they encountered Linda and Silvertop Gordon. The four halted a minute, speaking low-toned in the silent street.

". . . there doesn't seem a thing we can do," Linda was saying. "But why should Uncle Jimmy, who never harmed a soul in his life, be picked out for their killing—?" Her voice broke suddenly. In the faint light from the stars, Murragh saw that her eyes were moist, outraged, frightened. He said quietly, "You mention killers, Miss Gordon. Would you suspect who they might be?"

"Do you think I'd be standing here, doing nothing about it, if I knew, Mr. Murragh?" she demanded scornfully.

"I reckon not," he agreed, humbled, wondering at the same time exactly what course she'd pursue if she knew the identity of the killers—was there more than one?—and if she possessed suspicions, or even a far-fetched surmise, she wasn't putting into words.

"Now, girl," Silvertop advised, "no use you getting too stirred up over this business. What's done's done. There'll be a reckoning, one of these days. Meanwhile, we'd best get on home to bed. There's another day coming."

They said good night, their forms blending into the gloom as Henley and Murragh continued their progress toward the undertaker's. A dim light burned in the window when they arrived. The front door stood unlocked, and Henley pushed inside, with Murragh on his heels, toward a bright light burning in the back room. They passed a tier of coffins reaching to the ceiling, opened another door which stood partly ajar, and entered. Here Murragh met Dr. John Bradley and the undertaker, who was named, appropriately enough, Graves. Bert Echardt and Graves, a spare man in a collarless white shirt and suspenders, stood beyond a long wooden table on which was stretched the lifeless form of Uncle Jimmy Cochrane, stripped to the waist.

The doctor's coat was off, his sleeves rolled up; he was middle-aged, somewhat grizzled, with heavy eyebrows. His open bag of instruments stood on a nearby chair, and he was working about an ugly wound that showed in the cold, stiffened flesh. Murragh shook hands with Graves and remarked to Echardt that he'd made good time. The doctor had again resumed work after pausing to nod to Murragh.

"Probably could have made better time," Echardt said, "but after I'd loaded Uncle Jimmy into the stage wagon—he was dead; there was nothing I could do for him—I went on to Dry Bone. Wanted to know who this hombre was who had took Zwing's place."

"Could he tell you anything?" Murragh asked.

"Wa'n't nobody there. The horses Uncle Jimmy brought in hadn't been took care of. I did what I could, then pushed on back to Lanyard." He yawned. "Well, I should be getting some shut-eye if I'm aimin' to take out the stage at seven o'clock."

The doctor raised up from his task. "I surely wish you could stay for the inquest I'm calling this afternoon, Bert. That inquest has to be held, and the sooner the better. Your testimony—"

"Look, Doc, we've been through all this before,"

Echardt said aggrievedly. "I thought that was settled when Miss Linda was here. Her stage is got to go out. I've told you exactly what happened. You can testify for me. There ain't nothing much going to come out at your inquest, anyway. You know that well's I do. It's more important that stage go through on time. You wouldn't aim to make Miss Linda any more trouble than she's already got."

"I reckon not," Bradley conceded with a sigh. "All right, take out your stage. If anybody objects to the way I'm handling this coroner's job, they can have it and welcome."

Murragh followed Bert Echardt to the street. "What side of the road was Uncle Jimmy lying on when you found him, Bert?"

"Why, no side at all. He was stretched, face down, right between the ruts—sort of layin' across 'em. I had a lantern, and I looked the road over some. A mite beyond where I found Uncle Jimmy the earth was scarred plenty in places and chewed up from them runnin' hoofs. Those horses were traveling all right."

"You didn't note anything unusual at Dry Bone when you went there?"

"Unusual? Don't you call the place being deserted unusual? And the horses not havin' been took care of?"

"But nothing else?"

"What do you mean?"

"I'm asking you."

Echardt pondered a moment, then shook his head. "Nope. It was just like I said. And that's enough. I'll be driving through Dry Bone around ten this morning, and— Dammit"—struck by a sudden thought—"I'm going to have to do my own harnessin' and waterin'."

"All right," Murragh nodded. "That's all I wanted to know. Good night—good morning, rather."

Echardt stamped off down the street. Murragh returned to the undertaker's rear room. Cass Henley and Graves stood watching the doctor. Murragh said, "Is that Uncle Jimmy's shirt and hat on the chair yonder?" Graves raised his head long enough to reply in the affirmative. Murragh crossed the room. On the chair were also the dead driver's undershirt and knotted bandanna, together with some other odds and ends: a tattered envelope, a Barlow knife, a partly consumed plug of tobacco, a much-worn wallet.

Murragh examined the undershirt, stained darkly at one spot, with a hole in the center of the stain. The outer shirt had a hole at the same point, but there was little blood to be seen. Finally Murragh came back to the men at the table. "He didn't bleed much, looks like."

"Most of the bleeding was internal," Bradley grunted, not looking up from his probing.

"Some bones broken, I reckon?" Murragh pursued. "A fall like that should bruise a man plenty, if nothing else—"

"No bones broken either," Bradley said, continuing his work. Finally, "There it is," he said, holding up for their inspection a chunk of dull-colored lead. "A mite battered where it struck a rib after piercing the heart."

"Looks like a forty-five," Murragh said. Henley added, "That's my guess, too." Murragh went on, "Dr. Bradley, what sort of a course did that slug take? Go in from the side, sort of, or—"

"Looks to me like it went straight in. Didn't seem to range to any extent, neither up nor down, until it glanced off a rib—I figure it was a rib." He placed the bullet carefully on a corner of the table. "Well, there's Exhibit A for the inquest. I doubt it will do much good, but there's always some darn' fool on a jury wants to look at the bullet. Downright morbid curiosity, I figure it." He went to a basin of water and started to wash his hands, saying over one shoulder, "It's yours now, Graves. You can start cleaning up and laying out any time."

A step was heard at the doorway, and Alonzo Vaiden entered. "What's all this I hear about Uncle Jimmy stopping a slug through the heart?" he demanded. "I was—" He stopped short, looking at Murragh.

Cass Henley said, "This is Mr. Murragh—'Lonzo Vaiden."

The two men shook hands. Vaiden was a good inch taller than Murragh; his grip was hard, aggressive; his whole make-up seemed to express extreme strength and vitality. "Glad to make your acquaintance, Murragh." He turned to the others. "Now what about Uncle Jimmy?"

Graves gestured toward the table. "You can see for yourself."

Vaiden glanced at the still form. "Who did it?"

Cass Henley said, "You know as much as we do. Who told you about it?"

Vaiden didn't lift his eyes from the body of the dead driver. "Damned if I could say, now, who it was—

somebody in Pudge Ryan's saloon. I'd dropped in for a drink—I just got in, y'know." He looked up now, smiling somewhat sheepishly. "I was up to Millman City and missed the stage, like a damned fool. Had to hire a horse to get to Sulphur Tanks, then got a second mount there. Seems I missed something else, along with the stage. Somebody said there'd been a runaway and Uncle Jimmy had fallen off. I didn't get the straight of it, except that Linda Gordon and a passenger had had a hell of a ride, and that the stage had been nigh wrecked—"

Murragh broke in, "I remember seeing you in Millman City. You were atop the stage, then got off before it left."

"That's right," Vaiden nodded. "I don't remember seeing you, though. What's Linda going to do for a driver for today's trip?"

"Bert Echardt's taking over," Murragh said. "Didn't you meet him on the street before you got here?"

Vaiden said no, he hadn't seen Echardt, then changed the subject. "That reminds me, when I came though Dry Bone I stopped to water my horse. I wonder if Linda knows there's nobody in charge there?"

"I reckon Echardt told her," Cass Henley said.

Vaiden asked, "Anybody know exactly what happened to Uncle Jimmy—anybody got any theories, that is?"

"Not yet," Henley replied.

Vaiden frowned. "It's a damn' shame. You couldn't find a more likable old cuss. I suppose Sheriff Farley has gone seeking evidence."

Henley shook his head. "Jake don't even know it yet. There's nothing he could do right off. He might as well have his sleep out."

"I don't agree with you," Vaiden said coldly. "We pay taxes for decent law enforcement. If Jake Farley can't be on the job, maybe we'd better elect another sheriff—"

"Oh hell," Henley snapped. "I'm getting awful sick of that old song. Maybe you'd rather see Senator Welch in the sheriff's office."

"Lanyard County could do a lot worse than Max Welch."

"Or maybe even your watchdog," Henley continued.

"Who do you mean?" Vaiden's eyes narrowed.

"That shadow that's always with you—leastwise until right now—that thing on two legs that always looks to me like he'd just crawled out from under a rock, and him with his gun with the two notches—"

"You talking about Claude Balter?"

Henley laughed. "I see you recognize the description. Just where is Claude Balter? I just remembered something—'bout a year ago it was, Uncle Jimmy used his whip on Balter when he caught him beating a horse. And Balter would have shot Uncle Jimmy right then if a couple of us hadn't grabbed on to him."

"Don't talk like a fool, Cass. Claude's no murderer. How do I know where he is? He's probably at the ranch, where I left him." Vaiden broke off and smiled suddenly, showing even white teeth. "Look, Cass, there's no use you and me getting into an argument. What sort of an opinion will Mr. Murragh have of Lanyard's citizens?" He turned to Murragh. "You here on business—if you don't mind my asking?"

"I don't mind, not at all," Murragh replied. "Yes, in a way, I reckon you might call it business." He didn't however, mention the nature of his business.

Vaiden tried another tack. "I seem to remember somebody named Murragh doing something with the Texas Rangers a few years back. It was in all the papers. I've forgotten the details."

"I used to be with the Rangers." Murragh smiled thinly. "If the incident comes to your memory, let me know and I'll tell you if I'm the same man."

"I don't figure it's important enough to give it any more thought," Vaiden said evenly. "At any rate, I doubt you'll find any crime hereabouts equal to your talents."

"Meaning," Murragh smiled, not missing the other's sneer, "you calculate I'm just wasting my time in Lanyard?"

Vaiden shrugged his wide shoulders. "That," he said, "depends on what business brought you here. Without knowing—and I'm not interested, mind you—I couldn't say, Murragh." His face had taken on a dark flush during the exchange of words.

"Suppose we drop it at that, then," Murragh proposed quietly. "If—and when—I run across anything you might be interested in, I'll come to you—direct to you."

Momentarily Vaiden lost the firm check he'd held on himself. His eyes blazed. "Say, what in hell are you hinting at, anyway?" he demanded testily.

Murragh looked surprised. He laughed softly.

"Hinting? I didn't know I'd been *hinting.*"

Abruptly Alonzo Vaiden recovered his composure. "My mistake, Murragh," he said carelessly. "Let's forget it."

The others had been eying Vaiden and Murragh in frowning concentration, sensing, rather than actually hearing, the definite challenge each man had hurled at the other during the brief duel of words. One thing was clear to every man in that room: between Hoyt Murragh and 'Lonzo Vaiden no friendship could ever exist.

By this time Vaiden had turned the conversation to the dead man stretched on the table, but wasn't saying anything of importance. After listening a minute, Murragh looked at Henley. "Cass, I think I'll run along back to bed. What time you setting that inquest for, Doc?"

Bradley replied, "Around three o'clock. I'll want you there, Mr. Murragh."

"I'll be on hand."

"Wait a minute, Hoyt," Cass said, "I'll go with you."

Murragh said, "Good night, gentlemen," and he and Henley headed for the street. Outside, they paused a moment to roll cigarettes. A gray horse stood at the hitchrack, head down, straddle-legged.

Henley said, "Looks like Vaiden had rode the hoofs off that pony."

They started back in the direction of the hotel. A minute later Vaiden emerged from the undertaker's, mounted, and rode out of town. Murragh, catching the sound of hoofbeats, turned around.

"Is that the direction Vaiden takes for his ranch?" he asked the deputy.

Henley nodded. "He'll have a twenty-mile ride, due west, if that bronc don't play out on him before he gets there."

"He's probably heading for home then," Murragh said, half aloud. "I wonder if . . ." He let the words remain unfinished.

Unconsciously he had slowed pace. Cass Henley eyed him curiously, then quoted, " 'Speak to me as to thy thinkings, as thou dost ruminate.' "

The archaic words, spoken with such solemn cadence on the lips of this native son of the western cattle country, brought a smile to Murragh's face. "You don't overlook many chances to spill a quotation, do you? *Othello*, wasn't it?"

"Correct. But what's on your mind?"

"Cass, do you suppose you could get me a saddle horse this time of night—or morning? Does the Gordon Stage Company hire out horses?"

"Not the kind you want, but the Blue Star Livery does. I leave my horse there." He paused, then asked, "You aiming to ride up to Dry Bone and look around?"

"You made a good guess."

"I'll go with you. The Blue Star's just about a block farther—on the corner of Hereford Street."

They awakened the sleeping liveryman in charge, and while the deputy was saddling his own pony Murragh inspected two horses by the light of a lantern with a soot-darkened chimney. One was a sorrel gelding, the other a paint pony. "There's the horse for you, Mr. Murragh,"—the man indicated the paint. "You won't even need to do more'n leave the reins hang on one finger. Just shift your weight and he'll turn on a dime."

"I know, and give back seven cents change, I suppose. No," Murragh refused. "I don't like that coffin-shaped head. Besides, I don't want to work cows. I just want a horse that can cover distance without folding up."

"That's your horse, Mr. Murragh. Gentle like a kitten too."

"I'll take the sorrel," Murragh said.

At that moment Henley came up, leading his own pony. He said, reprovingly, "Tony, you should know better than to try to hire out a horse that's likely to buck so early in the morning. You'd better sell that paint. Nobody with any sense ever takes him."

"Can't blame me for trying," the liveryman chuckled. "All right, the sorrel it is. What kind of a saddle do you like, Mr. Murragh? You'll want spurs too, won't you?"

Five minutes later Henley and Murragh were riding through the wide door of the livery. "Let's swing over to Deming Street," Henley said. "I'll stop at Sheriff Farley's home and tell him where I'm going. He'll have to hear about Uncle Jimmy too. It's not out of our way."

6

Vaiden?

They didn't push the horses too hard. Ahead of them lay a round trip of nearly sixty miles. It was broad daylight by the time they stopped for a snack of breakfast at Peyote Flat Station, provided by Echardt's assistant and his wife. There was a certain amount of conversation, during the meal, relative to Uncle Jimmy's sudden death, then the two men tightened cinches and started the long upgrade ride to Coyotero Pass.

As the going became steeper, the horses slowed their gait; the sun was rising fast now, though the riders moved in shadow up the shoulder of the mountain. Murragh had appeared lost in thought during most of the journey so far, and the deputy had been reluctant to break in. Some distance to the east the range was flooding rapidly with bright light. Henley muttered something about " '. . . morning, like the spirit of a youth . . .' " and glanced hopefully at Murragh. Murragh failed to rise to the bait. Henley tried another tack: "Hoyt, are you figuring Vaiden had anything to do with this business?"

Murragh shifted in the saddle, surveyed the gaunt face with its shrewd eyes. "What makes you ask that?"

"I don't know, for certain. Only when you and Vaiden were talking at the undertaker's, it seemed like you were tryin' to prod him into an admission of some sort."

"If so, I didn't have much luck," Murragh said

moodily. "Cass, who else knew when you woke me at the hotel that Uncle Jimmy had been shot through the heart? Who was around when Echardt arrived with the body? Think hard, this is important."

Cass frowned. "Let me see . . . well, a little after you went up to your hotel room, the hotel bar closed and I moseyed back to talk to Silvertop Gordon. Then Linda came over to see if we'd heard anything yet. The three of us sat and *habla-ed* for probably fifteen-twenty minutes before Echardt arrived with Uncle Jimmy. We took the body right over to the undertaker's—had a mite of trouble waking up Graves. Just as we arrived there Doc Bradley passed, returning from a night call. He come in with us. Echardt had already left to take the stage wagon and horses to the stage company's stables—situated right back of the hotel. Bradley helped me carry the body inside. I just stayed long enough to hear him say, 'Shot plumb through the heart.' then I lit out to get you. On my way to the hotel I met Echardt heading back to Graves' place—"

"Then the only ones Echardt might have mentioned the shooting to are men at the stables?"

Cass nodded. "Unless he met somebody else on the street. There wasn't anybody moving around at that time that I noticed."

"And yet," Murragh pursued, "practically the first thing Vaiden said, when he came in the undertaker's, was something about Uncle Jimmy's having stopped a slug *through the heart*. Why those words, exactly, if he didn't already know how Jimmy had been killed? Of course, the men from the stables might have dropped in the same saloon for a nightcap that Vaiden did. That's probably what happened. But did they know any more than that Uncle Jimmy had been killed? I don't think so."

Cass said, "Vaiden might have met Echardt—"

"But he didn't," Murragh cut in swiftly. "Don't you remember I asked Vaiden if he'd seen Echardt, and he said no."

"By God, that's right, he did! Hoyt, you've got something."

"I haven't got a damn' thing," Hoyt said bitterly, "unless I can get proof of my suspicions. I've got to admit that what Vaiden said might have been said through mere chance. Only it started the wheels to rolling a mite." He told of being greeted by Wyatt Holliday the previous morning and of how shortly later Vaiden had alighted from the stagecoach.

"Vaiden recognized your name, of course," Henley said. "Naturally, if he's up to anything shady, he'd wonder why you were heading for Lanyard."

Murragh didn't answer that. The riders had reached a more level stretch and spurred the horses ahead, making time when they could. To the right, pine trees marched along the shoulder of the mountain, though as the horses climbed higher the trees were gradually left below. When the next level stretch was reached, the horses drew together again.

"Cass," Murragh said, "how much chance would Vaiden have had yesterday to leave the coach, hire horses, and get to Dry Bone before the coach did?"

"It could be done," Cass replied. "He'd have to keep

his horses pushing right along, but he'd save time by cutting straight across country to Dry Bone, while the coach road curves in a sort of arc to touch all the stations and avoid tough upgrade pulls. You think that's what he did—cut ahead and then shot Uncle Jimmy, hoping to wreck the coach and you with it?"

Murragh's brow wrinkled. "Somehow I can't just believe that. It would have been slicing his time pretty fine. It requires time to arrange anything like that. Vaiden couldn't have known I was going to be taking passage on that particular stage."

The subject was dropped while the riders climbed higher. The road twisted and turned; the pines and piñons below became dwarfed to view. At certain points the road was hoof-chopped and scarred. Occasionally a patch would be scraped bare, showing where the coach wheels had skidded precariously around a turn. Eventually a fresh excavation at the edge of the road drew Murragh's attention. He jerked one thumb toward the spot. "The coach knocked a big rock off that point yesterday."

Henley craned his neck to glance to the tree-tangled depths far below. He said, "You're lucky there was a rock there to bounce you back on the road."

"You don't need to tell me how lucky I am."

The horses swept ahead again and finally reached the crest of the pass. Here Murragh and Henley halted to rest their mounts, which were breathing heavily. Precipitous rock bluffs closed them in on either side. The two men dismounted, dropped to sitting positions at the side of the road, and started to manufacture cigarettes.

Murragh said, through a cloud of gray smoke, "Cass, who'd have anything to gain if Linda Gordon had been killed in a stage wreck yesterday?"

Henley frowned. "We'ell, Silvertop would sell the stage company, doubtless. That's where Vaiden and Senator Welch would come in."

"Would they be interested in buying?"

"Would they be interested? Hell's bells! They've been trying to persuade Linda to sell for some time. Look here, are you figuring that Vaiden tried to arrange a wreck so—?" He suddenly slapped one knee. "By God, it fits in! To forestall suspicion in his direction, Vaiden booked passage on the stage yesterday, then missed it a-purpose. If any evidence ever arose pointing to Vaiden, he could just laugh it off with a remark to the effect he wouldn't fix it to wreck a stage he intended to ride on. Any jury would see sense in that."

"Let's forget that for a moment. Why does Linda refuse to sell?"

"She figures Vaiden's and Welch's offer isn't large enough. There's a lot of money tied up in the Gordon line. There's two extra coaches, stage wagons, freight wagons, horses. There's the expenses, too, men to be paid, feed for the horses, new harness when necessary—things like that. But this past couple of years Linda has been making a profit, not only on the coaches, but with her freight wagons that make trips from the T. N. & A. S. Railroad at Lanyard and from the Kansas, Midland & Southwest Railroad that comes into Millman City. You see, the Gordon stage line is the connecting link between those two railroads."

"I understand that."

"What you probably don't know is that the K. M. &
S. Railroad was planned originally to come clear
through to Lanyard. On the strength of such plans, the
K. M. & S. got a mail-carrying contract from the United
States Post Office. That mail contract pays the railroad
a good-sized sum of money."

"A mail subsidy, I reckon. 'Most all railroads get that
from the government."

"That's the word—subsidy. To collect that subsidy
each year, the K. M. & S. has to deliver the mail to Lanyard. Howsomever, the railroad never did build rails as
far as Lanyard—lack of capital, or something of the
sort. Meanwhile, the Texas Northern & Arizona
Southern Railroad was building fast in the direction of
Lanyard, and it put in a bid to get that mail subsidy
away from the K. M. & S. All this is quite a few years
back, of course, but I remember folks talking about how
the nation had gone railroad crazy."

"Crazy is the right word for it," Murragh nodded. "I
was reading about it one time. There were too many
roads building through the West—more than the popu-
lation could support. The government got behind 'em
with subsidies and so on, but even that didn't provide
enough money. The big financiers promoted roads, and
they had to keep pouring cash into 'em. One road—I
think it was the Northern Pacific—dragged a big
banking house into bankruptcy, and I've heard tell it
was that brought on the panic in '73—but I'm interrupting you."

"It was in the seventies that the K. M. & S. decided

70

Millman City was as far as it wanted to go. But the road wanted to hang onto that mail subsidy and not lose it to the T. N. & A. S. It was about that time that Angus Gordon stepped up with his idea of operating a stage line—"

"Who's Angus Gordon?"

"Silvertop's dead brother—Linda's uncle that was. Silvertop's name is Robert, but nobody ever calls him that—his hair turned that way when Linda's mother died. Anyway, Angus Gordon had made money in mining, and he went to the K. M. & S. and offered to open a stage line from Millman City to Lanyard and carry the mail, if the railroad would give him a part of that subsidy. The railroad jumped at the idea, and it's that subsidy pays Linda's expenses today—most of 'em, leastwise. It's more money than the actual carrying of the mail is worth, but it keeps the T. N. & A. S. from getting the mail contract. I guess one railroad will do 'most anything to keep a rival road from getting ahead."

Cass ground his cigarette under one heel. "Angus had it right tough at the beginning. Other stage companies were formed and tried to crowd him off the road in the hope of scaring him out so they'd get the business, but they finally quit when Angus proved he was tough enough to stay."

"Where do Silvertop and Linda come in on this?"

"Angus tried to get Silvertop to come in with him when the company was formed, but Silvertop wasn't interested. He had itching hoof, or train whistles in his head, or whatever you want to call it. Howsomever, that

71

hadn't stopped him from getting married, and after Linda was born he seemed to settle down quiet enough. Later the stage company was formed and Silvertop worked for Angus, off and on, until Linda's mother died. When that happened, Silvertop took Linda and lit out of town. Him and Linda roamed all over the West, Silvertop making a living for 'em playing poker and dealing faro wherever they happened to light. One minute they'd be rolling in cash, the next they'd be scratching gravel. And that's the way Linda grew up. Meanwhile Angus took sick with some sort of sickness there wasn't any cure for. When he died, he heired the stage company to Linda and Silvertop. By that time the line was run down some. Linda was sick of traipsin' around the country, and she was all for coming back and operating the line—"

Cass Henley paused, then went on: "You understand, Silvertop wa'n't enthusiastic about running stage-coaches, but I guess he felt he owed Linda something, so he allowed himself to be persuaded. They came back, borrowed some money from the Lanyard bank, and started to put the line in good operating condition again. Since then they've built up gradual, though it's all Linda's doings. Silvertop is willing to help any way he can—like when he rode shotgun when they were short a guard and got shot—but his heart isn't really in it. Something happened to him when Linda's ma died that he's never got over."

Murragh smiled. "You know quite a bit about their affairs."

"Cripes, why shouldn't I? I've known Linda since she

72

was a button. When I wa'n't but knee-high to a clump of buffaler grass, stagin' talk was all I used to hear at the supper table. My dad drove for Angus until he died— my dad, that is—and he had it in mind for me to tool stages when I got older, but somehow I never got into it. Angus was forever trying to train stage drivers. He even tried to make a driver out of Linda when she was growing up."

"I'd say he did."

Henley nodded. "Angus used to take her out driving with him. I've heard tell that once, up in Utah, when Silvertop's gambling wasn't producing the way it should, Linda took a job as relief driver for a stage company. But even when Linda was still small, I remember Angus would line out six wood chairs for her, then he'd tie a rein to each chair and put a rein between each of her two fingers. Then he'd tell her which chair to tilt without wiggling any of the other five. Yeah, she learned to drive all right." Henley's eyes were lost in space, his mind conjuring up visions of bygone days.

Murragh brought him back to the present. "How much farther did you say it was to Dry Bone?"

Henley got quickly to his feet. "That's right, we were headed someplace, wa'n't we? Oh, say 'bout five miles farther."

Murragh drew a last drag from his cigarette and stepped on it. The two men tightened cinches and climbed back into saddles. Once more dust rose from their ponies' hoofs.

7

The Empty Shell

They had gone a trifle over two miles when Henley asked, "What you thinking about, Hoyt?"

"Not thinking exactly. Just looking the country over. We're getting mighty close to the spot where the horses started to run yesterday. Just before that happened the coach had slowed down and I had a chance to look the country over now and then. There's one or two landmarks that look familiar farther on—see, where those big boulders are stacked one atop the other?"

While not as close to the road as at Coyotero Pass, high granite bluffs rose on either side. Here and there small clumps of cottonwood or oak struggled up through the loose rock that lined the roadside. Overhead a few drifting wisps of white cloud formed ever-changing patterns against the turquoise sky. The horses had been slowed to a walk by this time.

The men proceeded slowly, eyes intent on the earth. Henley said suddenly, "Wow! Looks like the stage really took off here!"

Murragh's gaze followed the pointing finger and saw a wide gash at the side of the ruts. There were deep hoof cuts in the gravelly earth. Farther along, more skid marks showed.

Murragh guided his pony to the edge of the road and climbed down from the saddle. Henley followed suit. The two men progressed on foot, finding tangible evidence now of the swiftly running spans of the previous day. Henley shook his head. "Look how far apart those hoofmarks are. Don't seem like those horses were doin' much more than just touchin' feet to the ground to take off again. Given feathers 'stead of manes, and I'd bet a plugged peso they'd been flying."

"I thought they were," Murragh said dryly. A few minutes later he pointed out, "Look here, where the wheels left the ruts. You can only find wheel marks on the left side. That coach was sure tilted plenty at this point."

A little farther on they came to the end of such indications of the wild ride. "The coach was riding easy here," Murragh observed. "I guess this is about the point where Linda suggested that Uncle Jimmy speed up a mite. And that brought on that horse lashing." He paused and retraced his steps a short distance, followed by the deputy, then stopped and looked about. "Those horses had just started to really move about here . . ."

At the right side of the road grew an ancient live-oak tree with wide branches, one of the boughs extending well out over the road. Without speaking, Murragh nodded toward the tree.

Henley glanced up at the overhanging bough. "I'd sure like to have a dollar for every time a Gordon stage has passed under that limb," he commented idly.

"You'd have a lot of money," Murragh nodded. He approached the tree, scuffed through the heavy accumulation of years of dead leaves at its base, and started to clamber up the thick trunk. Once up in the tree, among the glossy-leaved foliage, he called to Henley to

75

join him. The deputy came clambering up to stand beside Murragh on the overhanging bough, bracing themselves by a grip on still higher branches. Here they'd be lost to view of anyone passing beneath. They exchanged quick looks.

Murragh said, after a few moments, pointing to a freshly broken twig, "There's some evidence. Did you notice that jagged slash on the bark just before you came over here?"

"Guess I was too busy climbing," Henley said.

"Looked to me like somebody's foot might have slipped and his spur cut the bark. Or the end of a gun barrel might have gouged it. Anyway, whatever it was, it happened recent."

"Holy smokes, Hoyt!" Henley's eyes were wide. "That's what Vaiden did—left the coach before it pulled out of Millman City, hired horses and rode here, climbed the tree and hid among these leaves until the coach came along, then plugged Uncle Jimmy with his forty-five! Jimmy fell off, and the horses started running. Vaiden couldn't miss from here; it's that close, he could just about reach down and knock off Uncle Jimmy's hat—only that"—the deputy's eyes blazed wrathfully—"only that wouldn'ta resulted in the horses runnin' away—that dirty son of a— Say, he planned to kill Linda in a stage wreck—and what better place to plan a wreck than at Coyotero Pass? Then Vaiden'd get the stage company from Silvertop at the first price he offered. By God, Hoyt, a man like Vaiden should be—"

"Let's get down out of this," Murragh interrupted the

76

tirade tumbling from Henley's angrily white lips.

They scrambled down to earth, Henley still cursing wrathfully. "Come on, let's get going. I'm aiming to arrest Vaiden the minute—"

"Hold up a bit, Cass." Murragh smiled grimly. "If I could only think of it, right now, I'm certain Shakespeare must have said something about jumping to conclusions."

Some of the fire died from Henley's eyes. "What do you mean?" he asked, frowning. "Damn it, that's the way it could have happened."

Murragh nodded. "Could have, yes. But it's a far cry between a theory and a proved fact. You can't act without proof, Cass. Come on, let's ride to Dry Bone."

They walked, silently now, back along the road until they'd reached the waiting horses, then climbed up into saddles. Five minutes later Henley reined his mount close to Murragh's. "You're right, Hoyt. I think it was Desdemona in *Othello* who said, 'A most lame and impotent conclusion.'"

"You admit you jumped without thinking?"

"I reckon. Y'see, I got to wondering why you didn't hear Vaiden's forty-five when he shot Uncle Jimmy— Wait! Maybe you did hear the explosion and mistook it for the crack of the whip."

"Those whipcracks sounded more like rifle shots."

Henley said disgustedly, "Lord, you can be a disappointin' man at times." He brightened momentarily. "You didn't notice a rifle on Vaiden's saddle when he left Graves' place this mornin', did you?"

"I didn't see any rifle, and if I had it's too late for us

to do anything about it now."

The horses spurted ahead again and about twenty minutes later carried their riders into Dry Bone Station, where they dismounted. As they stepped down, the door of the adobe hut opened and a man peered out cautiously. Then he pushed into full view. "Oh, it's you, Cass."

"You're back, eh, Zwing?" Henley greeted. "How's your mother?"

"Oh, Ma's all right—was last time I drove to Sulphur Tanks—that's two weeks ago Sunday, but there's something else—"

"Hold on a minute," Henley said unbelievingly. "You say your mother's all right?"

"Certain." Zwing hitched up his overalls, spat a long brown stream of tobacco juice, and pushed his sombrero back on his stringy blond hair. He cast a questioning look at Hoyt. A faded woman in gray calico had emerged from the house and was looking at Hoyt too.

"Mr. and Mrs. Zwing," Henley introduced, "Mr. Murragh." The introductions acknowledged, he got back to business. "You weren't on duty when the stage came through yesterday, Zwing, and your wife's brother said you'd been called to Sulphur Tanks because of your mother being took bad."

The woman said, "I haven't any brother."

Zwing swore angrily. "So that's what! I was planning to come to Lanyard this morning, soon's the stage passed, to see you about this, Cass."

"You see me, now. Let's get this straightened out."

Zwing explained: "Early yesterday morning, before

78

we were up, a knock came at the door. When I opened it a gun was stuck in my belly and I was told to keep my mouth shut. I figured it was a holdup, but wa'n't really bothered, 'cause we haven't any money here. The men were masked, with bandannas tied across their faces. They—"

"How many were there?" Murragh interrupted. "Even with the masks, did any of 'em seem familiar to you?"

"Couldn't recognize 'em. Can't say for sure how many—four or five. It was dark, and they weren't all in the house to oncet. They told us if we did as ordered we wouldn't be hurt, so naturally we done as they told us. They made me'n Martha get dressed, then I had to hitch up that light stage wagon, and we got into it. Two of 'em rode horses alongside, and we druv a right smart piece—"

"Along the stage road?" Henley asked.

"No, back in the hills and down toward Marijildo Canyon. The two riders made us pull up at that little stream there—and there we stayed all day."

"But what happened?" Henley pursued.

"Nothing. We just waited there. Daylight come, and they give us some biscuits and beef, the same at noon—no supper, though. Must have been round eight o'clock last night they said a mistake had been made and we could go home, but they warned us not to hurry. By that time of course I knowed the stage had gone through, so there was no use of me hurrying—"

"Besides," the woman put in, "I was skeered. I expected to find the station burned when we come back, but I didn't want to hustle none—"

"I'd tried my level best," Zwing said, "to make those fellers understand I should be at the station to take care of the southbound stage, but they didn't pay me any mind, just kept us there all day and into the night. They maintained they'd left somebody to take care of the stage. That worried me, 'cause I didn't know what they intended. But everything looked all right. The horses had been took care of—"

"Bert Echardt did that," Henley said. "He was out here last night. Couldn't have been gone long when you got back."

"But—but what's the idea?" Zwing demanded.

Henley explained that he hadn't figured the whole thing out himself, but "there was a scheme to wreck the stage, and those fellers wanted you out of the way, Zwing."

"Th' hell you say. What happened?"

Henley explained that Uncle Jimmy had been killed. No, he couldn't give any details. Martha commenced weeping at this point and retired to the house. Zwing said apologetically, "She thought a heap of Uncle Jimmy—knowed him all her life." From that point on, he deluged Henley with questions.

Murragh left the pair talking and wandered around to the back of the station. He scrutinized the earth as he moved, but quickly gave up hope of finding any clues there. There were hoof- and footprints both—so many of them in fact that nothing definite could be ascertained in that direction, so jumbled together were they.

He passed the corrals and headed farther back to the

hay barn and stables. Here he entered. There wasn't much to be seen here, either, except a number of horses waiting quietly in stalls. At the far end of the barn was a small door leading to a lean-to built against the outside wall.

Sunlight gleamed between cracks in the boards as he stepped into the lean-to, which was empty except for a rope lariat hanging on a nail in one wall, beneath the low-slanted roof, an old burlap sack which had been slung in one corner, with, nearby, several lengths of rawhide thongs. Considerable hay and straw was strewn across the dirt floor. Murragh picked up the burlap sack, shook from it the wisps of straw clinging to its sides, and examined it closely. Finally he dropped the lengths of rawhide into the sack, folded it as flatly as possible, and stuck it between his shirt and his belt, beneath his coat, where it wouldn't be noticeable unless someone were on the lookout for something of the sort.

For a long time he stood, pondering. Finally, as he turned to leave the lean-to, his gaze was attracted by a glint of sunlight shining on a small metallic object on the floor, near the doorway. Stooping, he picked it up and found himself holding an exploded cartridge case from a forty-five six-shooter. Murragh studied the empty shell's round, brassy form. From the lack of dust on its surface, he judged it hadn't been long on the floor where he'd found it. After a time he slipped the shell in his pocket and joined Zwing and Henley at the front of the station.

"Find anything to interest you, Mr. Murragh?" Zwing asked.

"Nice arrangement for a station here. I like the way you keep the horses. Everything seems well taken care of."

"Thankee." Zwing tossed away his old cud and took a fresh bite from his plug of tobacco. "I always give my best to an owner when I work horses for him."

The men talked a little longer before Henley said, "We won't delay you any more, Zwing. 'Twon't be long before Echardt is due in with the stage, and you'll be busy. We'll see you again." The men shook hands, and Murragh and Henley got into saddles.

Neither said anything until they were some distance along the road, heading back to Lanyard; then Henley spoke, "Zwing wanted to know who you were, what you were doing with me, and so on. Finally he asked flat out if you were a detective."

Murragh smiled. "What did you tell him?"

"What would I tell him? If you're a detective, you never told me about it. No, I just said I didn't know for sure, but that I had a hunch you'd been sent by some company that was thinking of buying the stage company from Linda, and that you were just sort of looking around."

Murragh gazed straight ahead. Finally, "I don't know, Cass, but that's as good a reason for me being in this part of the country as any I can think of. Maybe it would be a good idea to build up that thought in people's minds. You might spread it around a mite."

"It won't need much spreading, once Echardt gets back to Lanyard tomorrow."

"How come?"

"Zwing will tell Echardt, and Bert never has been known for his reluctance to talk."

They rode on, and had nearly reached Coyotero Pass when they saw the stagecoach coming. The horses were swung aside to let the coach pass, but Echardt had spotted them and pulled to a momentary halt. "What in Nick's name are you two doing 'way off here?" he demanded in surprise.

"Just takin' a little early morning ride," Henley laughed.

Echardt nudged the shotgun guard seated next to him. "Listen to that, will you! An early morning ride!"

Murragh, meanwhile, had shifted his horse around where he could look into the coach. Within were a man, a woman, and a little boy. They looked like easterners. Murragh touched fingers to the brim of his sombrero, said "Good morning," and reined his pony around to the opposite side of the stage. The shotgun guard was a stranger to him.

". . . yeah, you'll find Zwing at Dry Bone," Henley was saying to Echardt. "Him and his missus had quite an experience yesterday—no, I'll let him tell it while you're changing horses. We've got to be pushing on. See you again."

Echardt's whip cracked, and he spoke loudly to the six bays. The animals lunged forward, and the coach rolled off, throwing up great clouds of dust in its wake.

Murragh and Henley touched spurs to their ponies as the stage vanished at their rear. Murragh said, "Linda wasn't riding shotgun this morning."

"Not necessary," Henley replied. "He was the regular

guard out of Lanyard. He'll ride clear through to Millman City this morning, though ordinarily he'd be relieved at Sulphur Tanks, when Zach Decker relieves Bert Echardt. Starting tomorrow morning, on the southbound, there'll be a new guard—friend of Wyatt Holliday's that wanted a job. You see, Linda was just substituting for a guard who had quit, until she could get another man."

"Do all stage lines work their drivers and guards the same way?"

Henley shook his head. "Different companies have different methods. Some companies, on a stretch like from Lanyard to Millman City, would have the same guard all the way through. Linda figures it's a long ride any way you look at it, so she has both guards and drivers relieved at Sulphur Tanks, which is approximately halfway. Some companies even have shorter drives, but Linda pays good wages, and nobody's kicked on her ideas so far."

The ponies drummed on. They slowed a bit just after the crest of Coyotero Pass was reached, and Murragh said, "Tell me something about Vaiden's cow outfit—what sort of setup is it?"

"Well, like I told you, he and Senator Max Welch are in pardners. I got to admit," Henley added somewhat reluctantly, "that Vaiden knows his business when it comes to cows. He runs a right big herd and makes a paying proposition out of it."

"They're all his own cows?"

Henley nodded. "If there's any rustling goes on, I don't guess we can lay it to Vaiden's outfit. We don't get many complaints on cow thieves any more. At one time there was considerable rustling in Lanyard County, but Jake Farley pretty much cleaned that up. Nope, whatever he is, 'Lonzo Vaiden's no cow thief."

"What sort of an outfit does he have?"

"Mostly run-of-the-mine cowhands; good, bad, and indifferent; loyal to the man who pays their money, like a good cowpoke should be. His foreman, Quent Hillman, is something of a slave driver, I hear. Can't say I care for Hillman, but I don't know anything against him. Kind of a hot-tempered cuss and boils over easy."

"You mentioned something at Graves' place, when you were talking to Vaiden, about his shadow—I think that's the word you used. Who's that?"

Henley frowned. "Feller named Claude Balter, undersized, but poison-mean I figure him. Got a couple of notches cut in his six-shooter butt. Don't know when he put 'em there, though. Generally when you see Vaiden, you can count on Balter being with him."

"Sort of a bodyguard?"

"He's supposed to draw cowhand wages, but I figure him as something more—I don't know what. Yeah, I might call him a bodyguard, if Lanyard was a real tough town, if Vaiden needed a bodyguard, which same I don't see why he should. I've never had any real trouble with Balter. Once or twice he got sort of sneery about law officers in general, but before I could take the matter up with him, Vaiden quick hushed him up." Murragh made no instant response, and Henley changed the subject, "Hoyt, what do you make of that business at Zwing's?"

"What do you know about Zwing?"

"He's straight as a die. Used to fight the bottle pretty hard when he worked at the livery in Lanyard, but Linda gave him the job at Dry Bone, and I don't think he's touched a drop since. You can count on what he said."

"All I can say, then, it's a mystery to me. Somebody wanted Zwing away from Dry Bone for some reason connected with Uncle Jimmy's killing—but I haven't yet got it figured out. It'll stand some thinking."

"Look, Hoyt, we're due to give testimony at Doc Bradley's inquest this afternoon. I won't have much to offer, unless—well, are we going to tell about this Zwing business and about Uncle Jimmy being shot from that live-oak?"

Hoyt said, "I'm not your boss, Cass. What's in your mind to do?"

"I'm willing to string along with you on this."

"We-ell, I look at it like this. I've a hunch Doc Bradley won't be too strong for the legal technicalities—not when he's willing to do Echardt's testifying for him—and if we don't tell all we know, right now, I can't see as it will make much difference. This inquest isn't going to decide much, one way or the other, aside from the fact that Uncle Jimmy was murdered—and maybe not even that much. After all, we're supposed to give the facts relating to death as we know them. Surmises, guesses, conjectures, speculations—call 'em whatever you like—from any one or two witnesses, when proved facts are lacking, haven't any place at a coroner's inquest."

"In other words, you figure to keep your mouth shut."

"For the time being, yes. There's no need to let Vaiden know what we've learned, if he's the man we're gunning for. Anything told to a coroner's jury eventually becomes public property."

Henley said again, "I'll string along with you, Hoyt." He added, a trifle awkwardly, "You've got me wondering just why you take so much interest in this business."

Murragh evaded that with a slight smile and, "Why shouldn't I? If that coach had been wrecked yesterday, I might have been killed. I never have been able to get over being interested in my own safety."

The deputy didn't pursue the subject further as they pushed their horses in the direction of Lanyard.

8

Killer Unknown

Murragh and Henley reached town in ample time to testify at Dr. Bradley's inquest—the deputy's testimony being required only because he had been on hand when Uncle Jimmy's body arrived. The inquiry was held on the second floor of a weather-beaten two-story frame building, located a block east of the hotel on Main Street, which bore the imposing title, Lanyard Court House, painted in sun-faded letters across its front wall. The jury had already "viewed the remains" at the undertaker's, and the hearing and

87

giving of testimony required almost as little time as the jury devoted to returning a verdict to the effect that "death had come to the deceased James Cochrane as the result of a bullet wound inflicted by some person unknown." Further, the jury recommended that Sheriff Jacob Farley take steps at once to apprehend the murderer. Having thus dumped the problem in Jake Farley's lap, the jury, clothed in the warm glow of a civic duty satisfactorily discharged, at least in its own estimation, adjourned to the nearest saloon with all speed and dispatch, where it assumed once more the mantle of ordinary civilian status and immediately fell to arguing as to what actually had happened to Uncle Jimmy.

Murragh and Henley emerged from the courthouse just behind Linda and Silvertop Gordon. Linda wore a tight-bodiced dress of some soft brown material, with touches of white at the throat and wrists, that accentuated her slim, firm figure and established in Murragh's consciousness as definite an impression of the girl's femininity as had been his amazement, the previous day, at her handling of the shotgun-guard job and efficient driving. The warm, late afternoon sun cast bright highlights in Linda's maize-hued hair drawn smoothly back from the brow, waved loosely over the ears, and gathered in a thick, shining knot at her nape.

Murragh fell quickly in at the girl's side as the four of them sauntered toward the corner of Main and Bowie streets, where the Lanyard Hotel, with the stage office next door, was situated. Henley and Silvertop were discussing the inquest: ". . . it's about what I calculated the verdict would be," the deputy was saying.

Murragh nodded agreement. "No coroner could be expected to produce more on the evidence we gave."

Linda darted him a quick glance from her long-lashed dark eyes. "But is Uncle Jimmy's murderer to get off scot-free?" she demanded indignantly.

"That," Murragh replied quietly, "depends."

"On what?"

"On such further evidence as may be uncovered," Murragh replied.

"And who is to uncover it?" Linda wanted to know.

Silvertop said, "If I was Jake Farley I can't say I'd know just where to start looking for evidence."

Linda sighed. "You men . . ."

"Well, girl," Silvertop smiled, "if you were sheriff just where would you commence?"

Linda accepted the challenge. "First, I'd try to learn if Uncle Jimmy had made any enemies recently. Then"— she considered a moment—"then I think I'd head my pony up toward Dry Bone and look the ground over pretty thoroughly at the point where the body was found. There might be some sort of evidence in the brush at the side of the road, or—or someplace— showing where the killer had hidden, waiting for the coach to come along. There might be footprints to be followed."

The girl paused, not having missed the quick look that passed between Murragh and Cass Henley. Her dark eyes widened. "I'll bet a 'dobe dollar that's just where you two have been," she exclaimed tri- umphantly. "I've seen neither of you all day, you were covered with dust when you arrived at the inquest—"

Henley chuckled, quoting, " 'I have no other but a woman's reason: I think—' "

"You look here, Cass Henley," Linda interrupted, "I won't be thrown off by any of your Shakespearean sayings. I've listened to them—been forced to listen to them—too many times now. Come, own up, Mr. Murragh. You did ride up there, didn't you? What did you learn?"

Murragh laughed softly. "Why, now, Miss Linda, you heard Cass and me give testimony at Doc Bradley's inquiry. Are you accusing us of withholding evidence?"

By this time the four had reached the hotel corner and halted, receiving nods, now and then, from passers-by. Linda was about to press further for information relative to Murragh's and Henley's ride to Dry Bone, when there arrived an interruption in the person of a woman of around twenty-five, wearing a close-fitting dress of maroon silk and a small hat, trimmed with a curving ostrich feather of scarlet, which was perched on one side of her head of glossy black curls. In her right hand she carried a sun parasol to shade her flamboyant, too highly colored elegance from the rays of the southwest sun. Her eyes were large and melting; her full red lips, voluptuous.

"Linda, dear!" she cried, approaching. "Do tell me about the inquest. What was decided? Hello, Cass, Silvertop." She paused, waiting.

"Miss Fanchon . . . my friend, Mr. Murragh," Linda said in chilly accents. Murragh removed his sombrero and bowed. Linda continued, before the other woman could speak, "The verdict was what everyone expected—killer unknown."

"It's a shame, don't you think, Mr. Murragh?" Miss Fanchon, purred. "Uncle Jimmy was such a dear old man. Everyone loved him. I can't see why—"

"Nor can anyone else," Linda agreed stiffly, interrupting.

"Linda! You're not wearing a hat. You must come into the shop. I have just the thing for you. It will do so much for your hair."

"I'm sure it would." Linda was suddenly all sweetness. "Is it something you've tried yourself?"

Miss Fanchon's coloring heightened. "Oh no, I don't think we could wear the same things."

"I'm sure we couldn't," Linda agreed in saccharine tones.

"Well, I must be going on. So glad to have made your acquaintance, Mr. Murragh. You must have Linda bring you into my shop." Murragh again bowed, and the girl concluded, "Good day," and swept on her way, head high beneath the parasol.

For a few moments there was silence, then Linda drew a long breath. "Since when am I 'dear' to Isabel Fanchon?" she commented distastefully.

Silvertop was shaking with silent laughter. "Linda, you were downright brutal."

"I wasn't at all, Dad, but I can't understand this sudden cordiality, unless—unless—" She paused and looked at Murragh. "*You* were the reason she stopped. She wanted to meet you."

"If so," Murragh laughed, "she succeeded—though I

91

thought for a moment the atmosphere might freeze out whatever she had in mind."

Linda crimsoned. "It all came as such a surprise. We never do more than nod. Besides, I've heard that she said it wasn't ladylike for me to work with horses and men and stages."

"The idea being," Silvertop explained gravely, "that on the other hand Linda considers Isabel Fanchon to be a hussy."

"I never said that, Dad," Linda exclaimed. To cover her embarrassment she turned to Murragh. "Isabel Fanchon is the East's contribution to style-and-fashion as it exists in Lanyard." Linda paused and added, "So Isabel thinks."

"If I was twenty years younger," Silvertop chuckled, "I'd say she was a demned handsome woman—maybe I will, anyway."

"Dad!" Linda protested. She turned to Murragh again. "She came here about eighteen months ago and opened a hat-and-bonnet shop. She really does—or did do—quite a bit of business."

"Did her business fall off?" Murragh asked, surveying Linda with amused eyes.

There was an awkward silence for a moment. Linda said, "I've always done my buying at the Bon Ton. I couldn't say exactly what business she does do." Her confusion heightened. "Dad, we must get back to the office. We'll see you later, Mr. Murragh, Cass." Seizing her father's arm, she hurried him on and entered the stage office.

Murragh was suddenly conscious that he was weary

and dirty and unshaven. "I reckon I'll go up to my room, Cass. See you at supper, maybe, if you eat at the hotel."

"Don't make it too early. I have to stay in the sheriff's office while Jake goes home to his supper. He'll be back around seven."

"That suits me. *Adios.*"

"S'long."

As he stepped into the hotel lobby, the clerk hailed Murragh: "The man you were asking about last night was here, inquiring for you."

"Russ Kennard?"

"That's him."

"Is he up in his room?"

"No, he went out again—said he'd come back later, when I told him you weren't in. I did say he might find you at the coroner's inquest."

Murragh nodded and started for the stairs. "If he comes in again, tell him I'm waiting to see him."

9

Russ Kennard

Three quarters of an hour later, shaved and washed, Murragh was stretched out on his bed in the hotel room, hands clasped behind his head, wide-open eyes abstractedly fixed on the bare wood ceiling. His forehead, beneath the triangular slash of black hair, was wrinkled with speculation. "Dammit," he muttered, irritatedly, "it just couldn't have been Vaiden. The time element doesn't altogether knock out that idea, but a man of Vaiden's height would—"

A knock at the door interrupted his thoughts. Murragh swung his legs to the floor, but didn't get off the bed. "Who is it?" he called.

From beyond the closed door: "It's me, Hoyt—Russ! Open up." The knob rattled.

Murragh crossed the floor in quick strides and opened the door.

"Hoyt! God, man, it's good to see you."

Russ Kennard was a smooth-shaven man with light hair. His eyes were blue, and he was around twenty-eight years of age. By some he might have been termed handsome. He wore sombrero and boots; otherwise, his togs were what is known as "citizens' clothes" in the Southwest. He looked rather pale and drawn; the hand he extended to Murragh wasn't quite steady. Murragh hesitated a moment and then shook hands.

The smile vanished from Kennard's face. "What's wrong. Hoyt? Aren't you glad to see me?"

Murragh closed the door, came back into the room, pushed one of the straight-backed chairs toward his visitor and sat down on the bed. Only then did he reply: "What makes you figure anything's wrong?"

Kennard settled uneasily to the chair. "I can't say you look overjoyed to see me," he accused pettishly.

"I wanted to see you," Murragh said quietly. "I asked for you the minute I got in last night—"

"And ever since I heard you were here I've been trying to find you," Kennard defended himself. "You weren't at the hotel all day. The clerk couldn't say where you were. I went to Jake Farley. All he knew was you'd gone someplace with the deputy sheriff. What's the idea? Don't you think I can handle this job?"

Murragh considered before making a reply. He took out a cigarette paper, sifted tobacco into it. His movements were slow, deliberate. Then he looked up. "I'm not sure you're handling it, Russ." He finished rolling the cigarette, scratched a match, touched flame to the brown cylinder of tobacco and inhaled deeply, then deftly snapped the dead match toward a slop jar standing next to the dresser.

"I don't understand what you mean," Kennard said, frowning.

"I think you do, Russ," Murragh said coldly. "You came here to do a job. As we arranged, you were to pose as a cattle buyer. Have you done one thing to convince anybody you're out to buy beef?"

"Why, sure, I've let it be known—"

"Don't be a fool," Murragh said harshly. "You might be able to pull the wool over somebody's eyes, but not over mine—and I doubt there's any other person in Lanyard who doesn't know exactly what you are, what you're here for—though your lack of interest in the subject may have thrown them off the track. I couldn't say."

"Sure, there you are," Kennard said eagerly, "if I went too direct, looking for information, I'd tip my hand."

"Don't stall with me, Russ." Murragh's voice was hard. "You haven't been near one ranch since you came here. No, don't lie. I know what I'm talking about. Who in hell do you think you've fooled?"

Kennard said nastily, "You seem to know it all, so there's no use my answering that. Maybe I can do a little kicking myself. Do you think it was smart to come here under your own name? God! Talk about me being careless. A man with Hoyt Murragh's rep doesn't—"

"That," Murragh snapped, "was something that couldn't be avoided. I was recognized. There was nothing else for me to do."

Kennard laughed insolently. "And you set yourself up to criticize my behavior—"

"Your behavior is something else I don't like. You've been drinking pretty hard since you've been in Lanyard, Russ."

Kennard's features tightened. "Sounds like you'd been keeping cases on me."

"Maybe that became part of the job too."

"Anybody told you I was drinking heavy is a damn' liar."

Murragh said again, "Who in hell do you think you've fooled?" He took a deep breath. "Russ, I know your failings better than you do, so it's no good trying to put me off."

"Nobody's trying to put you off," Kennard said angrily, and he drew a flask from his hip pocket. "There's no man telling me when I drink and when I don't drink." He laughed a bit shakily. "Come on, Hoyt, forget it. We'll have a drink together." He glanced at two empty glasses on the dresser and started to get them.

The next instant he found himself flung back in the chair, and Murragh was standing over him. "I'm one man who's telling you you can't drink," Murragh stated savagely. He snatched the flask from Kennard's surprised grasp, drew the cork and started to pour the contents into the slop jar. "You're going to stay sober while I talk to you."

"Damn you, Hoyt!" Kennard was up, pawing at Murragh, trying to reach the flask.

Murragh swore, dropped the flask into the slop jar, and whirled on the other man, who paused and started to back away before the look in Murragh's eyes. Murragh's right hand came up, smacked smartly against Kennard's left cheek, leaving the white imprint of sinewy fingers. The back of his hand caught Kennard across the lips, then crashed again on the man's cheek. Kennard staggered under the onslaught, gasped for breath, and collapsed on his chair, trying to shield his face with his arms.

Murragh stood looking down on him a moment, disgust sweeping the anger from his face, then returned to the bed. A full minute passed with neither speaking. Kennard first broke the silence: there was almost a sob in his voice as he said, "God, Hoyt, you're hard!"

"That's more than I can say for you," Murragh snarled. "You're soft, Russ—soft as hell. This shows me how far back you've gone. Three months ago you'd have put up a fight—at least, tried to put up a fight. Now you take it and whine that I'm hard. What else do you expect me to be? What sort of pardner do you call yourself? Drinking! Woman chasing! Did you come here to do a job or didn't you?"

"What do you mean, woman chasing?"

"Isabel Fanchon."

A trace of belligerency showed in Kennard's eyes. "You leave her out of this."

Murragh rose from the bed. Kennard cowered back. "You can't blame nothing on her—" He broke off, flinging his arms in front of his face.

Murragh rasped, "Won't anything make you fight? Is your backbone entirely gone?"

"What do you want me to do? I can't fight you, Hoyt. Why—why, we're pardners."

Murragh took a deep breath and settled on the bed again. "Pardners," he said wearily. "All right, Russ, we're pardners. But there was a job to do down here. You've been here almost three months. The job hasn't been done, has it?"

"I can't see what you're kicking about. We're getting good money—"

"And you've been spending a hell of a lot more than you can afford, too, from all I hear. And no progress to date."

"Don't say that, Hoyt. I've accomplished more than you think."

"What, for instance?"

Kennard's blue eyes slipped sidewise. "Well, I don't want to go into it right now, Hoyt, until I'm sure I'm on the right track, but I'm really—"

"You're lying," Murragh said quietly.

"Don't say that."

"You're lying." Murragh took a final drag on his cigarette and extinguished it. It had grown dark in the room while they talked, only a faint light entering the window from Main Street. He rose, struck a match, and lighted the lamp. He didn't sit down again, but stood leaning against the dresser, looking down on Kennard. Finally he spoke, the words coming hard:

"We took a job down here, Russ, and passed our word that we'd handle it. If I'd known how you were going to work out, I'd never have gone into this business, but I've passed my word and I'm aiming to see it through—with your help or without it. If you get in my way, so help me God, I'll smash you!"

"How could I get in your way? I'm here to help. I could have handled this alone. There was no need for you to come here—"

"Handled it alone," Murragh said scornfully. "You've been here three months. Can you point your finger at one man—just one—and say, 'He's responsible,' or even 'I think he's our man.' Can you do that?"

Kennard sat looking down at the floor. Finally he replied, "You should know better than I do, Hoyt, it takes time to make progress in these things."

"*They've* made progress—in the time you've been here, the stage has been held up four times—three times successfully. Once the guard—old Silvertop Gordon— had guts enough to prevent them getting the Silver Belle pay money—but three times out of four looks pretty black for us. The K. M. & S. doesn't like it at all. They won't put up with this forever. They'll be demanding somebody else take over the stage line, and on the strength of these holdups they can break the contract with the Gordon company."

"Maybe another stage company could handle things

better, so there wouldn't be holdups. After all, what does a girl know about running a stage line?"

"Have you heard any complaints in that direction?"

"Plenty."

"That's right interesting," Murragh said quietly. "Just exactly who have you heard complaining?"

Kennard was evasive. "You know how it is—you hear things, now and then, without paying any attention. . . . I can't say I remember just who it was now—"

"You said you'd heard plenty complaints," Murragh reminded coldly. "I'm asking for just one name."

"I don't remember."

"Vaiden?"

"Who?" Kennard looked up sharply. "Oh, 'Lonzo Vaiden. No, it wasn't him. What made you think of him, Hoyt?"

Murragh shrugged carelessly. "I can't say—probably because he's the only one in Lanyard I've met who rides the stage—aside from Miss Gordon herself. And Vaiden didn't ride yesterday."

"Got off just before it started, didn't he?"

"Where'd you hear that?"

"There's talk around town. From all I hear, Vaiden considers himself lucky. You made a drive, I understand. If I knew Vaiden, I could have told him Hoyt Murragh can handle any proposition he tackles—"

"Never mind greasing my hubs, Russ. You've been here three months and you don't know Vaiden, you're telling me?"

"Oh, I've seen him around town." Kennard was vague.

"Where?"

"Bars here and there."

"Drunk with him too, I suppose."

"Hoyt, what makes you say things like that?" Kennard said testily. There were small beads of perspiration on his forehead.

Murragh said blandly, "Why, what's wrong with that? Is there any reason you shouldn't drink with Vaiden— anything against him?"

"He's foursquare as far as I know," Kennard spoke quickly, "though I don't like the looks of a fellow that's always with him."

"Claude Balter?"

"That's the man. What do you know about him?"

"Not much. I understand he wears a notched gun."

Kennard studied his boot toe. "I hadn't noticed that," he said carefully—too carefully. "I just don't like his looks."

"Had any trouble with him?"

"Well, I—er—no, Hoyt. Why should I have trouble with a man I scarcely know?" He was still concentrating on the boot toe.

Murragh studied him a moment, waiting for Kennard to continue. Kennard remained silent. Murragh manufactured another cigarette. Smoke drifted through the room. Murragh produced a cigar from his vest, rose and stuck it under Kennard's nose. Kennard accepted it between his teeth, one hand fumbling at his pocket. Murragh gave him a match. Kennard drew the match head across the bottom of the chair seat. On the third try it ignited. His hand was shaking, as though palsied, when he finally succeeded in bringing the flame to the end of the cigar. He looked appealingly up at Murragh. "I need a drink."

Murragh resumed the seat on the bed. "I could wish that's all that's needed to fix you up."

Kennard laughed nervously. "You called the turn, Hoyt. I've been fighting the bottle considerably," he admitted.

"And losing the fight. It's not worth it, Russ. There are two kinds of drinkers: those who can take a drink in the morning, and those who have to take a drink in the morning. Where does Balter notch his gun—on the side or edge of the butt?"

"On the side—uh—" Kennard's hand started shaking again. "Well, you see, I don't know. I never—"

"You utter damned fool," Murragh said savagely. "What makes you think you can lie to me? A few minutes ago you said you'd never noticed Balter's gun butt, and now, damn you, Russ—"

"Now wait a minute," Kennard said shakily. "Don't jump to conclusions. I guess I wasn't thinking—somebody must have told me, or I heard it someplace."

"Save it," Murragh snapped. "If you've had some trouble with Balter, that's your own business if you don't want to tell me. I thought I had a pardner. Maybe I didn't. Maybe you can handle your own affairs, and that's your business too. But the job that brought you down here is my business, and if you can't handle it, you'd better take the first train out of Lanyard and let me take care of it."

"God, Hoyt, I'm willing to do anything you say. I'll admit I've been slow here, but I've done my best. I've got feelers out, I've picked up some information and—"

"Will you quit lying? We'll forget what's gone and done and start fresh. Just say you've bungled so far and let it go at that. Maybe together we can get something accomplished."

"You're a white man, Hoyt." Kennard's voice quivered. "Just tell me what to do. I'll pull myself together, I swear I will. What do you want done?"

"I want the stealing of the Silver Belle pay roll stopped. Yesterday a driver was murdered—"

Kennard cut quickly in, "Do you think that had anything to do with the pay-roll bandits?"

"I don't know who did it. We've got just one thing to work for—that stage has to go through without trouble."

"Why you so worried about the stage line? The Gordon company doesn't have to make good those pay-roll losses."

"The K. M. & S. does. How long do you think the railroad will put up with that?"

"I don't know. I can't tell you anything."

"I haven't asked you to tell me anything. From now on I intend to find out things for myself."

"Where do I come in?"

"You're going to ride stage every time the coach carries a pay roll for the Silver Belle. You'll ride as a passenger—"

"Say, that's a good idea." Kennard brightened considerably. "Hoyt, it takes you to think up plans. I never was any good, but you—"

"You'll ride as a passenger. You'll carry your six-shooter. If a holdup occurs, start shaking lead out of your barrel. Keep your eyes open, try to identify any bandits possible. When they've left—in case they get away with the money—get off the coach and read sign on any hoofprints you see."

"You've hit on the idea for stopping them."

"The pay roll leaves on the southbound coach on Friday. You'll take the stage north Thursday. And you be on that Friday coach."

"I'll be there. What will you be doing meanwhile?"

"I figure to stay in Lanyard and get acquainted with people. I might pick up something around here."

"Yes, you might, but"—Kennard looked dubious—"I'd say Millman City would be the better town for that. The holdups always occur more up that way. I've a hunch it's a gang up there that's doing the jobs."

"You might be right. Howsomever, I figure to look over Lanyard first." Murragh drew out his watch and glanced at it. "Time for supper. Come along and I'll buy you some chow."

"Geez, I'd like to, Hoyt, but I made another date—"

"Isabel Fanchon?"

Kennard nodded. "I got a supper date with her. Now look here, Hoyt, don't you get any wrong ideas about Isabel—"

"Why should I?"

"There're a lot of snooty folks in Lanyard that look down on her, but she's all right."

Murragh slipped on his sombrero, brushed some dust from his coat lapel. "I'll take your word for it," he said, even-voiced. "You'd better get to bed early tonight, Russ. What room you got here?"

"Number 11—just two doors from yours."

"All right. I'll see you tomorrow. And remember, there's a lot of whisky made that was never meant to be drunk—by you."

"Sure, I know what you mean. I'll go easy."

In the hall, outside Murragh's room, Kennard went to his own door. "Got to brush up a mite first. I'll see you tomorrow."

Murragh waited until the door of Number 11 had closed, then moved close and listened with his ear to the door panel. He heard the clink of a bottle against glass. His face was drawn into a tight scowl as he moved down the stairs.

10
Gambling Blood

When he reached the hotel lobby Murragh found Cass Henley waiting for him. Henley saw him coming down the stairs and approached smiling. " 'Here comes a man of comfort,' " he quoted.

"Rather," Murragh replied, unsmiling, " 'a wretched soul, bruised with adversity.' "

Henley smiled delightedly. "*Comedy of Errors*, isn't it?"

"You should know better than I do, Cass. To tell the truth, I'm not sure. . . . I'm sorry I'm late getting down. Something came up—"

"I just came in a couple of minutes ago. Looked in the dining room and didn't see you. Decided to wait. What's wrong? I can see that something's rubbed your fur the wrong way."

"It's nothing." Murragh forced a smile. "Let's forget it. I'm hungry enough to eat anything that doesn't get first bite at me."

"Linda and Silvertop just went in. Silvertop said to tell you he figures he owes you a supper for saving Linda's life."

"Saving Linda's life?"

"Your driving yesterday."

"Cripes, I was saving my own life! I'm still not sure I'd have done it, either, if she hadn't taken over the reins."

They left their guns and belts with the clerk at the desk and entered the dining room, which ran along the inner wall of the hotel building. There was carpet on the floor and linen covers on the tables, all but one of which was occupied. Silvertop and Linda sat in a corner at the far end. Silvertop raised his uninjured arm to attract their attention, and Henley and Murragh started in that direction, passing on their way another table at which sat Vaiden and two other men. Vaiden nodded shortly as they went by.

Murragh hung his sombrero on a nearby hook as Linda and her father greeted him and Henley. "What's this I hear," Murragh asked, "about you putting the price of a supper on your daughter's life?"

"Well," Silvertop said gravely, "I reckon that is putting a rather high value on her, now you mention it, but I've always been right indulgent with Linda. Sometimes I suspect it's not good for her."

Henley grinned. "'O, what damned minutes tells he o'er, who dotes, yet doubts; suspects, yet strongly loves!'"

A faint smile appeared on Linda's serious features. "You, Cass Henley, sit down and keep quiet."

"I'm sorry about that 'damned,' Linda," Henley chuckled.

"It's not the profanity I mind, it's the Shakespeare."

Murragh and Henley sat down. A waitress arrived, took orders, and returned shortly with the customary beef, potatoes, and coffee. The guests had their choice of pie or canned peaches. Obviously something was troubling Linda: she substituted for her father's injured arm by cutting his meat, then started to eat in silence. The others kept the conversation going, though Murragh took small part in it, he, too, being partially lost in his abstractions.

Chairs scraped at Vaiden's table as he and his companions concluded their meal. Murragh glanced toward them, then asked Henley the identity of the two men with Vaiden. Henley said, "The tub of lard is Senator Max Welch. The other is Claude Balter."

Senator Welch was well overweight for his height. He was middle-aged, with rather flashy clothing of eastern cut. His fancy vest and watch chain stretched taut across his prominent abdomen. An unusually wide-brimmed sombrero, fawn-colored, and fancy-stitched high-heeled boots were his sole concessions to southwestern custom. His florid jowls bulged over a wilted, starched collar. His eyes were small, porcine, sly.

Balter, in range togs, was thin, with muddy-hued hair, stringily plastered back from a narrow forehead. In a country where well-tanned men are the rule, Balter's sickly-white face, with its pale eyes hard as agates, seemed definitely out of place. The tight, vicious mouth above a not too pronounced chin contributed to the man's unprepossessing appearance. To Murragh he resembled a chalky-hued spider that had stayed too long hidden from the sunlight. "So that's Vaiden's shadow," Murragh commented.

"More like a ghost than a shadow," Silvertop said. "And a dangerous little rat if I ever saw one."

"Do you know anything definite against him?" Murragh asked.

"Not yet," Silvertop replied.

Murragh said, "I wonder what Welch is doing here."

"Your guess is as good as mine," Henley said. "I was down to the depot when he came in on the eastbound T. N. & A. S. this evening. He makes frequent trips out to the Rafter-AV, but never stays away from the capital long."

Murragh studied the three men as they left the dining room, then turned back to his food. Silvertop said, "Linda, you might as well perk up. What can't be helped can't be helped."

"I know, Dad." Again that faint smile which quickly disappeared. "I just can't help thinking about—things."

"Linda got a letter that sort of upset her," Silvertop said.

"I don't want to appear curious" Murragh offered,

"but is there anything any of us can do to help, Miss Gordon?"

"I'm afraid not," the girl sighed. "The letter really came down on yesterday's stage, but I was so worried about Uncle Jimmy that I put it to one side and didn't find it again until late this afternoon. The fact of the matter is,"—she was speaking directly to Murragh now—"the K. M. & S. Railroad doesn't at all like the holdups we've been having on the stage line. What they're referring to, of course, is the various thefts of Silver Belle pay-roll money."

"How about the mails?" Murragh asked.

"The bandits never touch mail sacks."

Murragh's eyes narrowed thoughtfully. "Those holdup men are smart. They don't want the government on their trail. Do they take express packages?"

Linda shook her head. "All they seem to go after is the Silver Belle pay-roll money. You see, the present contract I have with the K. M. & S. provides for the railroad being responsible for stolen moneys. They've made good in the past. It's not widely known, but the K. M. & S. is part owner of the Silver Belle Mine. Now the railroad is suggesting that I insure against pay-roll losses to bandits. I'm willing to do that if the railroad will increase the subsidy it pays the Gordon Stage Company. That, however, the railroad refuses to do."

"It looks to me," Murragh observed soberly, "as though you're in a rather tight corner."

"And it's growing tighter every minute," Linda replied testily. "Now the railroad wants the contract abrogated. If I refuse to comply, they threaten to take the matter to court and get the contract set aside on the grounds that the Gordon Company is incompetent. Lord knows, we're not strong enough to get into litigation with the K. M. & S. They'd wear us down." The girl added with sudden sincerity, "I must admit they have a case against us, if they want to push it. We wouldn't stand a chance."

Murragh considered a few moments. "How much time does the railroad give you?"

"We have to reach some sort of decision by July the first."

"You've got a good many weeks ahead of you yet, Miss Linda," Murragh pointed out.

"The time will pass too quickly to suit me."

"I imagine," Murragh nodded.

"Now, Linda, there's no use you fretting about this until the first of July," Silvertop said. "What if you do lose the contract? You can always sell out to Vaiden and Welch."

"And then what?" Linda asked.

"I'd like to see some more of the country again," Silvertop replied.

Linda slowly shook her head. "And take what we'd get from Vaiden and Welch and ramble from one gambling place to the next. No, Dad, I've gone through that once. It may be what you'd like, but what would I do— especially if you had a run of hard luck?"

"I could teach you to deal faro," Silvertop suggested genially. "There are other games too."

Linda's chin came up. "I won't sell to Vaiden and

Welch," she stared doggedly. "We've come this far; somehow, I'm going farther. Once we get over this present difficulty, things will smooth out, I'm sure. We can expand the road north of Millman City. I might even get a tie-up with the Falls-Largo Express. You know they suggested it one time, if we could make certain expansions. The bandits have just got to be stopped, that's all. Cass, you're a deputy. Why don't you do something?"

Henley said, "I've talked that over with Sheriff Farley, but so long as the holdups don't occur in Lanyard County, there's nothing much we can do. I keep a lookout, of course, to see if I can pick up any evidence showing who the bandits are, but I don't seem to have much luck."

"I know, Cass, I know." Linda's voice softened. "I realize it's out of your jurisdiction. The sheriff up north is doing all he can, too, I think. The cards just seemed stacked against us."

Silvertop said, "You know, Linda, you could get a better price for the line now than you could after you didn't have a contract with the railroad. Once your contract's gone, you'd have only our stock and coaches to sell."

"I'm willing to chance that," Linda said hotly.

Murragh studied the girl without speaking, then turned to Silvertop: "What's the biggest game you ever sat in—in stakes, I mean."

"That's easy," Silvertop replied enthusiastically, "I took thirty-eight thousand out of a stud game one time. That game ran for two weeks. We just knocked off long enough, now and then, to grab a few winks or a bite of food. Players dropped out gradually, but I stayed on when new men bought chips. I outlasted 'em."

"And dropped the thirty-eight thousand in various games over the next two months," Linda reminded him.

"True," Silvertop nodded carelessly. He went on, "Another time, I was fooling around with roulette. At one point I stood to take out better than fifty-three thousand, but I stayed in and when I quit I was broke. Once, up in Nevada—"

"That's enough," Murragh cut in. "I'll admit you haven't fooled with any tinhorn games. You know what you're talking about. But any game you ever entered, you had a fair chance of winning, didn't you?"

"Certainly." Silvertop looked sharply at Murragh. "I'd refuse to draw cards in a game that was crooked. 'Course, if I ever got caught in such a game, I'd do my dangdest to teach the crooks a lesson. Just what you aiming at, Hoyt?"

"You'll see in a minute," Murragh said reflectively. "I'd like to tell you about a game bigger than any you ever got into, and of a gambler who gambled for bigger stakes than you ever played for. The player I'm talking about could have pulled out with small winnings, but preferred to stay in and play for the whole pot or nothing."

"That's my kind of a gambler," Silvertop nodded approvingly.

"On top of all this," Murragh continued, "the cards were stacked against this player. It was a crooked game, but rather than quit cold, the player stayed on for the one lone chance—and there was a chance. A time came when this player's chips were running low. A relative of the player could have lent a hand then, but he wasn't very enthusiastic about it. Or maybe he didn't care for that kind of gambling."

"That's a hell of an attitude to take," Silvertop said indignantly. "Anybody that won't lend to his own kin—"

"Dad!" Linda protested.

"Hush, girl! A little hell isn't going to hurt anybody. . . . Go on, Hoyt. How'd the game come out?"

"We don't know yet," Murragh said quietly. "It's still running. But the player is still in there, playing the lone hand as cool and steady as she knows how."

"She? A woman player?" Silvertop frowned. "What sort of a game is it—stud, draw?"

"Neither," Murragh replied. "Coaches—stage-coaches."

"Stagecoaches? I never heard of that—" Abruptly Silvertop paused as he realized what Murragh was saying.

"Linda's got your gambling blood, Silvertop," Murragh went on, "only it's taking you a long time to see it. She's the one that's playing for big stakes. You talked about playing for thousands. Her game has a chance of running into hundreds of thousands. And you can't call that a tinhorn layout by any means."

There was a queer, baffled expression on Silvertop's face. He said slowly, "It's a big game all right."

Murragh laughed suddenly. "Shucks, I seem to be doing all the talking." He looked at Linda. The girl's eyes were bright, excited. Unusual color had come into her cheeks. "It—it is, sort of like a game, isn't it?" she said.

Henley was looking at Silvertop, who seemed to have fallen into a deep study, a frown creasing his forehead. The waitress arrived with peaches and pie. The coffee cups were refilled. The men lighted cigars. Silvertop's promptly went out. The supper was finally over; still Silvertop hadn't spoken. They rose from the table. Linda started out, followed by Henley. Silvertop caught Murragh by the sleeve and held him back a minute.

"Y'know," Silvertop said earnestly, "it never struck me this way before. Just hit me all of a heap, the way you explained it. I'm just a plain damned fool. Biggest game I ever had a chance to sit into, and here I been shying off like a half-broke bronc runs from his shadow. Linda would be foolish to sell now."

Murragh laughed softly. "That's the way it looks to me, too. It's a big game—but it's going to be tough."

"I've been in tough games before. And—and thanks, Hoyt."

"Forget it. I probably stuck my nose into something that wasn't any of my business."

"Sure you did," Silvertop grinned suddenly. "But I'm glad of it."

Linda's voice reached them from the doorway into the dining room. "Are you two coming, or do you intend to stand there talking the rest of the evening?"

"We—we were just talking about a game," Silvertop replied. "A game I figure to sit into."

As they strode out of the dining room, Silvertop still

clutching Murragh's arm, Murragh saw Russ Kennard and Isabel Fanchon sitting at a table against the wall. He hadn't noticed them enter. Kennard said, "Hello, Hoyt." Isabel said something in bright tones. Murragh wasn't sure what it was. Kennard looked as though he expected Murragh to stop, but he only bowed and continued on his way to the lobby. The scowl had again settled on his face.

11

Shadow

The lighting from buildings was spaced raggedly along Main Street when they emerged from the hotel. A few people made their way along the plank walks; a couple of wagons and several ponies still stood at the almost unbroken line of hitchracks that ran from one end of Main to the other. Linda said, "Well, I've got to get back to the office. There's work to do."

"I'll go along, Linda," Silvertop said. "Two heads will be better than one."

Henley said, "Funeral arrangements made for Uncle Jimmy yet, Linda?"

Linda nodded. "Tomorrow morning at ten. There'll be quite a turnout for the burial, I imagine. Uncle Jimmy was popular in Lanyard."

Murragh had lost track of the conversation for a moment. Across the street, on the corner diagonally opposite to that on which the hotel stood, was located a hay-and-feed store, closed at present. Murragh's attention had been drawn by a brief, pinpointed red glow that showed momentarily in its shadowed entrance. An instant later that small bit of light appeared a second time and again vanished. Someone was standing in the darkened entrance to the feed store, smoking a cigarette. Murragh asked himself why.

If the man, whoever he was, was waiting for a friend, he could have stood openly on the corner. As it was, he was keeping himself hidden from view, or thought he was. Therefore he must be watching someone's movements. Murragh considered. The hidden man was standing too far back in the doorway to be watching along the street. However, from that concealed position a watcher would have a clear view of anyone emerging from the hotel lobby or the side door of the hotel which opened from the bar. Therefore it must be somebody coming from the hotel for which the man was looking.

Murragh turned back to Henley and the Gordons. Henley was saying, "Well, I got to be getting back. Walk down to the sheriff's office with me, Hoyt."

"Might as well," Murragh nodded. "There's not much of anything to do. I figure to turn in early tonight. It's been a long day."

"That reminds me," Linda said, "you two never did tell me where you went this morning early."

"Hoyt wanted to try out a horse he hired," Henley put in.

"But did you learn anything?" Linda persisted.

"A little," Hoyt replied.

"What?" Linda wanted to know.

"It's quite a good horse." Murragh smiled. "Sorrel—

nice clean legs and a world of stamina—"

Linda interrupted, "Come on, Dad, let's go work for the Gordon Stage Company. We're not learning anything here." Taking Silvertop by the arm, she guided him into the stage-office entrance, next to the hotel.

Henley grinned widely as he and Murragh started west on Main Street. "We've sure got Linda on the run. She always was that way, from a little tyke, curious as all get-out if she thought something was going on that she didn't know about."

Murragh wasn't listening. He had cast a quick glance back toward the hay-and-feed store and observed a man leave the entrance and also start west on Main. Murragh took a few more steps and again shot a look over one shoulder. This time, in the light from Joe Low's restaurant, he recognized the fellow. It was Claude Balter. Balter wasn't walking fast, nor was he just sauntering along either. He was just proceeding at a rate that would keep him within sight of Murragh and Henley—if it was Murragh and Henley he was spying on. Of that, Murragh wasn't yet sure.

Reaching the corner of Main and Carson streets, Murragh and Henley crossed over. Again Murragh managed to get a quick glance to the rear through the ruse of stepping out to the hitchrack and examining a pony tethered there. "Nice bit of horse," Murragh commented.

Henley surveyed the animal, a quite ordinary-looking chestnut. He scratched a match and, before it flickered out, said, "Circle-Bar bronc." Murragh nodded carelessly and turned away from the hitchrack. Henley asked curiously, "Exactly what do you like in a horse, anyway?"

Murragh could almost feel the shrewd eyes as they probed at the reason for a delay. "My mistake, Cass," he said quietly. "It wasn't quite the horse I thought it was."

"And now I'd say you wasn't even interested in the horse from the beginning."

"I reckon you're right," Murragh admitted.

Henley swore softly under his breath. "I wish you were a prisoner of mine for about five minutes."

"*Por qué?* Why?" Murragh looked puzzled.

"I'd take you into a cell and beat out of you the reason why you stopped near that horse." He added, "I got a notion to do just that, anyway."

Murragh noticed that Henley hadn't said "stopped to look at that horse." Henley had sensed that the horse had nothing to do with the pause. Murragh smiled, " 'There is no terror, Cassius, in your threats.' "

The deputy's scowl vanished and he chuckled, "*Julius Caesar.*"

Any reference to the Bard of Avon was always a sure-fire method for switching Henley's mind from any subject on which he became too inquisitive. For the remainder of the distance to the sheriff's office, Henley made no further mention of the horse. Jake Farley was seated at his desk when they entered. He glanced up briefly, grunted, "Evenin', gents," and continued working.

"How you making it tonight, Sheriff?" Murragh replied.

The sheriff's office contained a desk, straight-backed chairs, and a cot with neatly folded blankets, against one wall. Above the cot a pine shelf held a complete red-bound set of the Shakespearean classics in small, pocket-size volumes. Directly opposite, the wall was decorated with a calendar from a meat-packing company and a topographical map of Lanyard County. A third wall held a rack of guns and handcuffs with, near by, a row of wooden pegs driven into the adobe. At the rear a closed door opened the way to the cell block beyond. An oil lamp, suspended from the ceiling, reflected light on the desk. Henley said suddenly, "What are those clothes on that chair?"

Farley replied, without looking up. "Graves brought them in a spell ago. Uncle Jimmy's duds. Graves figured the bullet holes might be needed as evidence or something. If so, I don't know when." He looked at Murragh now. "Cass tells me you picked up a mite of evidence around an oak tree that overhangs the stage road near Dry Bone."

"Maybe we did." Murragh sounded noncommittal.

"What do you figure we can do about it?"

Murragh shrugged. "I'm not sheriff of Lanyard County—nor deputy, either."

Farley said flatly, "You're a cold-blooded proposition, Murragh."

"Because I refuse to outline your duties for you?"

Farley didn't answer that. He said, "I could ask you what you're doing here, you know." Murragh conceded the truth of the statement. Farley continued heavily, "But if you didn't feel like telling, you wouldn't. I'd like to know why you were so interested in making that ride to Dry Bone, but I won't ask you that, either. I keep remembering that a man named Murragh did good work with the Texas Rangers. Not only that. Cass thinks you're on the level."

"Cass," Murragh smiled thinly, "doesn't know any more about me than you do, Sheriff. Don't take his word for anything that bothers you."

Farley's eyes narrowed, but he didn't say anything. Finally he made a sort of grunting sound and resumed working.

Henley had been looking at Uncle Jimmy's shirt. He said, abruptly, "That gun was sure close. The cloth is all powder-burned around this bullet hole." He glanced sharply at Murragh. "Did you notice this at the undertaker's?" Murragh nodded shortly, impatiently. Henley went on, his voice bitterly self-accusing, "The feller that invented insomnia medicine didn't have me in mind. Hoyt, is this what gave you the idea for that ride this morning?"

Murragh nodded again and once more turned toward the street window through which he'd been watching a cigarette end glow and die away in a narrow passageway between two buildings across the way. After a moment he faced back, explaining, "I knew the shot must have been fired from a point closer than the side of the road."

"That's clear," Henley agreed, and added, "now." He dropped Uncle Jimmy's shirt back on the chair and said, "What you working on, Jake?"

"I'm trying to total up the amount paid out for prisoners' meals last month. Added it up three times, and each time it's different—"

Henley interrupted to say, "How's the missus tonight?"

"Poorly—like always," Farley grunted.

"You slope on home, Jake," Henley proposed. "I'll take care of those papers."

"Don't like to be puttin' on you that way, Cass."

"Forget it. Mrs. Farley needs you more than this job does, right now."

Farley looked grateful. "I reckon I'll do it then, Cass." He rose, got his hat from one of the wall pegs, and departed, saying over one shoulder a gruff, "G'night."

Murragh turned to the window again. As the sheriff stepped out to the street, Murragh caught the quick withdrawal of a shadowy form into more dense gloom on the opposite side of the thoroughfare.

Henley said, "Jake's having himself a worrisome period of late. Ailing wife, and now this Uncle Jimmy business to occupy his mind. And of course there's always a faction that wants a different sheriff in office, no matter who's in."

"Men with worries shouldn't hold public office," Murragh commented, "though I don't know how it can be stopped. The minute they get into office their worries start, even if they never had any before." He glanced from the window again, but there was no one to be seen now. "I guess I'll saunter around a spell and then turn in," he finished, stifling a yawn. "I'll see you tomorrow, Cass."

"S'long, Hoyt." Henley gestured toward the cot against the wall. "I won't be out of the hay so long myself."

Murragh emerged from the doorway and walked west a block, past a Mexican rooming house, a real estate office, a small clothing store, and a barbershop—all dark, at present, except the rooming house, which showed a light from the rear, where a soft tenor voice, accompanied by a guitar, was raised in the nostalgic strains of "El Sonoreño." Half a block farther on, the houses were spaced still farther apart, and Murragh crossed the street and started back toward the center of town.

He strode easily along, the fingertips of his right hand occasionally brushing the leather gun holster at his thigh. Ahead of him a man turned into a Mexican saloon. The swinging doors were still in motion when Murragh came abreast of the place. That was Balter, all right, Murragh mused. Now just why is he keeping tally on me? Must be Vaiden got curious as to what I'm doing here.

The next building was a Mexican restaurant, with beyond that a shabby-looking, two-story frame structure on the dirty window of which, silhouetted against the light from within, were the words, Cowman's Rest Hotel, with below, in smaller letters, Rooms—Day or Week. The building stood on the corner of Main and Tombstone streets; on a sudden impulse Murragh pushed open the door and entered.

Within, a tired-looking elderly man sat at a table which held a stack of newspapers, an oil lamp, and a dilapidated register. A few stiff-backed chairs stood about the room, which was evidently intended as a lobby. As Murragh closed the door behind him, the man raised his head from a pink-sheeted magazine and peered across the tops of his spectacles. "You lookin' for a room, mister?" His tone seemed to convey the idea that he hoped Murragh wasn't and that he was too weary to be bothered right now.

Murragh shook his head. "Looking for a man," he replied. "Thought he might be staying here. Name of Nicodemus Jabberwocky?"

The weary man's jaw dropped. "Would you repeat that name?"

"Jabberwocky—Nicodemus Jabberwocky."

The weary man made a sound like a ghostly chuckle. "Sounds just like you was sayin' Nicodemus Jabberwocky."

"That's the name."

"'Tis?" A certain indignation crept into the old man's words. "What next won't be comin' into this country? Nope, mister, he ain't here. No furriners ever stay here. Just cowhands—and then, mostly, just at beef shippin' and when they're drunk. You'd best try the Lanyard Hotel."

Murragh thanked him and asked, "Mind if I leave by your back door? I want to short-cut over to Deming Street."

"Don't make no mind to me. The door works out's well as in. Just close it tight after you. Go right down that hall yonder."

Murragh nodded, entered an open doorway across the room, and found himself in an unlighted hall that ran straight through the building. At the end of the hall was a door. Murragh opened the door, then slammed it shut without going outside. He stood there in the darkness, listening.

After a few moments he heard the front door open and shut. Voices sounded in the lobby, but Murragh couldn't distinguish the words. Again the door opened and closed. Murragh made his way back to the lobby.

The elderly man looked up in some exasperation. "Thought I heard you leave."

"I changed my mind. Wasn't that Nicodemus Jabberwocky in here a minute ago?"

"Cripes A'mighty, no! That was a feller named Balter. There's no Jabber— Say, what is this?"

"What did Balter want?"

"Wanted to know what you come in here for. I guess he was lookin' for you. I told him you'd already left by the back way."

"Why didn't you tell him it was none of his business?"

"Not me! Folks don't talk that way to Claude Balter. He irritates plumb easy." Concern crept into the elderly tones. "Look, mister, if you and this Jabber—Jabber—whatever that name was—is havin' any trouble with Balter, will you please to kindly quit usin' my doors? I don't want no ruckus here."

"Leaving right now," Murragh told him and stepped once more out onto Main Street. He took quick strides to the corner and glanced down Tombstone Street. It was too dark to see anyone, but he caught the sound of running footsteps.

After a moment the footsteps ceased. Then they recommenced, this time approaching rapidly. A thin smile crossed Murragh's face. Nothing like giving a man a run for his money, he told himself. The footsteps slowed to a walk, while Murragh stood on the corner waiting for Balter to come up with him. There weren't many people on the street now, so Balter spied Murragh almost at once.

The two exchanged glances in the uncertain light shining from the Cowman's Rest. If there was any expression of surprise in Balter's hard, agate eyes, Murragh failed to detect it. The man gave him a brief unrecognizing look and continued on across Main Street. Reaching the opposite corner, Balter halted and stood looking in Murragh's direction.

Murragh rolled and lighted a cigarette. He knows I outguessed him, Murragh speculated, but he's not sure if I did it purposely or by accident. Probably he thinks I left that Cowman's Rest joint, stepped out in the alley, and returned here—and he's wondering why. Or maybe he doesn't wonder, or think, which is what a man might judge from his face. No more expression than a chunk of gray granite. Anybody with a face like that should make a good poker hand. Well, we'll try it again and see if he's got sick of his job.

Murragh started out, walking east on Main. When he had gone a half block he stooped down, as though picking something from the sidewalk, and managed to glance toward his rear. Balter had again taken up the trail and was moving along, keeping close to the buildings he passed. As Murragh neared the Gordon stage office, where light still showed in the window, he crossed over and turned down Bowie Street in the direction of the T. N. & A. S. Railroad Station.

Reaching the station, a frame structure on a raised-dirt platform, Murragh entered a door at one end, stood for a minute scrutinizing the chalked figures on a blackboard timetable, nodded to the stationmaster behind the ticket window, and departed by a second door at the opposite end of the building. As he stepped once more into darkness his ears caught a slight sound from beyond a stack of packing cases on the station platform.

Murragh considered, He's sure a bustard to hang on. I've had enough of this. He walked swiftly back along Bowie Street, then, nearing Main, broke into a run and dashed around the corner. Once he'd made the turn, Murragh halted and wheeled into the shadowed doorway of the hay-and-feed store where he'd first spotted Balter watching him. By now the light in the stage office was gone, though a certain amount of illumination showed through the windows of the Lanyard Hotel diagonally across the way. A block to the east, Pudge Ryan's Bar still remained open. The street was in half gloom for some distance, and no one was in sight.

Murragh hadn't long to wait before he again heard running footsteps along Bowie Street. The footsteps slowed as they approached Main, then rounded the corner. Balter was just opposite the darkened recess where Murragh was concealed, when Murragh said, even-toned, "You looking for me, Balter?"

Balter halted in mid-stride. Slowly his head came around and the hard eyes probed at the shadow. Murragh drew on his cigarette, the resulting glow bringing his features into strong relief. "You shouldn't ever smoke a cigarette, Balter, when you're tailing a man," Murragh advised in the same quiet tones.

Balter ignored that. There was a kind of leashed violence about him that contrasted strangely with his flat voice when he replied, "Why should I be looking for you, Murragh? I don't even know you."

"You know my name."

"Why should I be looking for you?" Balter repeated.

"You've been following me all over town, watching my movements, ever since I left the hotel."

"You've got too much imagination for your own good, Murragh." The tone didn't rise or fall. It was flat, expressionless, non-resonant, yet hard like the man's opaque, agate eyes seen dimly now in the light from the stars.

"It wasn't my imagination that sent you into the Cowman's Rest to learn what I went in there for," Murragh said patiently.

"Anybody in the Cowman's Rest that told you that is a liar," replied the toneless voice.

Murragh continued, "Why did Vaiden tell you to trail me? What's he want to know?"

"Vaiden don't tell me what to do."

Murragh snapped away his cigarette butt. It cut a short crimson arc through the darkness, struck the road in a shower of tiny sparks and was extinguished. Murragh went on quietly, "Where's Vaiden at present?"

"I don't know, Murragh." Balter didn't seem anxious to get away. Murragh could almost sense the cold hate rising in the man, throwing out a challenge that couldn't be denied.

Murragh said again, "Where's Vaiden?"

Still there was no change in the dead voice as Balter called Murragh a name and added, "I don't know."

The back of Murragh's hand swept savagely across Balter's mouth. Balter swayed back, then his right hand darted with incredible speed to the holster at his hip. At the same instant Murragh's left hand closed on Balter's right wrist, twisted hard, and the heel of his other hand caught Balter under the chin. There was a brief, violent struggle before the gun clattered from Balter's fist and his body went sprawling across the sidewalk.

There'd been no outcry from the man, even though the wrenching of his right wrist had been extremely painful, laming. Just as Murragh retrieved Balter's gun from the sidewalk, Balter came scrambling up to hurl himself on Murragh. Murragh stepped back, swung the gun barrel in a short vicious arc that terminated on the crown of Balter's sombrero.

Balter's legs sagged, his knees struck the sidewalk. His outstretched hands saved him from going all the way down. For, a minute he crouched there on hands and knees, shaking his head as though to clear it from the effects of the blow. Then once more he clambered slowly erect and closed on Murragh again.

Murragh pushed him away without any trouble now. The man was groggy, only half conscious of what he was doing. Murragh said, "Your hat saved you that time. Next time I'll strike lower."

"Let me have my gun." Aside from being slower, there was even now no perceptible change in Balter's speech.

"Where's Vaiden?" Murragh demanded again.

"Told you I don't know. Give me my gun—"

Once more Murragh knocked him sprawling. "I can keep this up as long as you can, Balter," Murragh said, standing over the prone figure stretched half on the sidewalk, with the legs beneath a hitchrack at the edge of the road.

Balter lay without movement. Murragh flipped back the loading gate of the man's forty-five and, revolving the cylinder, removed five cartridges. When he came to the empty shell on which the hammer rested, he shoved it out with the ejector rod and dropped cartridges and shell into his pocket. By this time Balter was again struggling to his feet. "Give me that gun," he commenced.

"I'll keep on giving it to you all night long, if you insist," Murragh told him harshly. "Now it's up to you."

Balter hesitated, swaying uncertainly on his shaky legs, the milky, agate, expressionless eyes fixed on Murragh. Even now there was a viciousness about him that couldn't be disregarded. Murragh went on grimly, when Balter took a tentative step toward him, "You want some more of the same?"

"Just let me have that gun, Murragh," Balter persisted doggedly.

Murragh again raised the gun. Balter stood there, unflinching, waiting for the blow to descend. Murragh swore disgustedly: "God damn it, Balter, use your head. I can keep this up longer than you can. This gun barrel's tougher than you are. Take my advice and talk. Where's Vaiden?"

Unexpectedly, Balter gave in. A hint of sullenness entered his tone as he said, "Down to Pudge Ryan's Bar."

"That's better. All right, lead the way."

"What you want to see Vaiden for?"

"Get moving, Balter. My patience is pretty much gone. You wouldn't want to get hurt, would you?" Grim humor in that last.

Balter turned after a moment and, followed by Murragh, negotiated a wobbly-legged progress along Main Street. A pedestrian passed, glanced curiously at the pair, but kept going, without comment. At the corner of Main and Hereford streets, Balter stumbled up a flight of three steps and through the swinging doors into Pudge Ryan's Bar. Only a few customers stood within, among whom were Vaiden and Senator Welch. As Balter staggered in, Vaiden swung around and saw him. "Good God, Claude! What happened to you—?" He broke off upon catching sight of Murragh, just behind Balter; his features tightened, he said, "What's up?" Balter fell against the bar and reached for a drink that stood there. Vaiden repeated, "What's up, Murragh?"

Murragh said quietly, "I don't like being shadowed, Vaiden. Maybe you didn't realize that, or maybe Balter didn't. I don't want any more of it."

"But I don't understand—" Vaiden commenced.

"Balter works for you. He's been trailing me around town all evening. He caught himself a couple of bumps on the head and a lame wrist that will probably take a couple of days to grow strong again. If I hadn't taken his gun away somebody might have got hurt—and it wouldn't have been me. Now is it clear to you?"

"Not quite. What have I got to do with Balter's actions?"

"He's under your orders."

"Not always." Vaiden turned to Balter. "What's all this about, Claude?"

Balter, clutching the bar with one hand, swayed unsteadily. For a moment the hard agate eyes focused on Vaiden and a look passed between the two. Without speaking, Balter turned his head and reached for another drink. Senator Welch said pompously, "Well, I can't make head nor tail of this, but I'd say charges for assault are in order."

"Are you somebody I'm supposed to know?" Murragh fixed Welch with a sharp look. "Where do you come in on this business?"

Vaiden said, "This is Senator Welch—Hoyt Murragh."

Murragh nodded. "Welch, if you know any more about this than Vaiden, start talking fast. Otherwise, you'd better leave it to him."

Welch's already florid features went purple. He made certain sputtering sounds that failed to resolve themselves into words. After a moment, Murragh ignored him and turned back to Vaiden.

Vaiden said, "I can assure you, Murragh, that I know nothing—"

"You can't assure me of anything," Murragh said harshly, "so long as Balter's on your pay roll. If you want me shadowed, you'd better hire somebody with know-how—somebody I've never seen."

"Why in hell should I want you shadowed?"

Murragh snapped, "If you've forgotten, probably Balter can tell you."

"But I still can't understand what this—"

"Then maybe we're both wasting time," Murragh cut in coldly. He drew from the waistband of his trousers the six-shooter he'd taken from Balter and tossed it to the bar, where it went sliding along the already scarred surface. "When Balter regains his senses—if any—tell him to keep that gun in his holster and he won't get hurt."

Even as Murragh turned away, he heard the quick movement at the bar and then the sound of a gun hammer falling on an empty cylinder. There were further sounds of a scuffle and Vaiden's sharp, "You, Claude!" Murragh didn't look back. The men were still struggling with Balter as Murragh pushed through the swinging doors and headed toward his hotel.

12

Fighting Spirit

Uncle Jimmy Cochrane was buried the following morning. A long line of buggies and riders formed a procession and moved from the Graves undertaking establishment slowly out Tombstone Street until it reached the wire-fenced area of earth north of town known as Lanyard's Boot Hill. The services were brief, and before long the buggies and horses were hurrying back toward Main Street. Stores that had closed commenced to reopen.

Murragh hadn't attended the funeral. He was passing the Blue Star Livery when he saw Cass Henley just emerging, after having left his pony. The two men greeted each other. Cass said, "Didn't see you out to the graveyard."

Murragh shook his head. "Didn't feel called on to go. I didn't know Uncle Jimmy personally. There were a couple of other things I had to do. For one thing I slept late. Maybe there'll be some other way I can honor Uncle Jimmy to make up for not attending his funeral ceremony. It won't make any difference to him, now, either way."

"What do you mean by that?"

"Simply that Uncle Jimmy is dead and buried and—"

"No, I meant what you said about honoring him some other way."

Murragh shrugged his shoulders. "I haven't figured that all out yet."

Henley's shrewd eyes studied Murragh's face. The deputy said slowly, "As I see it, there's just one way you could honor Uncle Jimmy now. That's by discovering who murdered him. Do you mean you know?"

Murragh said again, "I haven't figured it all out yet." Henley frowned thoughtfully, but didn't say anything. Murragh went on, "Who all went to the funeral?"

"Old friends of Uncle Jimmy's. He was pretty well known in Lanyard—helped settle the town, back in the old days, you know. Linda and Silvertop were there, of course. Even 'Lonzo Vaiden."

"I saw Vaiden and Balter in saddles this morning."

"Balter didn't attend—probably he was heading back to the Rafter-AV. Senator Welch drove out to the cemetery in a buggy. That was purely for political purposes, of course. Trying to build up votes, so the next time he runs for something—" Henley broke off disgustedly. "Welch even had the nerve to give out like he'd just come to Lanyard for the funeral. Maybe he fooled some people, I don't know. Hell's bells! He couldn't have heard about Uncle Jimmy's death in time to get here, but some folks'd never stop to think about that."

"Were you talking to him?"

Henley shook his head. "I never talk to him if I can avoid the fat windbag. No, I heard it from some other people. Just to make it look good, he spread it around how he had to hurry back to the capital on the seven-ten train tonight. You'd think he had cares of state, or something, to take care of, in the interests of Lanyard County. S'help me, I'll bet half the people in this town think Welch has some sort of political appointment up there." Henley paused, frowning. "So far as concerns Vaiden being at the funeral, that was just for appearances. He don't care anything about Uncle Jimmy."

It was hot along Main Street now. The midday sun broiled down, drawing pitch from the plank sidewalks and making black shadows in the passageways between buildings. Cow ponies slumped at hitchracks, switched desultory tails at myriad flies buzzing about. Murragh watched Henley mop at his face with a blue

134

bandanna and said, "No need for us to stand here in the sun. Had your dinner yet?"

"No. I figured to eat at Joe Low's place before I went back to the office."

"Come on. I'll eat with you."

Three quarters of an hour later, as the two men walked west on Main Street, Henley said, "There goes Welch now. Looks as if he'd been in talking to the sheriff. Wonder what he wanted."

When they entered the office, the sheriff was leaning back in his desk chair, thoughtfully surveying the ceiling, a half smile on his face. Henley said, "Somebody been tickling you with a feather, Jake?"

Farley surveyed the two with amused eyes which rested longest on Murragh. He said, "Well, now, you'd never consider Senator Welch a feather, would you, Cass?"

"We saw him leaving here," Henley said. "What did he have to offer that was funny?"

"Welch claims," Farley explained, "that somebody beat the living daylights out of Claude Balter last night, and done it with Claude's own gun barrel."

"Th' hell you say!" Henley exclaimed.

"It's the sort of news I've been wanting to hear for a long time," Farley went on. "Welch wants me to arrest the feller on charges of assault and battery, and when I pointed out that Balter just got what was due him, Welch damn' nigh made a political speech to the effect that a new sheriff was needed in Lanyard."

"The son of a—! So now he figures to get your job," Henley growled. "But, say, who beat up Balter?"

Farley gestured toward Murragh. "Ask him. He can probably tell you more than I can. Besides, I'd like to hear it again."

Henley whirled on Murragh. "Did you—did you—? Cripes A'mighty! Why didn't you tell me?"

Murragh smiled. "Do you expect me to go boasting how I beat up a man smaller than I am? I didn't feel so good about it, to tell the truth, but—"

"Smaller than you hell!" Henley said. "Maybe in poundage, yes, but he's a heap stronger and more wiry than he looks."

"I know, I tussled with him some. He's tough. I thought he never would give up."

"But just what happened?" Henley wanted to know.

Murragh supplied details. When he had finished, Henley said, "Well, I'll be damned." He looked serious. "You'll have to watch out for Balter from now on. I wouldn't put it past him to shoot you from the rear. But why should Vaiden want you shadowed?"

"Probably curious to know who I was seeing in town, and why, if possible."

Farley asked. "Is there any particular reason you know of, Hoyt, why Vaiden should want such information?"

"Why don't you ask Vaiden?" Murragh said.

Farley swore. "That reminds me—Cass, do you know anybody named Jabberwocky in Lanyard?"

"Who?" Henley frowned.

"Well"—Farley looked apologetic—"it sounded like Jabberwocky. That's what Welch came in here first for—to ask if I knew anybody named Jabberwocky. I told him I didn't naturally. Then he started telling me about Murragh and Balter. The more he talked the madder he got, and he ended up by demanding I arrest Hoyt. I told him to get Balter to swear to a warrant and I'd serve it to the best of my ability, but I gathered that Balter didn't want to bother with a warrant of any sort. He probably figures to even the score in his own way. You'll have to keep your sights primed for that snake, Hoyt."

"Jabberwocky—Jabberwocky," Henley was saying. "I never heard of such a name." He looked quickly at Murragh. "What you chuckling about? Is this Jabberwocky got something to do with you?"

"I reckon it has. Last night when I wanted to make sure Balter was shadowing me, I dropped into the Cowman's Rest and asked if they had anybody staying there by the name of Jabberwocky. It was the first name that popped into my head—danged if I know why. Anyway, I was no sooner gone than Balter came in and asked who I'd been looking for . . ." Murragh furnished more details from that point on. He concluded, "If that doesn't prove that Balter was keeping cases on me, I don't know anything that does."

"You've made a bad enemy, Hoyt," Farley said.

"I'm not sure I'd want Balter's kind for a friend, anyway," Murragh said quietly. "I've got to admit he can take punishment, and he kept coming back for more. And all the time, no change in his voice, no expression in those dead eyes of his. It was like when you're putting a snake out of the way. The snake doesn't make any noise, and its eyes watch you just as deadly and it fights the same way when it's cornered."

"Balter always did remind me of a sidewinder," Henley observed.

They talked a while longer before Murragh prepared to leave. Farley said, "Just in case there is an assault warrant served for your arrest, Hoyt, do you figure to come quiet?"

Murragh's smile matched Farley's. "We'll worry about that problem when it comes up," he said. "I don't figure Balter will swear to any warrant, though."

He cuffed his sombrero at a straighter angle on his head and left the building. Half a block along Main Street he saw Vaiden and Welch approaching. Welch looked as though he intended to stop and talk, but Vaiden seized his arm and with a short nod they hurried past.

Murragh continued on until he'd reached the stage company's office. Here he turned in. Linda and Silvertop were there. Silvertop was seated at the desk behind the counter partition. Linda was standing near the doorway, talking to a tall muscular man, in overalls, with an unshaven face and shifty eyes. The girl spoke to Murragh when he entered and then she turned back to the man.

"It's no good, Twitchell," Murragh heard the girl say. "You had your chance. No, Bert Echardt will be taking Uncle Jimmy's place. Later, if I need a station attendant, I'll let you know—if I decide to use you."

That was all Murragh heard. Silvertop hailed him, "Glad to see you, Hoyt. Come back and rest your boots a mite." He shoved a chair in Murragh's direction. Murragh heard the door close, then Linda came back and joined him and her father. Silvertop said, "What did Twitchell want?"

"A job driving stage. He thought with Uncle Jimmy gone there'd be a place for him. . . . How are you today, Mr. Murragh?"

"I'm doing very well, Miss Gordon."

Silvertop snorted. "Miss Gordon! Mr. Murragh! Seems to me if you know a girl well enough to save her life it's time to drop the formalities. Saying 'Hoyt' and 'Linda' would be simpler and a heap more friendly-sounding."

Murragh said seriously, "What do you think, Linda?"

"Sounds all right to me, Hoyt," the girl smiled.

Silvertop said, "I hear you had a little run-in with Claude Balter last night."

"Where'd you hear that?" Murragh asked.

"With Balter?" Linda looked surprised. "Dad, you didn't tell me about that."

"You're so busy with the stage business you probably wouldn't have had time to listen." He turned back to Murragh. "Friend of mine was telling me. He was in Pudge Ryan's place last night when you come along, herding Balter in front of you. I guess you must have talked turkey to Vaiden too."

Murragh briefly sketched what had happened and then answered questions. No, he hadn't any idea why Balter should have been following him around.

A small frown appeared between Linda's eyes. "Well now, if you were a detective and were looking for somebody in Lanyard and if Vaiden or his men had

139

committed a crime," she speculated, "I'd say there was a reason."

"When you tell me what crime Vaiden and his men have committed," Murragh smiled, "maybe we can go to work on that theory. And if I was a detective I'd probably be asking for information on everybody around Lanyard. For instance, I might ask who that was you were talking to when I came in here."

"That was Barney Twitchell," Linda replied. "He drove stage for us at one time, but I had to fire him for being drunk. He was hard on the horses too—always ready to use his whip. No driver that knows his business overworks a whip. No, Twitchell will never get a chance to work for us again."

"What does he do now?" Murragh asked.

"Not much of anything, so far as I know. Said he hadn't been able to get a job. Trying to work on my sympathy, I imagine. He may not have a job, but his breath smelled like a distillery."

"Whisky isn't free, so he gets money someplace," Silvertop pointed out.

"I suppose he gets odd jobs here and there," Linda said carelessly. "Let's forget Twitchell and tell me how I can assure the Silver Belle pay roll going through intact Friday. That's what's worrying me right now."

"And every Friday," Silvertop added.

Murragh said, "A few years back, down in Texas, there was one stage line that made a business of carrying valuables frequently. It always had a guard with it—twelve riders, fully armed and ready for trouble."

"That was probably one of the Butterfield divisions,"

Linda said. "The Butterfield lines can afford that sort of expense. The Gordon company is small potatoes compared to Butterfield. My grief, Hoyt, do you realize what I'd have to pay for such a guard?"

"Never gave it much thought."

"Think it over. Twelve riders, with a change of horses at each station. We'd use the men only two days a week—a trip up and a trip back—but such guards don't come cheap. They run certain risks, and as the two days' work prevents them taking any other job, we'd have to pay for the whole week. That would wipe out profits. And we need every cent of profit. No, Hoyt, some way has simply got to be found to stop those holdup men, break up their gang. If not, the Gordon company is finished." The frown that had gathered on her brow vanished suddenly, and she said, "Have you any more bright suggestions for operating a stage line, Hoyt?"

"If so, I'd better keep 'em to myself. I'm learning I know less and less about your business. I'm no authority—"

Silvertop chuckled. "You could at least give us a testimonial regarding the safety and good riding qualities of our coaches. That's something you've had experience with."

"I reckon you're right. At that, there is one thing that puzzles me. Why do you use those leather thorough braces in place of steel springs? Surely, steel springs would hold up better."

"That's just where you're wrong," Linda replied. "Those thorough braces are cut from mighty tough hide. They allow the coach to swing back and forth and sidewise, as well as up and down. That helps take some of the strain from the horses too. No steel spring has yet been invented that will do the work or stand up under the roads in the West . . ."

From that point, Linda fell into a discussion of coach and wheel construction, drivers she had known, horses, the speeds that had been made over various routes. Murragh found his respect for the girl's knowledge increasing. The minutes flew rapidly past.

Suddenly the girl paused, her color heightening. "I guess it's just about time I called a halt and let somebody else talk for a while."

"You certainly know your subject," Murragh congratulated her.

"I should. Uncle Angus—he used to own this company, you know—drilled the business into me from the time I was a small girl. I wish you could have heard him talk. And the fight he had on his hands when he first started this stage line! Other companies tried to crowd him out. Then suddenly all the trouble stopped, and he had clear going from then on. But for a time the competition was pretty fierce, until the rival lines were forced to quit." Her chin came up determinedly. "And that's just the way we're going to hang on, too. Nothing's going to stop the Gordon line from operating."

Murragh's heart warmed to the girl's fighting spirit. "Don't worry too much about next Friday's Silver Belle pay roll, Linda," he advised. "I've a hunch it's going through all right."

The girl eyed him narrowly. "It that hunch based on anything in particular?"

"Maybe."

"Meaning what?" Silvertop cut in, looking curiously at Murragh.

"Suppose we let it go as is," Murragh suggested. "I'll know more after Friday." He changed the subject. "How about you two eating supper with me tonight?"

"Not tonight," Linda said. "We always stay in the office until the stage arrives. The time varies. Sometimes it's late." She smiled. "But don't think we won't accept the invitation for some night when the northbound trip is on. A free meal is a free meal, and nobody of Gordon blood ever passes one up."

"Meanwhile," Silvertop said, "I don't know of any particular reason, Hoyt, why you and I shouldn't step around to the hotel bar and try some of its beer. It's a hot day, and beer's mighty satisfactual when the sun's streaming down."

Murragh smiled. "I never had to use the sun for an excuse. Let's try it under those conditions."

13

Secret Departure

Murragh was at the T. N. & A. S. station when the seven-ten train departed that night, carrying with it Senator Welch on his way back to the capital. Alonzo Vaiden had accompanied Welch to the depot to see him off, but neither man appeared to notice Murragh. There were several men standing about the platform—the usual loungers who managed to meet every train—so Welch and Vaiden may have failed to see him, though Murragh thought otherwise. When the train had pulled out on its westward journey, Vaiden turned and walked swiftly up Bowie Street, toward Main.

One by one the other people headed back to the center of town until only Murragh was left standing on the platform, lost in thought. It was growing dark now. To Murragh's right, beyond the distant peaks of the San Xavier Mountains, the setting sun still reflected a faint crimson glow, but overhead faint stars were already winking into existence. To the south, across a vast expanse of sand and alkali, cactus and greasewood, a low-lying range of mauve ridges marked the existence of Old Mexico.

The light from kerosene lamps shone through the station windows. Murragh turned and entered the building, after a time, and wrote out a telegram. The station agent took the paper, read it through, then glanced at Murragh. "You're not the deputy sheriff," he said.

"Did I claim to be?" Murragh asked quietly. "Cass couldn't get down here right now. He'll be looking for the reply."

The agent nodded. "I'll send him word when it comes in."

"You don't need to bother. Cass will be around to pick up the answer." He paused, then, "It's something we wouldn't want mentioned."

The station man said stiffly, "There'll be no talk from here."

"That's the way I figured it would be."

Murragh left the depot and sauntered through the gathering gloom to Main Street. Here the illumination from several windows cast yellow rectangles of light across sidewalks and dusty roadway and reflected upward, throwing into faint relief, against the darker sky, the false fronts of the various buildings.

Entering his hotel, Murragh ascended to the second floor. He knocked first at the door of Number 11, Russ Kennard's room. There was no answer. Murragh went into his own room then and waited for a time. He rummaged through his satchel, closed it again, and returned the grip to its place beneath the bed. Leaving the room, he closed and locked his door and again knocked at Number 11. Still no answer.

Murragh descended the stairway, his sardonic features set in a scowl. On the street once more he started to make a round of the saloons. Kennard wasn't to be found in any of them, though in Pudge Ryan's Bar Murragh saw Vaiden talking to the man whom Linda had been conversing with that afternoon. As Murragh entered, Vaiden and the man—his name, Murragh remembered, was Twitchell—immediately separated, and Twitchell hurriedly departed from the saloon.

Vaiden made his way along the bar, where Murragh was buying a bottle of beer. "I'd like to see you a minute, Murragh."

Murragh deliberately poured beer into a glass, studied

145

the amber liquid and foam a moment, tasted it, and replaced the glass on the bar. Only then did he glance at Vaiden. "You see me," he said quietly.

"About that misunderstanding last night," Vaiden commenced. "That could have—"

"What misunderstanding?"

"Why, that little trouble you had with Claude Balter."

Murragh said flatly, "It wasn't a misunderstanding—and it wasn't any trouble for me, either."

"But you've got Claude all wrong."

"Could anyone get him any other way?"

"Now if you're going to take that attitude—" Vaiden commenced.

"I didn't open this conversation."

"I'm just trying to make you understand that Balter's a good man—he's no troublemaker." Vaiden's face was getting red.

"All right." More of the beer vanished down Murragh's throat.

"I seem to be having a hard time"—Vaiden's words came awkwardly—"making you understand exactly what I mean."

"That's all right, too," Murragh said quietly. He finished his glass, left the remainder of the beer in the bottle, and headed toward the swinging doors, leaving Vaiden muttering resentfully at the bar.

Murragh returned to the hotel. He asked the clerk, "Has Kennard been up to his room recently?"

The clerk shook his head. "I haven't seen him since suppertime."

"He was here then?"

"He and a young lady—Miss Fanchon—ate in the dining room."

Murragh left the hotel, cursing his own stupidity. "Why in the devil," he muttered, "didn't I think of looking in the dining room in the first place?"

He made his way down the street until he'd reached the sheriff's office. Farley wasn't there. Cass Henley sat at the desk, the suspended oil lamp casting light on the open pages of one of his red-bound volumes. He closed the book as Murragh entered and sat down. "I was wondering where you were."

"I've been around town, one place and another. Cass, I took the liberty of signing your name to a telegram tonight."

"'He that filches from me my good name—'" the deputy commenced, smiling.

"I didn't filch your name, Iago," Murragh said dryly, "—just signed it as deputy sheriff of Lanyard County. Some information I wanted and didn't care to sign my own—not knowing anything about that fellow down to the depot."

"Joe Phelan? Oh, he's all right. Keeps his mouth shut pretty much."

"That's good. I'll appreciate it if you'll collect the answer to the telegram I sent off, if I'm not here."

"Where you going?"

Murragh didn't answer that. Instead, "I'd like to get out of town without being noticed. If I come riding out of the Blue Star Livery on that sorrel gelding—"

"Better let me get that horse and meet you someplace. No, wait." Henley frowned, considering.

"What's on your mind?"

"It wouldn't fool Tony, down to the Blue Star, if I took out that sorrel. He'd figure it was for you. If anybody got inquisitive, Tony might talk."

"And what do we do about it?"

"You take that gray pony of mine. He wouldn't have the speed of the sorrel in a short dash, but over a long ride I think he'd have a shade more stamina."

"Who said anything about a long ride?" Murragh demanded.

"Nobody." Henley's shrewd eyes twinkled. "There's no law against a guess, is there? When do you want the horse?"

"About ten or ten-thirty tonight."

Henley consulted his watch. "You want to slip away without anybody knowing it. All right, I'll have the gray waiting for you in the alley between the hotel and the Gordon stage barns, shortly after ten."

"Will the hombre at the Blue Star think anything about you taking the horse out?"

"It's my horse. Just to keep his mind quiet I'll tell him the blacksmith at the Gordon barns is going to do a job of shoeing for me first thing in the morning. That blacksmith always takes care of my pony's hoofs, so it will sound all right."

"And do you always saddle up to take your horse a block away, when you could lead him just as well?"

"Cripes, yes! Ever know a horseman to walk—even a block—if he could get out of it? No, Tony won't think anything about that. We can adjust the stirrup straps, if necessary, when I meet you with the gray."

" '*Sta bueno*. When I get back, Cass, maybe I'll be able to explain all this—"

" 'Tain't necessary. What I don't know, I can't spill accidentally."

Murragh left the sheriff's office, crossed Tombstone Street diagonally to the other side of Main, and continued east. Half a block farther on, he came to Isabel Fanchon's hat shop. Murragh glanced through the window. A lamp, turned low, burned on a table within. There was a varied assortment of hats and bonnets on stands and on a long shelf at one side. A carpet of a neutral gray covered the floor. At the rear of the room a nearly closed door showed a crack of light from Miss Fanchon's living quarters.

Murragh tried the front door and found it locked. Then he knocked. Through the glass in the door he saw the inner door open and shut quickly, as Isabel Fanchon appeared, dressed in a loose dress covered with a large pink floral pattern. The black shiny curls were piled high on her head. Murragh heard the lock click. As the door started to open, he pushed on in, then closed it quickly behind him.

Isabel Fanchon sounded startled at the abrupt entrance. "Who—who is it? Oh, it's you, Mr. Murragh. Why, how nice of you to call." She laughed softly, self-consciously. "Isn't it a little late, though? People in this town have a habit of talking . . ." The words died into silence and she came a little closer. A strong perfume filled the room, making Murragh conscious of her warm vitality. She went on, "I really don't think you should stay. Some other night, when we can plan—"

"This isn't exactly a call, Miss Fanchon." Murragh stood, hat in hand. "You see, I thought perhaps you could tell me where Russ Kennard is."

"Have you tried the hotel? We had supper together, and then—" She paused, looking at Murragh. Murragh's nostrils twitched as he sniffed at the air. The girl laughed. "You've noticed my perfume. Do you like it? It's a new kind—in fact, a present from Russ."

"Not perfume—tobacco," Murragh said.

"I guess I'll have to confess," Isabel Fanchon laughed throatily. "I do enjoy a cigarette when no one's around to see me."

"Except friends, of course."

"Except friends," the girl admitted.

Murragh said dryly. "I hadn't noticed any cigarette smoke—just cigar smoke."

Before she could stop him, Murragh had reached the door to the living quarters and flung it open. It was rather cozily furnished, with a bedroom and kitchen beyond. At a table, near a window with the shade drawn, sat Russ Kennard. There was a bottle of cheap wine, a whisky flask, and two glasses on the table. Kennard put down his cigar as Murragh entered.

"Hello, Hoyt," he said, rather shamefaced.

"Thought I might find you here," Murragh said quietly.

Isabel Fanchon put in, breathlessly, "Mr. Murragh, what will you think of me? I should have told you Russ was here, but it was getting late, and a lady doesn't entertain— Oh, you know what I mean. I can't bear to think what your opinion of me—"

"Don't give it a thought, Miss Fanchon," Murragh said. "My opinion formed the first day I met you, hasn't changed in the slightest."

"It's so nice of you to say that. You're really gallant."

"Thank you." Murragh turned to Kennard. "I take it you're about ready to leave."

"I'd been gone in another five minutes," Kennard said. "Be right with you, soon's I get my hat."

The hat was found after a few minutes, and Isabel Fanchon followed the two men to the front door. "May I hope you'll call again, Mr. Murragh?"

"I'd like to, thanks."

"Just have Russ bring you any time—or come alone if Russ happens to be busy."

Kennard looked jealously at the woman, but he didn't say anything, beyond "Good night," in which he was joined by Murragh. The door closed behind them, and the light in the shop was extinguished.

"Where we going?" Kennard asked sullenly, as Murragh started toward the hotel.

"You're going to bed. Don't forget, you're going to catch the stage to Millman City in the morning and come down with the Silver Belle pay roll Friday morning."

"I hadn't forgotten, Hoyt. I was about ready to leave Isabel's when you arrived. Do you think it was necessary to bust in on us that way?"

"Yes, I did. I had to make sure, Russ. I don't want you to miss that stage, come morning."

"You act as though you thought I'd get drunk or something."

"That's possible, isn't it?" Murragh asked dryly.

"Not tonight. I just had a couple of drinks at Isabel's—"

They broke off, upon reaching the hotel. Murragh said, "You'd better have the clerk wake you up at about a quarter to six in the morning."

Obediently, but still nettled, Kennard left word to be called. Murragh accompanied him up the stairway and waited while Kennard unlocked his door. They went in. Kennard was swearing under his breath while he lighted the kerosene lamp. Murragh said, "All right, get your clothes off and get in bed."

"Look here, Hoyt, you're getting mighty bossy."

Murragh's features went hard. "I can get a hell of a lot bossier, too, if you don't do as I say. I told you yesterday, Russ, that I wasn't going to stand any monkey business. I've been losing too damn' much sleep over your fool antics, and I'm sick of it."

"But I really intended to make that stage in the morning."

"That makes two of us agreed on that point."

Kennard subsided, undressed, and crawled into bed. Murragh drew a small flask of whisky from his pocket and placed it on the dresser. He smiled slightly. "I got this, thinking you might get thirsty during the night, Russ. There's just enough there to make you sleep sound, and not enough to do any harm."

"Geez!" Kennard brightened. "You're a pretty right hombre."

"Glad you think so." Murragh blew out the flame in the lamp chimney, then paused a moment in the

152

doorway. "But you won't think I'm a right hombre, Russ, if I wake up and find you still in Lanyard. I aim to sleep late in the morning, but you'd better be gone when I wake up. I don't intend to stand for any more of your shilly-shallying. We've got a job to do. Good night."

"Good night, Hoyt." Kennard's voice sounded very meek.

Murragh closed the door, went to his own door, opened it and slammed it shut again without entering. He moved softly back to the door of Number 11 and listened closely. Kennard was moving about. Murragh caught swallowing sounds, then the noise made by an empty flask as it dropped on the floor. Next came the creaking of bedsprings as Kennard crawled back.

Murragh straightened up and moved silently away from the door. A lamp burned dimly at the end of a passageway leading to the rear of the building. His feet made no sound as they carried Murragh to a window at the end of the passageway. He paused a moment, musing: I think that flask will keep him in bed until he's called.

He pushed up the window and glanced out. Just below was the roof of a shed built against the rear wall of the hotel. Murragh slipped through to the roof and closed the window as his feet touched the boards. Then he moved down the slanting roof and dropped to the ground in the alley. A few yards away Cass Henley and the waiting horse made a blurred mass in the gloom.

Henley spoke in a whisper: "A professional burglar couldn't have done that any better."

153

Murragh crawled up on the gray pony, turned up the collar of his coat. A chill breeze was blowing through the alley now. He settled himself in the saddle, gathered the reins after a moment. "You guessed right about the stirrups," he said.

"I'm glad to know some of my guesses are right."

"Cass, Russ Kennard is in bed in his room now. He's due to catch the stage for Millman City in the morning. If it looks as though he wouldn't make it, will you rout him out and put him on—?"

"If I have to kill him to do it. But what reason—?"

"I don't think you'll have to. If you do, just tell him it's a chore I gave you. If he wants to know where I am, tell him the first thing that comes into your mind. But I think he'll make it without any trouble. I just don't want to chance him missing it, that's all."

"I'll take care of it. Anything else?"

"Sort of keep tabs on Isabel Fanchon. Let me know where she goes, who she sees."

"Isabel—?"

"Didn't you tell me she was Vaiden's girl?"

"She was, until Kennard took over. Vaiden's not in the swim any more. I've been expecting trouble from that direction, too. I'll take care of it. Anything more you want?"

"Just want to say thanks for the help."

"Forget it."

Murragh nodded. "I'll be seeing you, Cass."

"S'long. I think you're going to like that pony. S'long."

Murragh turned the gray out of the alley and north on

Bowie Street. All the way to the edge of town he didn't see a soul. The street was dark and silent. Once away from the buildings, he touched the gray lightly with his spurs, and the animal picked up speed.

14

Holdup

Murragh rode steadily all night, swinging wide when he passed Peyote Flat Station. He wasn't pushing the horse hard; just traveling fast enough to put the maximum distance to his rear without tiring the rugged little animal. The stars wheeled overhead while the pony's steadily drumming hoofs left mile after mile behind. Dry Bone was passed a few miles to the east, but a short distance farther on a ranch house provided a rest and water for the horse. By this time Murragh was nearly opposite Cottonwood Springs. He was invited to eat breakfast with the cowhands in the ranch crew, but declined with thanks on the ground he was in a hurry, and again pushed on.

It was midmorning when he pulled into Sulphur Tanks. Here he directed the weary pony to a reliable-looking livery stable and, after giving directions for its care, hired another horse and changed his saddle. Smoke was belching from the stacks of the Silver Belle Mine smelter. A few miners were seen on the streets of the soot-smudged town, but not many of them; most had already been working for hours. Murragh stopped at a shabby-looking restaurant and wolfed down flapjacks, coffee and greasy bacon, then once more climbed into his saddle and took a course that would avoid his passing the Sulphur Tanks stage station. Once more in open country, he spurred ahead.

The new horse was cranky—a rawboned buckskin animal with wild eyes—and inclined to buck, and then to race. Once it bad been straightened out, under Murragh's firm reining, however, it proved to be a good traveler and finished the remaining distance to Millman City with only three stops for rest and water.

Late that night Murragh sat in the back room of a saloon with Wyatt Holliday, marshal of Millman City, a man both feared and trusted. His ready guns and indomitable spirit had brought law and order to the town months before, and now the better-class citizens were ready to give him anything he asked for. The two men had drinks before them. Murragh had lines about his eyes; he looked fagged from his long ride.

". . . and that's the story," Murragh concluded. "Will you help me out?"

"Cripes A'mighty, yes!" Wyatt Holliday replied promptly. "But does it have to be done that way?" Concern showed in the hawklike features. "You look pretty well beat down now, and by the time you've made the return trip—"

"Don't worry about me," Murragh cut in impatiently.

"You know best. Y'know,"—Holliday's words came awkwardly—"I keep thinking of that blunder I made that morning. Damned if I know what got into me, going up and calling you by name that way. I should have known you were on a job and didn't want to be recognized. I just didn't think, that's all, it was such a surprise seeing you. The words just popped out before I could stop 'em. I sure hope I didn't do any harm."

"No lasting harm." Murragh smiled wearily. "I had some notion of appearing in Lanyard under another name, but I figure it's best the way things turned out. Kennard hasn't fooled anybody, I believe, and if I was seen talking to him, folks could put two and two together. No, you recognizing me didn't bother me any. I like to play my cards the way they fall. Besides, you got my note that morning and that helps, so just forget it. I never did like sailing under false colors—even in a good cause."

"And you think Linda Gordon's got a good cause?" Holliday asked shrewdly.

"Never saw a better," Murragh replied promptly.

"She's a danged nice girl—and a fighter. Chip off the old block, and even more interested in stagecoachin'. I've run across Silvertop a few times. They don't come any better than Silvertop Gordon."

Murragh glanced at his watch. "If you're going to help me, Wyatt," he hinted, "I think we should get started."

Holliday's stern features relaxed a little. "Same old Hoyt," he commented, "always anxious to get going."

"I've told you how things stand," Murragh said irritably.

"Of course you have, Hoyt. I know what we're doing. You're just touchy 'cause you're fagged. You leave things to me."

"I'm sorry, Wyatt. I don't want to be critical. I just thought—"

"Stop thinking for a spell. I'm going to take you down to my place and see that you get into my blankets for a couple of hours. When things are ready, I'll come wake you up and we'll start—"

"You can handle it without me?"

"Maybe better. Quicker, leastwise. You'd have to do some talking. With me—well, folks in Millman City give me what I ask for and no questions. . . . Yeah, I'll get that bronc for you, too. From now on you don't think of a thing except the two hours' shut-eye ahead of you."

"I'm plenty appreciative, Wyatt."

"Don't talk like a damned fool. I haven't forgotten you lent a hand when you were with the Rangers, 'bout five years back. I'm just glad for a chance to return the compliment. Come on, we'll head for my place."

Murragh rose wearily and followed Holliday out of the saloon.

When the stage left for Lanyard from Millman City the following morning, Russ Kennard was seated on top, on the seat behind the shotgun guard. He had arrived in Millman City on the stage the previous night, went at once to a hotel, and spent the rest of the evening in the hotel bar, after leaving a call for early in the morning. He had imbibed more than his share of the juice that supposedly cheers, but managed to get down to the coach in plenty of time before it departed. At that time there were still seats within the coach, but Kennard, apparently, preferred the top for riding. Perhaps he felt he needed the air.

From his seat atop the waiting coach he watched with interest while two men staggered out of a bank across the street, carrying between them a heavy strongbox which was hoisted with some muscular effort to the top of the coach. The shotgun guard who accompanied them from the bank and who had watched alertly while the box was placed on top had kept his weapon ready for instant trouble, if trouble came. But none came, and the guard relaxed as he mounted to the top of the vehicle and dropped on the seat beside the driver, Zach Decker. Zach picked up the reins and prepared to depart. He had a world of faith in this new guard. After all, the great Wyatt Holliday had recommended the man to Linda Gordon, and anybody with Wyatt Holliday's recommendation simply had to be all right.

The coach rolled out of Millman City and into open country. Dust Creek and Fishhook Stations were reached and stops made to change horses in the usual manner. It wasn't until the coach was some twelve miles out of Fishhook, with Sulphur Tanks the next stop on the schedule, that trouble came.

At this point the road narrowed where it passed between two thick clumps of mesquite and sagebrush. There was a turn to negotiate a bend here, and to Zach Decker the first indication of trouble was two thundering gun explosions. Decker endeavored to manipulate the reins to check the horses, but his maneuver came too late: the span of leaders broke step, stumbled, and went crashing into the dust, the swing horses behind overrunning them as the wheelers crowded in from the rear. In an instant it was all a confused blur of tangled harness, snorting horses, and kicking hoofs. The coach jolted to a sudden stop in the road, and a voice came from the brush, harsh and demanding, "Up with your hands, you coach-ridin' sons!"

Decker had his hands full with the frantic horses. At the sound of the shots, the guard had started to swing his shotgun into action, but before he could move he found himself clasped around the arms from behind, and heard Russ Kennard's wild tones: "Don't shoot, don't shoot! They'll kill us!" Kennard cried in shaking tones. "Give 'em what they want. For God's sake, do as they say!"

The guard cursed and struggled, but taken unawares as he was, found the shotgun jerked from his grasp before he could prevent it. Kennard threw the shotgun behind him, out of reach, then flung both arms in the air. "Take what you want. Just don't shoot us," he begged hoarsely.

There were three passengers in the stage, below. They offered no resistance of any sort. Decker was still sawing on the reins, trying to quiet the horses. The shotgun guard glared furiously at Kennard, then resignedly raised his hands in the air.

"That's better," came the voice from the brush. "You fellers do as we say and nobody won't get hurt."

The guard was still cursing Kennard in low, monotonous tones. Kennard didn't reply, but glanced nervously on both sides of the coach, where gun barrels were sticking through the tangled brush. Here and there he could glimpse a sombrero through the leaves. He tried to determine the number of bandits that had ambushed the coach and managed to count eight gun barrels pointing through the mesquite.

Now, from the other side of the coach, came a new voice: "You on top, throw down that strongbox. We need it more'n you. Hurry up about it!"

The shotgun guard growled. "T'hell with you, you scut!"

"Throw it down pronto, or I'm boring you—"

"Don't be a fool," Kennard urged. "Do as they say. They'll kill us—"

"You got the right idea, mister," the hidden bandit said to Kennard. "You throw it down."

Kennard moved with alacrity, pushed the box to the edge of the railing, tugged it over the edge and gave it a push. The box landed on a corner, digging a triangular pit in the dirt at the side of the wheel ruts.

"That's good!" The first bandit spoke again. "You, driver, cut those dead animals from harness and get out of here."

Zach Decker climbed down and with his knife cut such of the harness as it was impossible to save. All the time he was working, he was receiving from the hidden voices in the brush instructions to "make it pronto!"

"God damn it," Decker swore, "I'm working as fast's I know how. If you scuts can do any better come out here."

"None of your lip, driver," a voice said ominously. "Just get a move on."

Zach sweated and tugged at buckled straps and swore. Finally he backed the wheelers and the coach retreated a few yards. Again he climbed up to the driver's seat and, with only four horses, swung the vehicle around the dead horses in the road, listlessly cracked his whip and again got under way. The instant he was out of view, two masked men slipped from the brush, seized the handles of the strongbox and quickly carried it out of the road.

Meanwhile, on top of the coach, the shotgun guard was bitterly cursing out Kennard: "You yeller-bellied, no-good, doublecrossin', gall-sored son of a—"

"Now look here," Kennard endeavored to placate the guard, "use some sense. If you'd started to shoot, we'd all been killed. Why should I—or any of us—risk our lives to save the Silver Belle pay roll? It isn't as though the miners will lose anything. The money'll be made good, and it won't be out of your pocket or mine. Best of all, we didn't get shot—"

"Damn your sneaking hide," the guard spoke savagely, "if you hadn't double-crossed me by yanking that gun outten my hands, I could've plugged a couple of them bustards—"

"If I didn't have my hands full with these ribbons," Zach Decker growled, "I'd kick your goddam face in—"

"You lousy, spavined, two-bit sneaking rat of a flea-bit sidewinder . . ." The shotgun guard was started again. His bitter flow of denunciatory invective continued the

162

remainder of the way to Sulphur Tanks, where guards and drivers, as well as horses, were changed.

There was considerable excitement about the stage station when news of the holdup was reported, and those standing about the stage cast contemptuous looks in Russ Kennard's direction. Before the stage resumed its journey, Kennard descended on the far side of the vehicle and slunk inside, to remain there the rest of the trip to Lanyard, the only other passenger in the coach eying him with undisguised disdain and refusing all attempts at conversation.

15

The Right Hunch

The coach had scarcely stopped in front of the Lanyard Hotel that evening before Russ Kennard had slipped out and hurried furtively into the building and up to his room. Linda had come out of her office the instant the vehicle halted. The shotgun guard and Bert Echardt hadn't yet climbed down when Linda asked, "Did the Silver Belle pay roll get through all right, Bert?"

Echardt shook his head. "Can't rightly say it did, Miss Linda. The stage was held up just the other side of Sulphur Tanks."

The guard, Obie Nordwall by name, had reached the sidewalk by this time. He growled bitterly: "Yeah, they got the strongbox."

Linda's slim shoulders drooped; she bit her lip, then forced a wan smile. "All right, boys, take the stage around to the stables and then come back and tell me about it."

As she turned back to the stage office, Silvertop met her at the doorway. "Did I hear 'em say the pay roll had been taken?"

Linda gulped and nodded her head. Silvertop swore under his breath. "The game seems to be running against us. I thought, maybe, after the way Hoyt talked—"

"I was counting on that too," Linda wailed. "I thought—I thought—oh, darn it, I don't know what I thought!" She brushed at her eyes, and Silvertop followed her, speechless, back into the office.

A minute later Cass Henley pushed open the door. Linda saw him entering, and her words burst forth, "The Silver Belle pay roll was lifted again."

Henley replied soberly, "Yes, I was just talking to Echardt. I didn't get the details. He said he'd be in and give us the story in a minute."

Silvertop said, "I'd like Hoyt to hear what happened. Haven't seen him all day. Where is he?"

"He's around someplace, I guess," Henley said vaguely.

Bert Echardt and Obie Nordwall entered a few minutes later.

Linda tried to smile bravely. "Well, boys, it looks as if that new guard, Steve Jenkins, didn't turn out so good. After the recommendation Wyatt Holliday gave him, I felt sure our strongbox would be—"

"Wait a minute, Miss Linda," Echardt said. "You can't blame him. Nor Zach Decker either. Obie and me talked to both of 'em before we took out the coach and . . ." From that point he gave the story as he had received it from Decker and Jenkins. ". . . so you see," he concluded, "with the leaders being shot and Decker having his hands full with the horses, and that Kennard coyote grabbing onto Jenkins thataway, there wasn't much could be done."

"It was Kennard's fault, then," Linda said. "I didn't see him get off the stage tonight. I knew he left yesterday morning—"

"The dirty scut sneaked off almost before we'd rolled to a stop," Echardt said indignantly. "I saw him tailing it into the hotel. He's so yellow that—" He turned to Henley: "Cass, couldn't you arrest him and hold him responsible?"

"Not unless you could prove he was working with the bandits. There's no law that prevents a man from getting scared that I know of. Besides, what he did was done up in Mescalero County. That's up to the sheriff at Millman City. It looks to me like you'd just have to blame it all on Kennard's losing his head, but I don't know what can be done to him—legally, that is. I have an idea of my own on the subject—"

"You should have heard Decker and Steve Jenkins," Obie Nordwall put in. "It wouldn't have taken much for those two to have plumb annihilated Kennard."

Linda shook her head. "We can't hold passengers responsible for what happens—not and stay in business. Whatever was done to Kennard, it wouldn't bring back two horses and that pay roll. I can forbid him the use of our transportation from now on, though."

Around eleven o'clock that night Cass Henley heard a noise at the doorway of the sheriff's office. Farley had long since left for home, and Henley was improving his time with a volume of *Macbeth*. He glanced up as a spur jangled against the doorstep, to see Murragh leaning against the jamb looking gaunt and unshaven and weary-eyed.

Murragh said gravely, "That little gray horse of yours is a good traveler."

"Thought you'd like him a lot. Do I have to ask where you've been?"

Murragh came in, closed the door behind him, and dropped to a chair across from the desk. "You don't have to ask. I'll tell you—Millman City."

Henley stared. "Millman City! I thought maybe that's—but still that's about two hundred fifty miles you've covered since you left here."

Murragh scowled. "My saddle muscles are flabby as hell. Stage and train travel will ruin this country yet. It's a long spell since I made a ride like that. I could have been back sooner, but I didn't want to kill your pony. . . . No, I didn't ride him all the way. Left him at Sulphur Tanks while I hired another horse. Your pony's down to the livery. There's nothing wrong with him that rest, feed, and water won't cure."

"At the livery? I thought you didn't want Tony to know you'd been out of town."

"It doesn't make any difference now. Anybody ask for me yesterday or today?"

"One or two people. I evaded the questions. There's a rumor around town that you're here to buy the stage

166

company. Vaiden asked me about it today."

"What did he have to say?"

"Asked me if it was true. He maintained he didn't think it was, that something else brought you here. He was fishing for information. I said good-by to him and said I had to meet you at dinnertime and that I'd ask you about it. So he thinks you were in town today."

"Good. What news on Isabel Fanchon?"

"Vaiden called on her last night, so maybe she's through with Kennard. Oh yes, Kennard left on the stage Thursday morning, so I didn't have to rouse him out—that reminds me, the stage was held up today and the Silver Belle pay roll lifted— Hey, you're not listening!"

Murragh had been staring at the floor. Now he looked up and smiled slightly. "I heard you. I had a hunch the stage would be stopped."

"Kennard"—Henley swore—"lost his head and grabbed the guard to prevent him from shooting. . . ." Henley told the rest of the story, adding, "You don't seem surprised."

Murragh said heavily, "Maybe I know Kennard."

"I'd like to kick his face in—oh yes, I got the reply to that telegram you sent. Who's Twitchell Barnett?"

"Let's see the telegram."

Henley produced a half sheet of blue paper with words written on it and signed with the name of a Texas county sheriff. It read:

Warrant still out for Twitchell Barnett, known as Twitch, who escaped from jail three years ago while

167

being held for trial involving implication in horse-stealing gang. Description: Six feet, two inches; hair, light brown and thin above forehead; eyes, blue; long jaw; powerfully built; drinks; chews, but does not smoke; generally works around horses. Reputation bad, but not dangerous. Advise if have information.

Murragh considered the telegram a moment, then folded and placed it in his pocket. "Maybe," he said half to himself, "this territory needs him worse than the State of Texas right now."

"Who's Twitchell Barnett?" Henley said again.

"I remembered hearing about him when I was with the Rangers, though I never worked on that case. I'm not positive, Cass, but he could be Barney Twitchell—"

"You mean the hombre who drove stage for Linda one time? By cripes, could be! The description fits. Now that I recollect, it was him driving the first time the Silver Belle pay roll was lifted. I never did like the feller, but just figured him as a no-good."

"He's chummy with Vaiden."

"What does that prove, Hoyt?"

"I don't know yet. I've got to think this over."

Murragh rolled a cigarette, lighted it, inhaled deeply. His features were set in a frown. Henley said at last, "Linda was plumb discouraged about losing that Silver Belle pay roll today. From something you'd said, she didn't think there'd be a holdup."

"I never said there wouldn't be a holdup. I said I had a hunch the money would go through all right."

Henley sighed. "We can't be right on our hunches all the time, can we?"

Murragh agreed. "However, I had the right hunch this time."

"Now I know you're dead for sleep. I just told you a few minutes ago the bandits got the strongbox. Didn't you hear me?"

"I heard you, Cass. All the bandits got in that strongbox was some rocks, put in to make it weigh heavy. The—"

"What! What are you saying?" Henley's eyes were wide, staring.

Murragh explained in weary tones. "I had a hunch another holdup was about due. I made that ride to Millman City to see Wyatt Holliday. Wyatt can get practically anything in that town he wants. I told him what I wanted. He roused the banker out of bed, got hold of the Silver Belle representative in Millman City. Wyatt and I drove that pay roll to Sulphur Tanks early this morning, in a light buggy. All the stage carried was a box of rocks which the Silver Belle representative turned over to the stage guard. The miners will be paid on time tomorrow."

"Well, I'll—be—goddamned!" Henley's eyes were bulging. "Say, why you so interested in all this?"

"It's part of a job I've got to do. Besides I had sort of given encouragement to Linda Gordon. I didn't want to see her disappointed."

Henley said narrowly, "Any particular reason for that last?"

Murragh studied the ceiling. Finally he said, "I don't

like to see any good fighter disappointed."

"Man alive, this is going to lift a load from Linda's shoulders! If I were in your boots I'd be over there now, telling her."

"She's probably home in bed."

"But not sleeping, I'll bet a plugged peso. That girl's worried nigh sick, right now."

"Cass, I'm dead for some shut-eye. You know Linda. I'll appreciate it if you'll drift over to her house and tell her the pay roll's safe."

"Cripes! I'm more than glad to do it." Henley rose from the desk and got his sombrero. "If you're heading for the hotel, I'll walk part way with you. Linda and Silvertop just live a mite over a block from the hotel. Say, is it all right to tell her how you worked it?"

Murragh paused, "Yes, I reckon."

"Lord, you did make fools out of those holdup men! Anything else I can tell her?"

"Yes, tell her to keep her mouth shut. Today isn't the last stage that will be going through."

The two men strolled up Main Street. As they passed Isabel's Fanchon's place, they noticed a dim light shining from the back room. Henley gestured toward the building. "Vaiden or Kennard?"

"What do you think?"

"I'm betting on Vaiden, especially if Isabel's heard how Kennard showed yellow today. A woman likes nerve in a man. Remember that line in *Othello*? 'She loved me for the dangers I had passed.'"

Murragh yawned. "Don't ask me to remember any Shakespeare tonight. Anyway, from what you tell me,

Kennard passed danger as fast as he could today."

The men said good night at the entrance to the hotel. Murragh went in, paused a moment to speak to the clerk, then climbed the stairs to the second floor. At the door to Number 11 he stopped and knocked. There was no answer from within. Murragh frowned, musing, "I never seem to have much luck finding Russ in his room." He examined the key to his own door. "Mostly, these hotel keys fit all the doors. Let's see . . ."

He inserted the key. It turned easily, and he stepped into Kennard's room and scratched a match. Clothing had been flung in helter-skelter fashion about the bed and chairs. The match flame flickered and went out. Murragh speculated, "Looks like Russ just took time to clean up and leave again. . . . No, I reckon it's not Vaiden at Isabel Fanchon's tonight—unless they're both there at once."

He emerged from the room, locked the door, then entered his own room. Undressing in the darkness, he wearily slipped between the covers of his bed and almost instantly passed into sleep.

16

Two Invitations

Slightly before eight the following morning Cass Henley found Murragh at breakfast in the hotel dining room. Cass slid into the chair across from him. Murragh said, "I can recommend the fried eggs, and the ham isn't so bad either."

Henley said, "That answers the question."

"What question?"

"'Who can cloy the hungry edge of appetite?'" Henley quoted, grinning. "I just had ham and eggs at Joe Low's."

"And on that flimsy excuse"—Murragh pretended disgust "you drag in *King Richard II.* Don't you ever think of anything but—?"

"Now wait a minute. It was thinking of you that brought me here."

"What about me?"

"I ran into something that might interest you. Seen Russ Kennard this morning?"

Murragh drained his coffee cup, set it down again. "Not yet. I think I heard him come in—I should say stumble in—about three or four this morning. When he's slept off his load, I'm aiming to take up that stage holdup with him. What about Kennard?"

"It looks like he's got the edge on Vaiden. I was making a round of the town before I turned in last night—it was after midnight—when I noticed the light still on at Isabel Fanchon's, and—"

"So you got snoopy."

"So I got snoopy," Henley admitted. "I crossed the street and listened at the front door, which was locked. I could see light coming from the rear, and I could hear voices. It sounded like an argument to me, but damned if I could make out the words. So I knocked on the door, and when Isabel showed up I asked her if everything was all right."

"Subtle, aren't you?" Murragh said dryly.

"Curious," Henley countered. "Isabel didn't ask me in, but I stepped in before she could say 'Scat!' Anyway, she assured me that there was nothing wrong. No, she hadn't realized there was any loud talking going on. She and a couple of her friends had been playing three-handed seven-up. They might have been laughing a lot, or arguing about the game. Anyway, that's what Isabel said. I know damn' well I didn't hear any laughing. By this time everything was quiet in the back room, and as Isabel had closed the door I couldn't see who was out there. So there was nothing for me to do except leave, which I did pronto, not wanting to freeze to death."

"Isabel acted rather chilly, eh?"

"Damn' nigh cut my head on an icicle when I left."

"What about the friends?"

"You know that hardware store across the street from Isabel's? Well, I stood in the doorway there for nearly an hour, before I saw Vaiden leave. He walked down the street a half block where he'd left his horse in front of the Pyramid Pool Parlor, got into the saddle, and rode out of town."

"What about Kennard?"

"I don't know. Isabel's light wasn't put out. I got sleepy waiting for Kennard to leave, so I went back to the office and turned in. But it sure looks like Kennard had ousted Vaiden from Isabel's favor for good."

"Or bad. . . . Did you tell Linda the Silver Belle pay roll was safe?"

"I was wondering how long it would be before you'd ask that."

"I was wondering how long it would be before you told me."

"Yes, I broke the news, right after I left you last night. She and Silvertop were plumb tickled. It'd have done your heart good to see Linda's eyes when I told her. She was that excited—well, she threw her arms around me and kissed me."

"I must be getting careless," Hoyt Murragh said dryly.

"What do you mean?"

"After this, I'll do my own breaking of good news."

"Shucks! Don't forget that Linda and I have known each other since we were buttons. Y'know,"—the words came awkwardly—"I asked Linda to marry me once—several years ago."

"Which same proves you have good taste, Cass. Marriage might have made a man of you, so you wouldn't have to spend all your time reading Shakespeare."

Henley assumed a hurt expression and called *Julius Caesar* to the rescue: " 'This was the must unkindest cut of all.' "

Murragh smiled and rose from the breakfast table. "All right, you've got me licked. Let's get out of here." They left the dining room. Murragh stopped at the desk to buy a couple of long black cigars, one of which he lighted; the other he passed to the deputy.

They paused a moment on the narrow gallery that fronted the hotel. Bright morning sun shone along the street, sending down early evidence of the greater heat to come later in the day. A buckboard drawn by two horses rattled into town and turned in at the hitchrack before Bainbridge's General Store. Two Box-90 cowboys passed and exchanged greetings with Henley. Murragh dropped into one of a row of chairs arranged along the gallery railing for the convenience of hotel guests.

"Why not," he proposed, "sit down and enjoy your cigar? The morning's too fresh yet to do anything except enjoy it. I might even stand for your quoting some Shakespeare."

"That's a real temptation, Hoyt, but I've got to get back to the office—"

"'Blessed is the man that endureth temptation,'" Murragh interrupted.

Henley paused, frowning. A troubled look crept across his features; his shrewd eyes challenged Murragh. "That's not Shakespeare, is it?"

Murragh said dryly, "No. That's something I learned in Sunday school."

Henley looked relieved. "Thought somebody else must have written it. . . . Well,"—reluctantly—"I've got to get going. Promised Jake I'd get back as soon as I'd seen you, so's he could send off a telegram he's composing at present—or it's probably composed by this time—"

Murragh said quickly, "You didn't mention that telegram we had about Twitch Barnett—or Barney Twitchell?"

Henley shook his head. "Figured you'd tell Jake when you got around to it. No, Jake's going to get in touch with some doctor in El Paso and take his missus there for an operation that Doc Bradley advised."

"What wrong with her?"

Henley shrugged his shoulders. "I don't know, exactly. Something uncurable that has to be cut out."

"When's the sheriff and his wife going?"

"When Jake can make arrangements—probably sometime in the next week or so."

"I suppose that means you'll act as sheriff while he's away."

"I reckon."

"Will another deputy have to be brought in?"

Henley shook his head. "I told Jake you and I could handle all the law-enforcing that would be necessary."

Murragh looked sharply at the deputy. "You did? How come you to include me?"

"Help me out if I got in a tight, wouldn't you?"

"Hmmm . . . yes, I reckon I would, Cass."

Henley smiled. "That's what I told Jake you'd say. Well, s'long."

"I'll see you later."

Murragh gazed after the deputy's loose-jointed figure as it proceeded down Main Street. He mused: A deputy badge might come handy, at that; and a little later: I wonder just how much Cass has guessed.

When his cigar was finished, Murragh rose and stepped next door to the stage office. Linda was alone when he entered. She looked up, then came swiftly from behind the short counter, hand outstretched, to greet him: "Hoyt!"

"Morning, Linda."

"Hoyt Murragh! Do you realize what a load you lifted

176

from my shoulders? Why didn't you tell me what you intended?"

"Wasn't sure it was going to work out. Didn't want to raise any false hopes." Her hand was cool and firm to his grasp. After a moment she released it, though the feel of her slim fingers remained with him for some time.

"I don't know how we're going to thank you, Hoyt— you and Wyatt Holliday."

"You'll see Wyatt one of these days. You can tell him then."

"And won't I just do it, too! I appreciate it like the deuce, what you did, Hoyt," the girl said sincerely. "After I went to bed last night I couldn't sleep. I lay there wondering what to do next. I was so discouraged. Then Cass Henley knocked on the door and told me the Silver Belle pay roll was safe. I couldn't believe it at first. And then, all of a sudden, I realized it was true. I was so overjoyed—excited—I didn't know what to do or what to say."

"Cass said you were plumb tickled," Murragh replied dryly.

Linda colored. "That," she said, "was what you might call acting under the stress of emotion."

"That's the way I figured it," Hoyt smiled. "Better hang on to your emotions next week. There'll be another pay roll going through."

"Darn it!" Linda exclaimed. "I hadn't thought of that. And what's to do next week? Those bandits are going to be mighty mad at the way you fooled them." She giggled suddenly. "Can you imagine their faces when they opened that strongbox?"

Murragh said quietly, "They probably weren't nice to see. And it will make them that much more eager to stop the next pay roll that goes through."

"Hoyt, what can I do? You and Mr. Holliday can't go on repeating that performance week after week."

"Look, Linda, we've fooled 'em once. Until I start worrying, there's no need for you to fret. Where's Silvertop?"

"He said he was going to go home and catch a little shut-eye. He was up early this morning to start the stage north, you know. But I wouldn't be surprised if he was in the hotel bar, having his morning bottle of beer. Oh yes, Dad and I would like to have you and Cass come to supper tomorrow night—say around five-thirty."

"Tomorrow night?"

"It's Sunday, you know. No stages go out. I have the whole day free. That's when I experiment with my cooking."

"Thank you." Murragh bowed slightly and smiled. "I'll be more than glad to be the object of your experiments—"

He broke off suddenly, having noticed through the window Isabel Fanchon passing along Main Street. He turned back, thanked Linda again for her invitation, and added, "If you'll excuse me, I've got to move along." He put on his hat again and started toward the door. "I'll see you later."

"Of course, Hoyt. And thanks again for that pay-roll business. Cass said you said to keep my mouth shut."

"Sort of a rough way to put it," Murragh laughed,

"but I guess you understood."

"Of course," Linda said again.

When Murragh had gone, she stepped outside to the edge of the sidewalk and managed to make out the man's tall form sauntering beside the smaller one of Isabel Fanchon's, a block east on Main Street.

Linda returned to the office, her brows knit in a frown. "Business," she told herself tartly, "certainly takes a man around." Brushing viciously at a stray lock of maize-colored hair, she returned to the papers on which she'd been working.

Murragh had caught up with Isabel Fanchon before she was a block away. The girl was dressed as she'd been the previous day, except that the hat and parasol were lacking. Murragh spoke her name: "Miss Fanchon."

The girl turned her large dark eyes on him, startled at first, then melting into a smile when she recognized Murragh. "Oh, it's you, Mr. Murragh."

Murragh fell into step beside her. The girl brushed at her face with a wisp of lace handkerchief. "It's going to be warm today, don't you think so?"

"Seems that way."

"I simply hated to go out, but I just had to have some ribbon—blue ribbon. Menzies' Dry Goods and Notions is the only place that handles what I want."

"Miss Fanchon, I wanted to apologize for the other night."

"The other night?"

"For breaking in on you at such an hour."

"Oh, when Russ Kennard was there. Just don't mention it, Mr. Murragh, or"—she looked archly at him— "should I call you Hoyt? Russ always does, and it comes so natural—"

"Hoyt's all right with me," Murragh smiled.

"But not unless you call me Isabel."

Murragh laughed softly. "We'll have to come to some sort of arrangement, won't we?"

"It really didn't matter, you coming in like that. But you see, I didn't know you, I didn't know what you'd think. And Russ shouldn't have stayed so late—"

"Meaning Alonzo Vaiden might not like it?"

"'Lonzo? Humph! Who cares what 'Lonzo Vaiden thinks? Just because I kept company with him for a time, that's no sign— Why, would you believe it, Hoyt, he came to my place last night, when Russ was there, and he started the most dreadful argument. There's no sense in such jealousy. Even Deputy Henley heard the voices and thought I was having trouble—oh yes, I suppose Russ told you?"

"Told me what?" Murragh added. "I haven't seen him today yet."

"Why, I thought it would be nice if Russ brought you to visit tomorrow night. I could have a little lunch, and I know you men like something to drink. We could play cards—or something; perhaps you'd care to look at some of my views of the Civil War. People who haven't seen them are always interested . . ." The girl appeared rather nervous now, and her smile was a bit too forced.

"Why, I think that's fine," Murragh accepted heartily, "if you don't mind my coming a trifle late. You see, I have a supper invitation—"

"At the Gordons', or I'm wrong. You men! If it isn't one girl, it's another. But come when you can, Hoyt. We—I'll be delighted to see you, and I know Russ will be pleased. Gracious, here's Menzies' now. I nearly walked past. Well, see you tomorrow night."

Murragh removed his sombrero and waited until the girl had entered the dry-goods store which stood a couple of doors from the corner of Main and Hereford streets. Then he resumed his walk, pondering the situation.

A mighty attractive woman and not quite so flighty as she'd like me to believe, he cogitated. And that argument between Vaiden and Kennard had nothing to do with her, either—else why did she start explaining? Probably figured that Cass had mentioned her guests . . .

At noon, when he went to his room to wash for dinner, he could hear Kennard snoring from beyond the door of Number 11. Later in the day, when Murragh once more went to seek the man, Kennard had awakened and left. Murragh entered his own room, opened his valise, checked the contents, and again descended to the street. He went down to the sheriff's office, talked to Cass Henley briefly, and started out again. Cass said, "All right, I'll remember. What do you think is up?"

Murragh shrugged carelessly and left the sheriff's office, saying over one shoulder, "I'll let you know when I find out."

He walked back and resumed his seat on the hotel gallery, from which he could see for quite a distance, in either direction, along Main Street. Being Saturday, there were more people than usual in Lanyard. Murragh saw Alonzo Vaiden ride past, heading east along Main. By leaning out over the gallery railing Murragh could see that Vaiden turned his pony in to the hitchrack near Pudge Ryan's saloon.

Ten minutes later Vaiden again rode past, heading west out of town. Whatever brought him in didn't keep him long, Murragh mused.

Twenty minutes passed, then Murragh saw Russ Kennard approaching the hotel. Kennard raised startled, bloodshot eyes when Murragh called to him and looked as though he was about to turn around and beat a retreat. However, he reluctantly ascended to the gallery and slumped into a chair next to Murragh's. Murragh rolled and lighted a cigarette, then offered the "makin's" to Kennard. Kennard refused with an irritable gesture. He kept looking at Murragh, waiting for Murragh to open the conversation. Murragh smoked in silence. Kennard grew more jittery every minute.

Abruptly Murragh said quietly, "Russ, you look like hell."

"Is that what you called me to say?"

"You're hitting the bottle too much."

Kennard turned suddenly to Murragh. "All right," he said testily, "get it out of your system. You didn't call me up here to say what you said the first day I saw you in Lanyard."

"Get what out of my system?" Murragh said mildly.

"You know damned well what I'm talking about. You're going to give me hell about that holdup."

Murragh looked surprised. "Why should I give you

hell about that holdup? You didn't get that Silver Belle pay roll—or did you?"

"That's it, that's it!" Kennard tried to whip himself into a rage. "That's the stand you take, eh? That I was working with those holdup men. I never thought you'd turn against me like that, Hoyt. You know damned well that's not true. I didn't get that pay roll, nor nobody— Hoyt, why do you treat me like this?"

"Lower your voice, Russ," Murragh advised quietly. "People on the street are commencing to look this way."

"What difference does it make? I haven't done anything to be ashamed of." Nevertheless he lowered his voice, and now it took on an apologetic tone. "You're right, Hoyt, I'm a coyote. I don't know what got into me, but those guns—there were eight of them pointing from the brush—just got my nerve. I thought sure as hell I was going to be shot—"

"You had your own gun, didn't you?"

"Yes, but I didn't dare pull it. All right, call me yellow if you like—"

"I'm not calling you yellow. You'll admit, yourself, that's a mighty queer way for you to act, though."

"I know it." Perspiration stood on Kennard's forehead. "I haven't a damn' thing I can say to defend myself. I'll go further than that: I'm admitting I'm to blame for that pay roll being stolen. Someday, when I get enough money, I'm going to square myself—"

"Getting sort of humble all of a sudden, aren't you?" Murragh asked dryly.

"God, if you knew how I feel! The story's all over

town. Men I used to drink with won't even stand at the bar with me."

"Can you blame 'em?"

"I reckon I can't, Hoyt. I expected you to jump all over me, though."

Murragh shrugged. "Anything I say doesn't seem to affect you. The money's gone. What's done is done. As Cass Henley might say, 'What's past is prologue.'"

Kennard scowled, "What do you mean by that?"

"It's something a man named Shakespeare wrote."

"Oh, some of that deputy's spoutings, eh? . . . What happened to you while I was up to Millman City?"

"Nothing much, I just boomed around looking for information."

"Learn anything?"

"Nothing to speak of."

"Y'know, Hoyt,"—there was a puzzled expression on Kennard's face—"I didn't expect you to take the holdup like this."

"Let's forget the holdup. Any man's likely to lose his nerve at least once in a lifetime. Maybe with that out of your system you'll get on with the job. If we can do what we came here to do, folks will forget the part you played in the holdup."

"God, Hoyt, you always did understand me—"

"Let's forget it."

"All right, we won't say any more about that. There's something else, though, I want to tell you. You know I've been seeing Isabel Fanchon quite frequently, and you know she used to keep company with 'Lonzo Vaiden."

"I've heard that."

"Well, I haven't wasted so much time as you think. Hoyt, don't mention this to a soul, but I've a hunch Vaiden has something to do with the stage holdups."

"What makes you think so?"

"Oh, little things that Isabel has dropped from time to time." Kennard was vague. "I'd like to have you hear her. Fact is, if you'll come, I got her to ask you to her place tomorrow night. Maybe you'll learn something—"

"I've already accepted that invitation."

Kennard looked surprised. "You have? Why—?"

"I ran into Miss Fanchon on the street this morning. She thought you'd told me, but I said I hadn't seen you yet."

"Well, that's fine."

"She's a darn' good-looking girl, Russ. I couldn't turn down an invitation from anybody like her."

Kennard cast a look of suspicion, tinged with jealousy, at Murragh. "Maybe you're getting to know how I feel, eh?"

Murragh laughed softly. "Ever know me to do any trespassing?"

"No, I can't say I ever did. I'm just wondering what's got into you—"

"We were speaking of Vaiden a minute ago. Look," Murragh interrupted. Vaiden was again passing on his pony. "That's the third time he's ridden past here in the last hour or so. Must be the horse needs exercise."

"Must be," Kennard agreed. "How about stepping into the bar, Hoyt? I could use a drink."

Murragh refused. "You go get your drink. I'm stiff from sitting. I'm going to walk around a mite."

He nodded to Kennard, settled his sombrero more firmly on his head, and stepped down to the sidewalk.

17

Double-Cross

The Gordon home on Deming Street was a neat rock-and-adobe structure with a white picket fence around it and an ancient cottonwood tree in the front yard. Cass Henley had also been invited to supper and had already arrived when Silvertop opened the front door for Murragh shortly before five-thirty. Murragh was ushered into the parlor and invited to partake of a bottle of bourbon which Silvertop and Henley had been sampling. Murragh accepted a small drink and asked after Linda.

"She's in the kitchen," Silvertop replied. "Can't you hear the pots and pans banging around? Getting a dinner is a serious business with that girl."

The parlor was a pleasant room with comfortable chairs covered with animal skins, a few pictures on the walls, and a flowered carpet. Instead of the iron stove, so popular the past few years, there was a rock fireplace and andirons manufactured from short sections of locomotive rails between which blazed a few mesquite knots to take the chill from the evening, semidesert air.

Linda entered a few minutes later in a large apron, her

face flushed from the heat of the stove, and greeted Hoyt and added she was ready for them in the dining room. Henley produced his inevitable quotation: " 'Come, give us a taste of your quality,' " and the men filed out to the dining room. There was fried chicken, mashed potatoes, beans, coffee, and two kinds of pie— dried apple and dried peach. Henley chose one of each and, when the supper ended with cigars passed by Silvertop, leaned back in his chair with a contented sigh of repletion.

Linda asked, "Did you all get filled?"

"Linda," Murragh said, "you're as good a cook as you are a driver. I can't think of any higher praise."

"Thank you, sir," the girl smiled. "Have enough chicken, Dad?"

"I never have enough of your chicken—but I've got as much as I can hold right now."

"As Shakespeare says,"—Henley beamed expansively—" 'Eating maketh a full man.' "

Murragh chuckled, "I knew you'd slip up if I waited long enough. Shakespeare never said anything of the kind. And the word is 'Reading,' not 'Eating.' "

A concerned frown fastened on Henley's features. "If Shakespeare didn't say that, who did—regardless whether it's eating or reading?"

"A man by the name of Bacon."

"Who's Bacon?"

"Francis Bacon—the man who wrote Shakespeare's works."

"What? What are you talking about?" Henley was really getting worked up now.

"That's what some people think, anyway," Murragh smiled. "I remember, when I was at college, there was a lot of talk about it. It was maintained that there was no actual proof that Shakespeare ever wrote a play in his life."

"Well, I'll be god—goshdarned," Henley said weakly. "Soon's I've got all of Bill Shakespeare committed to mind, I'll have to look up this Bacon hombre."

"Don't let it bother you, Cass," Murragh advised, eyes twinkling. "Whoever wrote 'em, they're darned hard to beat—those plays."

Linda was studying Murragh while he talked. She said, "You sound as if you'd taken your schooling seriously."

"I did, sort of," Murragh admitted.

"What did you take up?"

"The law—mostly. Passed my examination to practice, too, but,"—Murragh laughed self-consciously—"well, I reckon I never gave it too much chance. Got tired sitting around an office waiting for clients—had some, of course, and was making a fair living, but I felt sort of tied down. That's when I got the idea to join the Texas Rangers, and—well, here I am."

"Just where are you?" Linda asked.

"Even I'm not sure of that yet," Murragh replied with a slow smile.

"This town," Silvertop said, "could use a good lawyer, if you ever get the idea of settling down again."

"I'll keep that in mind."

Henley wanted to know more about Bacon and Shakespeare. Murragh satisfied him with such information as he had on the theory held during those times. Linda mentioned something about dishes having to be washed, and over her objection Murragh dried them for her, while Henley and Silvertop had recourse once more to the bottle of bourbon in the parlor. Linda and Murragh joined them there later. Inevitably the conversation turned to the pay-roll bandits. Murragh apparently had little more to offer in that direction; he listened while the other three talked.

About nine-thirty Murragh rose and stated he'd have to be going. Linda and Silvertop eyed him with some surprise. Silvertop said, "It's early yet—and we don't have the stage to get up for tomorrow morning. Just the southbound trip on tomorrow, y'know."

Murragh nodded "I'd like to stay, but there's some business to take care of." He turned at Linda's comment. "Yes, Linda, business even on Sunday. Cass'll keep you company. Try and get him interested in Shakespeare; he's a real good talker on that subject."

"I've heard something about that, I think," Linda said dryly. Murragh thanked her and Silvertop again for the supper, got his hat and left the house.

A lamp burned low in Isabel Fanchon's shop when Murragh arrived and knocked at the door. In a few moments, through the front-door glass, he saw the girl arriving from the rear part of the building. She opened the door, and Murragh was engulfed in waves of her strong perfume. She wore a green satin dress tonight, and even as he answered her greeting he found himself wondering if the shiny black curls were covered with some sort of varnish that held them in place.

"Oh, it's you, Mr. Murragh—Hoyt. We were commencing to think you weren't coming."

The door closed behind him. "Couldn't pass up your invitation, Isabel," Murragh said easily. "I'm looking forward to an interesting evening."

"We'll try to make it so. Just toss your hat on that chair there." Murragh followed her to the living quarters at the back and found Russ Kennard seated at the table near the side window. A lamp, two glasses, a partially filled whisky flask, and a deck of cards were on the table. Isabel Fanchon closed the door between the shop and the back room and pushed a third chair up to the table, while Kennard said, "Got here at last, did you, Hoyt?"

"Looks that way," Murragh said quietly. He sat down opposite the window, with Kennard and Isabel on either side of him. Kennard was far from drunk, but he had had enough to make him slightly ugly. Isabel had procured a third glass and reached for the flask. "Say when, Hoyt."

"Make it light."

The girl poured the glass half full. "Want a chaser? I've got some beer. Or you can have straight water."

"I'll take straight whisky," Murragh said. He lifted the glass to his lips, but barely tasted it.

"I thought we might have a lunch," Isabel was saying, "but if you've just come from supper at Gordons'—"

"Aw, Hoyt don't want anything to eat," Kennard hiccupped. "He just came here to see you, Isabel."

"Now, Russ, you mustn't talk like that," the girl laughed nervously.

"Talk any way I want," Kennard insisted. He lifted the glass to his mouth, set it down with a bang. "Good old Hoyt. What you want to do, Hoyt, play cards or something?"

"Whatever you two want."

"I know what you and Isabel want." Kennard leered at them. "You want me to leave."

Murragh said sharply, "Don't talk like a fool, Russ. You know what brought me here."

"I know, I know." Momentarily Kennard seemed placated. He kept sloshing the whisky around in his glass and finally succeeded in spilling some out on the table. Isabel said, "You'd better put that where it'll do the most good, Russ."

Silence fell for a time. A sort of tension seemed to exist in the room, as though Kennard and Isabel Fanchon were waiting for something. Murragh noticed that Kennard's hand on the whisky glass was trembling. Isabel rose from her chair, walked the length of the room, sat down again. She said, her voice sounding slightly strained, "This doesn't seem to be a very gay party, does it, Hoyt?"

"I hadn't thought much about it—" Murragh commenced quietly.

" 'Does it, Hoyt?' " Kennard mimicked sneeringly. "How about me, Isabel? You sick of me coming around? Does it always have to be Hoyt this and Hoyt that? You've talked of nobody else since I came here—"

"Hush it, Russ," Murragh said sharply.

Kennard subsided. "All right, excuse me for saying anything." He slumped down in his chair, sulking, with his head on his chest.

"Can I get you a bottle of beer, Hoyt?" Isabel asked. "You don't seem to be drinking."

"I'm making out all right," Murragh replied.

"Wouldn't think of asking me to have a bottle of beer, would you?" Kennard roused up from his chair.

Murragh said, hard-voiced, "Maybe you'd like one cracked over your head." The words were sudden, unexpected.

A look of fright crossed Kennard's face. He settled back in the chair again. "Now don't you get mad at me. Everybody's mad at me. Isabel's mad at me. Vaiden's mad—"

"Russ, you talk too much," the girl said sharply. "You know you scarcely know 'Lonzo Vaiden—"

"Aw, what difference's it make?" Kennard's tones were growing thicker every minute. "By morning, wonsh make bi' diff'nce. Let's all have lil' farewell drink—my ol' pal, Hoyt—" With an effort he focused bleary eyes on Murragh. "I liked you, once—'pon my word—did—"

"Russ!" Isabel said again, her voice strident.

Kennard stopped talking. He and the girl looked steadily at each other a moment, Kennard trying to keep his bloodshot eyes on her face. Again silence descended on the room.

"Rather warm in here, don't you think?" Isabel broke the quiet. "Hoyt, I never thought to tell you to take your gun off when I told you where to put your hat. Better unstrap your belt—"

"I'm comfortable," Murragh cut in. "I reckon we'd

192

better be going. I'll take Russ back to the hotel—"

"Ain' goin'—getsh ready," Kennard said thickly.

Isabel rose again, came back to the table with a small pack of cigarettes and opened it. She drew out a small card enclosed—a picture of a burlesque actress—tossed it on the table. Then she withdrew three cigarettes. "I get these sent from Chicago," she said. One of the cigarettes she tossed across the table to Kennard. The other two she stuck in her mouth, scratched a match and lighted them. After puffing a few moments she placed one of the cigarettes between Murragh's lips.

Kennard directed a look of hate at Murragh, then glared at the girl. A soft, nervous laugh left the girl's lips. Murragh drew on his cigarette a moment, then placed it on a saucer on the table, where it continued to send a spiral of smoke toward the ceiling. Isabel turned the lamp a trifle higher. The thought ran through Murragh's mind: It'll happen pretty soon now. I wonder what gun Russ is carrying?

Isabel complained, "God! It's hot in here. I'm going to open that window a minute. This smoke is choking me. Some fresh air will make Russ feel better, too." She moved around the table, back of Murragh. "Get up, Russ, so I can get at that window."

Murragh thought: Now it's going to happen. He watched closely while Kennard stumbled to his feet and stood swaying unsteadily at the side of the table. Isabel raised the shade, then pushed up the window and adjusted the sash peg in the proper hole to maintain the window at the right height.

At that instant Murragh moved. He whirled up and

193

away, kicking over the chair behind him, the maneuver taking him across the floor and against the wall at one side of the window. His gun was out, waiting.

Kennard commenced lamely, "Why, Hoyt, what's the mat—?"

Beyond the window a six-shooter roared. There came an instant, blinding flash from the darkness, and the air was tinged With the odor of black powder smoke. A stunned expression of mingled surprise and pain contorted Kennard's features as the bullet smashed in. For just a few seconds he remained erect, one hand clawing at his middle. Then, slowly, he bent forward from the waist as though making a formal bow. His head struck the table as he went to the floor.

Even as Kennard crashed down, a heavy steel object came hurtling through the open window to land, spinning, on the table beside the lamp. A scream, high-pitched, piercing, filled the room. Isabel backed away, shaking, eyes bulging, the back of one hand across her mouth as though trying to stifle the ululation-like sounds welling from her throat.

Running feet thumped, faded away on the packed earth beyond the open window, in the passageway between two buildings. Murragh, gun in hand, spun toward the rear door. It was locked, the key missing. He whirled back toward the open window. Isabel flung herself in his path, clutching at his body, pawing, gripping tenaciously at one coat sleeve.

"You won't escape!" she panted. "I won't let you—"

Hoofbeats drummed in the alley back of the house. Murragh flung the woman off, sent her staggering halfway across the room.

He leaned from the window, listening. The rapidly galloping hoofs were receding swiftly through the night. He relaxed and turned back to the room, replacing his gun in holster. Isabel had started screaming again, the sounds, shrill, strident, pealing from her lips in an unbroken cacophony. Murragh eyed her steadily for a moment and snapped grimly, "Cut it out." His lips tightened, and he glanced at the gun that had been flung through the window to land on the table. His eyes again came up to meet the woman's.

Isabel backed a step, eyes wide. "You killed him!" she cried over and over. "You killed him! You'll hang for this—"

"I told you to shut up." Murragh's voice was almost a snarl.

Isabel's eyes widened still further. A gasp of indignation left her mouth and she sank, trembling, into a chair, her dark eyes fixed as though hypnotized on Murragh. Then she commenced to sob. The black curls tumbled about her face; mascara streaked her cheeks.

Murragh knelt by the still form on the floor, which was huddled face down as though it had gone to sleep in that position. There came a sudden banging at the front door. Along Main Street running footsteps and voices made a confused din. Doors banged; windows were slammed up. Murragh rose, walked to the front door and unlocked it.

Cass Henley said, "What in hell is going on here, Hoyt?"

"Come back and see for yourself."

Henley closed the door and followed Murragh to the back room, nostrils twitching at the smell of gunpowder still in the air. He glanced at the dead man on the floor and said, "What happened, Isabel?"

The girl clutched at his sleeve. "Oh, Cass," she whimpered. "He killed Russ. Arrest Murragh, Cass. He killed Russ. Get his other gun—"

Murragh said brutally, "It's no good, Isabel. So just save your breath."

Henley stooped over the dead body, turned it on its back. He rose and said in flat tones, "Drilled plumb center."

Murragh said, "The shot came through that open window. I tried to get out in time to stop the killer, but couldn't make it. He made the getaway on a horse—"

"It's a lie, Cass, it's a lie." Isabel was commencing to shriek again. "Murragh killed him! I swear it. They got to quarreling and—"

"What were they quarreling about?" Henley cut in.

"About—about,"—the girl's head dropped—"about me. Russ was so terribly jealous—"

Murragh laughed harshly. "You're a better actress than liar, Isabel. That story won't stick."

The girl's eyes blazed. She looked from Murragh to Henley. "Cass, you've got to believe me! Murragh's the killer. There was no one else here, I swear to you—"

Henley interrupted, "Calm down now, Isabel. I want to get to the bottom of this. I can't make sense out of anything when you get to yelling like that. What was Kennard shot with?"

The girl pointed a shaking finger at the forty-four six-shooter lying on the table. Henley crossed over and picked up the gun. "You sure it was this weapon and not the one in his holster?"

"That's the gun," Isabel insisted.

"And Murragh didn't fire the gun in his holster at all?"

Isabel shook her head impatiently. "No, just that one on the table. I didn't see it on him when he came in. He must have had it hidden inside his shirt."

"Check that gun on the table, Cass," Murragh directed. "It was thrown through the window, after the shot was fired."

"You lie—!" Isabel commenced.

Henley said, "For God's sake, Isabel, keep calm. I'll decide what's what." He picked up the gun on the table, sniffed at the muzzle. "It's been fired right recent," he stated.

"Check the number," Murragh directed.

Henley glanced at the bottom of the frame and read off the digits, "Number nine seven nine three two . . ." He glanced at Murragh. "This is the gun you reported yesterday as being missing from your satchel."

Murragh nodded, withdrew the other six-shooter from his holster. "It's the mate to this. They're a matched pair. I bought them at the same time." He waved the muzzle of the gun beneath Henley's nose. Henley, a bit hastily, pushed the barrel to one side. "All right, it hasn't been fired. Let me see that number." Murragh gave him the gun. Henley glanced at the serial number and said, "Nine seven nine three one," then handed it back. Murragh dropped the weapon into its scabbard.

While they had talked they had become increasingly aware of many voices in front of the shop. Now there came a loud rapping on the door. Henley said, "I'll go open it."

While he was gone, Murragh said, "Isabel, just what kind of a game are you playing?"

"It's no game," the girl replied sullenly, "as you'll learn when you swing for murder."

Henley returned with Sheriff Farley and Alonzo Vaiden behind him. "Geez! You should see the crowd out front—"

"What is this—?" Farley commenced.

"'Lonzo!" Isabel rose and flung her arms about Vaiden's neck. "'Lonzo, he killed poor Russ—"

"What you doing here, Vaiden?" Murragh demanded.

"I got a right to be anywhere that Isabel's having trouble." He urged the girl back to her chair.

Jake Farley explained heavily, "'Lonzo came and woke me up. Said there was shooting over here and a woman screaming."

"You made mighty good time, Vaiden," Murragh commented. "A man might think you knew this shooting was coming off and were just waiting to get the sheriff the instant you heard the shot."

"What do you mean by that?" Vaiden scowled.

"Exactly what I said. Make what you like of it."

"Why, damn you, Murragh—"

"Cut it out, cut it out," Farley growled. "I'd like to get to the bottom of one mess before another gets started."

"Sheriff Farley!" Isabel was wailing again. "Arrest Murragh for murder. I saw the whole thing. I tell you—"

"What I said goes for you too, Isabel," Farley interrupted. "Now keep quiet. . . . Cass, do you know what happened?"

Cass gave the story as he had had it from Murragh. The sheriff shot a glance at Murragh. "Is that right?"

"It's a lie!" Isabel started once more. "Russ and Murragh got to fighting and Murragh shot him—"

"What were they fighting about, Isabel?" Vaiden asked.

"I hate to say it, but the argument was about me. Russ was so jealous—"

"Sheriff," Vaiden exclaimed, "I demand you place Murragh under arrest—"

"And I demand," Cass Henley interrupted hotly, "that you keep your mouth shut, Vaiden. Murragh's in the clear. The gun he's wearing hasn't been fired. Isabel herself said so. She claims the gun on the table there is the one that did the work. That's Hoyt's gun, all right— but he reported it as having been stolen yesterday. Whoever fired the gun threw it through the window, hoping to pin the killing on Hoyt."

"A likely story," Vaiden sneered. "Reported the gun stolen! Nobody but a fool would believe a yarn like that. He probably had the gun all the time and concealed it to come here. Things just came to a head between Murragh and Kennard, that's all. Murragh was here last Wednesday night, Isabel tells me, and insisted that Kennard leave the same time he did—hell, Jake, are you going to arrest Murragh, or have I got to appeal to the governor to send a real law-enforcement man down to Lanyard—"

"Now, look here, 'Lonzo," Farley growled. "No use you taking that attitude. Looks to me like Murragh's innocent—"

"I'm warning you, Jake," Vaiden interrupted harshly, "either you arrest this killer, or, by God, I'll—"

"You, Vaiden,"—Murragh's tones were sharp—"if you're so anxious for law enforcement, maybe this will satisfy you." He thrust a small metallic shield beneath Vaiden's gaze, then replaced it in his pocket.

Vaiden's face sobered. He looked at Murragh, then shrugged, trying to conceal his surprise. "I guess there's a mistake been made here tonight, and we'll have to take Deputy U. S. Marshal Murragh's word for what happened." Farley and Henley added their exclamations at the unanticipated statement. Vaiden turned swiftly on Isabel, saying, "You must be wrong if you say Mr. Murragh fired that shot. Probably, in the excitement, it just seemed that way, didn't it?"

Isabel looked bewildered. "Why—why, I guess that must be it," she stammered. "I'm real sorry, Mr. Murragh. I didn't realize—"

Murragh interrupted, "Drop it for now. But don't leave town, Isabel. There'll be an inquiry into this. I advise you to tell a straight story when you go before the coroner's jury." He reached to the table for his gun, then turned to the sheriff. "Jake, you and Cass do what's necessary here. I'm leaving for the hotel if you want me."

He strode out, got his hat from the other room, and stepped into the street. He didn't realize until he'd pushed through the crowd gathered in front of the building—and without answering any of its eager questioning—that Cass Henley had followed him. Cass caught up before he'd reached the hotel. "I'm heading for Doc Bradley's," Cass explained. "As coroner, Doc will have to know about this. So you're from the U. S. marshal's office."

"Put it that I have authority from that office." Murragh sounded bitter. "I didn't want that known, but Vaiden forced my hand. He'd have made a fuss if Jake hadn't arrested me. It was the only way to spike Vaiden's guns without making more trouble for Jake."

"I can't understand the business—Kennard killed and Isabel trying to fasten the job on you."

Murragh scowled. "A frame and a double-double-cross."

"That needs explaining."

"Russ Kennard was my pardner in a private detective agency. He came here to make an investigation into the stagecoach bandits. I didn't like the way things seemed to be shaping up. Before coming to Lanyard I got some additional authority from the U. S. marshal's office, though Russ didn't know that. Here's how I size up the situation: first, Kennard double-crossed me. If I'm not mistaken he was working with the bandits. Something went wrong. Maybe they suspected him of treachery when they failed to get that last pay roll. They decided to get rid of him and tie my hands at the same time. Isabel Fanchon worked on him until he was jealous of me—the fool. He consented to frame me; they told him I was the one to be shot. Then they double-crossed him, figuring I'd be arrested for the murder. Whether they'd be able to prove that on me didn't matter. What did matter was that they'd have me out of the way for a time. What they didn't figure on was having to contend with a deputy U. S. marshal. A private detective has little more legal authority than any citizen and, if suspected of a crime, can easily be placed in jail. The same doesn't apply to a man carrying authority from the U. S. marshal. See the scheme?"

Henley swore. "And you figure Vaiden is head of the bandits?"

"I haven't figured that far ahead—definitely." Murragh added soberly, "We'll talk it over tomorrow, Cass. I don't feel like talking now. It hurts when a pardner double-crosses you. You see, I used to think a hell of a lot of Russ Kennard."

18
A Baited Hook

A coroner's inquest was held the following day over the body of Russ Kennard, with Murragh and Isabel Fanchon—a much subdued Isabel—acting as the principal witnesses. Isabel told a story which corroborated Murragh's; she didn't attempt to renew the accusation that Murragh had shot Kennard.

When the verdict of the coroner's jury was returned, it carried the expected "Killer unknown," and once again the saloons of Lanyard were rife with gossip and speculation concerning the dead man, Isabel Fanchon, and Hoyt Murragh, now revealed as a deputy U. S. marshal. When the inquest had been concluded, Murragh arranged with Graves, the undertaker, to ship the body to Colorado, Russ Kennard's home state.

Shortly after dinnertime Murragh found Cass Henley in the stage office with Linda and Silvertop. Linda greeted him with a smile, "So now you're revealed in your true identity, Mr. Hoyt Murragh. You didn't fool us so much at that. Dad always said you were a private detective—"

"And so did Cass," Silvertop put in.

"Pure guesswork, of course," Cass Henley nodded.

Murragh said to Linda, "It was on your account I came down here in the first place."

"My account?"

"The Gordon Stage Company, then. Let's sit down a few minutes. It's about time I gave you folks an idea of what brought me here."

They retired to chairs back of the short counter. "As I told you last evening," Murragh commenced, "after I'd practiced law for a time, I joined the Texas Rangers. The Pinkerton Detective Agency made me an offer, and I went with that company for a time. It was there I met Russ Kennard. We happened to be working together on a bank-robbery case in Utah at the time. We cleaned that up, and then the Pinkerton people teamed us up on a few more jobs. I liked working with Russ."

"He was really a good detective, then?" Linda said skeptically.

"One of the best—when he stayed away from liquor. And Russ never could resist a pretty face, either. Those were his two weaknesses. But when he attended to business, he was a hard man to beat. Keen as a sharp knife. More than once he'd arrive at the solution of a problem while I was still thinking all around it. But it just needed a few drinks—or a pretty face—to throw him completely off the track, and then he wasn't worth a hoot."

Murragh rolled a cigarette and lighted it. "All in all, though, we made a pretty good team for Pinkerton. Finally Russ proposed that we leave the company and form our own private detective agency. What we could do for Pinkerton we could do for ourselves and make more money. Or so Russ maintained. I wondered if we could get enough jobs to keep us going. Russ had that all figured out. About that time, Linda, the Kansas, Midland & Southwest Railroad was getting right worried about the loss of pay-roll money on your stage route. A distant relative of Kennard's stood high in the K. M. & S., and when Russ told him of the detective agency we planned to establish, the railroad man offered us the job of an investigation down here."

"And so you got off to a flying start," Silvertop commented.

"It looked that way. The K. M. & S. gave us a good drawing account, so we had money to go on. Russ and I were coming down here together. Just as we were about to leave, another job was offered us—the running down of the murderer of a wealthy mine owner up near Coeur d'Alene, Idaho. Russ suggested I take that job and then come down here when it was finished. It required longer than I thought. I kept writing Russ, but his replies were vague, or he failed to reply at all. I didn't like it. Then I had a letter from the K. M. & S. people asking why our new agency wasn't getting results."

Murragh flicked ash from his cigarette and inhaled deeply. "As soon as I could clear up the other job, I headed for Lanyard. I suspected that Russ was indulging in one or both of his weaknesses. His last letter hadn't sounded friendly, he hadn't wanted me to come here, claiming he could handle the job alone. That told me that things were even worse than I'd suspected. To be on the safe side, I had the railroad fix it with the governor of the territory and the U. S. marshal to give me all the authority I might need. In addition, I'm down in the governor's books as an investigator and special prosecutor."

" 'A Daniel come to judgment!' " Henley exclaimed.

"Be still, Cass," Linda said. "That's not so appropriate. Just keep quiet and let Hoyt talk."

Murragh resumed, "I knew affairs were pretty bad the instant I saw Kennard. I sensed he wasn't playing on the level with me. He'd lost his head to Isabel Fanchon and was spending more than he could afford. I suspected he was sharing the stage bandits' loot, and of course he must have told them why he came here. Last week, when I suggested that he ride the stage with the next pay roll, I knew from the way he acted he was going to double-cross me. I offered no particularly good reason for him riding that stage—no reason he couldn't have thought out himself, had he been on the square—yet he jumped at the idea as though I'd suggested something really smart. He was altogether too eager to make that ride. That warned me."

Murragh paused to flip his cigarette butt into a nearby sandbox and went on, "Kennard had already gone out of his way to try to make me believe he scarcely knew Alonzo Vaiden. He overplayed his hand in that direction; I knew he lied. . . . There was just one thing I hoped for—up to the last I thought that Kennard might change his mind and decide to go straight. Had I known it was his death, and not mine, that was planned, I might have been able to do something. But he knew too much to suit the bandits; he had to go. Though if they'd known, last night when I went to Isabel Fanchon's, exactly the authority I carry, I'd have been the man to be shot through that window." He scowled at the floor, then glanced up, smiling thinly, "It's taken a little time to get you folks straightened out on things, but you were entitled to an explanation. Just don't let it go any farther."

Linda said, "You think Vaiden is at the head of the stage bandits?"

"I'm pretty sure of it—but I've got to have proof before I can act. There's more than robbery to be cleared up now. There's two murders to be squared."

Silvertop asked, "You suspecting all of Vaiden's Rafter-AV cowhands, too?"

"Not yet. I've circulated around town a lot since I've been here. I've talked to men in bars. I even ran across two of the Rafter-AV punchers and their foreman, Quent Hillman, in Pudge Ryan's one time. Somehow I've got a hunch they're in the clear. From all I can gather, the Rafter-AV's a profitable cow outfit. That means a hard-working crew. Any crew that gets a cut on a stolen pay roll doesn't work hard at cow business. The crew may or may not know what Vaiden is doing. I couldn't say as to that."

"How do you figure Claude Balter?" Henley asked.

"Balter's a different proposition. I don't think he claims to be much of a cowhand—"

"Speaking of Balter," Silvertop put in, "he don't seem to follow Vaiden around the way he used to. I haven't seen him for several days."

"Maybe he's giving Hoyt a wide berth," Henley laughed.

"I wish I could think so," Murragh said moodily, "but I'm still expecting trouble from that direction—"

"What I don't see," Linda broke in, "is how that gun was stolen from your satchel, Hoyt."

"I thought that was clear. Kennard took it, of course. His hotel key fitted the door to my room. He got the gun and turned it over to Vaiden—I think. When I know more about Vaiden I'll tell you for sure. I think Kennard had gone through my satchel before he took the gun. It wasn't quite as I'd left it on one occasion. After that I checked the contents of the satchel every day, expecting something of the kind from him."

"What's your next move?" Henley asked.

Murragh considered. "I'm figuring on baiting a hook for a certain man. . . . No, don't ask me about it. I haven't things all worked out in my own mind yet . . ."

That night the stage from Lanyard brought Murragh a letter from Wyatt Holliday, dated the previous Friday, the day the stage robbers had been foiled of their attempt to steal the Silver Belle pay roll from the strongbox. The letter read:

DEAR HOYT:

I hung around Sulphur Tanks until the stage arrived and heard all the wild stories of what had happened. That Kennard certainly played his part. By this time you probably know for sure that your hunch on him was right. Later on I went out and looked over the place where the stage was held up. I read sign on the ground and in the brush. All that talk about there being eight robbers is wrong. I could only find footprints of four men, and there was only prints of four horses back where they waited. There was evidence where several rifles had been laid on the ground. I even found one hat they forgot to take. It is my guess that the coyotes just stuck rifles and hats around through the brush so it would look like they had a big gang. I have to laugh when I think what their faces looked like when they opened that strongbox and saw the rock we put in for them. Well, this is all I have to write now. Let me know if I can help you on anything else. This town is so peaceful nowadays that I'd be pleased to see some excitement some place. Well, watch out and don't stop any lead.

Yrs. respt'y,
WYATT HOLLIDAY

After he had finished reading the letter, Murragh strolled out and found a seat on the darkened gallery of the hotel. His cigar dimmed and glowed in the darkness, while plans coursed his mind and were discarded for still other plans. Finally he tossed away the butt of the cigar and walked next door to the stage office. Linda and Silvertop were still there. Murragh asked, "Does Vaiden often make the trip to Sulphur Tanks?"

Silvertop frowned. "I don't know, exactly. Never paid much attention. Yes, I guess he does, come to think of it."

"He does, he does," Linda said excitedly. "I just happened to think that nearly every time the stage has been held up, Vaiden has made a trip to Sulphur Tanks anywhere from a day to three days previously. I'd noticed that before, but it just never struck me—"

"Thanks. That's what I wanted to hear." He doffed his sombrero and started to leave.

"But, Hoyt—" Murragh paused near the door, one hand on the knob. Linda continued, "What are we going to do about next Friday's Silver Belle pay roll? That has to be—"

"I'm going to deliver it myself."

"What! What did you say?"

"You heard me. I'll tell you about it later. Just don't worry about it. And"—he smiled—"keep your mouth shut."

The door closed behind him, and he continued on to the sheriff's office, where he found Cass Henley, alone, immersed in a red-bound volume entitled *Two Gentlemen of Verona*. Murragh said, without preliminaries, "Cass, if I were a horse thief wanted in Texas, and a sheriff there telegraphed you asking for information about me, and if I got a tip you received such a telegram, what would be my next move?"

"Get out of my county pronto," Cass replied promptly, "and lose yourself in some other town."

"What are the best towns hereabouts? Say, I don't want to get too far away from friends in Lanyard."

"Sulphur Tanks and Millman City. Millman City is a heap larger, but Wyatt Holliday's got that town so much in the hollow of his hand that crooks shy clear of it nowadays. That leaves Sulphur Tanks, unless you want to get completely out of the territory."

"Does Vaiden's Rafter-AV lie in Lanyard County?" Henley nodded. Murragh went on, "I'd better make it Sulphur Tanks, then."

"But what's the idea of tipping off Barney Twitchell and letting him get away?" The shrewd eyes narrowly studied Murragh's face.

"Who said anything about Barney Twitchell?"

"All right," Henley said good-naturedly, "don't tell me, then."

Murragh relented. "I'll explain everything, later, Cass. Right now I want to get back to the hotel and write a letter to Wyatt Holliday. I want it to leave on the stage in the morning. See you again," and he hurried off, but not before he'd caught the sarcastic quotation Henley sent after him, " 'What a spendthrift he is of his tongue!' "

At two-thirty the following morning Murragh knocked on the door of the sheriff's office. "It's me—Hoyt," he replied, in answer to the drowsy question that came from Henley's cot. There were bare footsteps on the floor, then the bolt shot back in the lock. The door swung open. Murragh stepped in quickly. "Don't bother to light the lamp, Cass. I'll be leaving in a minute."

Cass eyed him through the gloom. "Where you heading now? Looked like you had a satchel in your hand."

"I'm catching the three-fifteen train for the capital."

"My God, you get around places fast. Why the capital? You aiming to see Senator Welch?"

"Not if I can help it. On the contrary. It's some other business. That's not what I came to see you about. Cass, this stationmaster down to the depot—"

"Joe Phelan? He's all right. Why?"

"Phelan—that's the name. I want you to get him to do us a favor. Sometime Wednesday have him—accidentally, of course—just happen to run into Barney Twitchell around town someplace. It'll probably be a bar—"

"Twitchell can be found hanging around Pudge Ryan's place nearly any time."

"That's fine. We'll say that Phelan gets in conversation with Twitchell, buys him a drink and so on. Phelan gets careless and just innocently happens to mention a certain telegram from a Texas sheriff inquiring after one Twitchell Barnett. It's the similarity of the two names that brought the thing to Phelan's memory, something like that. Do you get what I mean?"

There was silence for a moment. Then Henley's voice came through the darkness. "If I know Twitchell he'll hightail it out of town if Phelan drops anything like that."

"That's what I'm hoping."

"You're baiting a hook, hoping Twitchell will take it and—"

"Lead me to other fish. I'm glad I don't have to explain everything to you, Cass. But will Phelan do it?"

"I'm sure he will. The main thing is for Twitchell to be tipped off, isn't it? If something comes up to prevent Phelan doing the job, I'll work it some other way. Just leave it to me."

"Good. But I don't want Twitchell to know before Wednesday. I'm playing a long chance, and my timing has to be right. I'll be back here by Thursday. S'long." And Murragh had stepped from the office to the sidewalk and was walking swiftly along darkened Main Street once more.

Henley crawled back between his blankets after relocking the door. "Now what the devil is he going to the capital for if not to see Max Welch?—and he said that wasn't the reason." For an hour Henley pondered the problem without reaching a solution. Finally he quoted sleepily, " 'The attempt, and not the deed, confounds us. . . .' "

During the next two days Henley found much of his time devoted to parrying queries relative to Murragh's whereabouts. Even Linda's questioning failed to elicit any information from the closemouthed deputy, who evaded her interrogations with cryptic quotations from Shakespeare, some appropriate, some not, which eventually discouraged the girl, and she gave up the attempt to learn where Murragh had gone.

Vaiden had cornered Henley, on Wednesday, in the hotel bar, and asked if Murragh had left town. Henley had shrugged his shoulders and suggested, "Why don't you ask at the hotel?"

"I did," Vaiden replied. "The clerk says he didn't give up his room yet."

"Then I bet you a dollar Murragh will be back," Henley had said blandly.

"But where's he gone?" Vaiden persisted.

Henley took refuge in the Immortal Bard: " 'Rest, rest, perturbed spirit,' " he said mockingly. " 'But that I am forbid to tell the secrets of my prison-house, I could a tale unfold, whose lightest word would harrow up thy soul, freeze thy young blood, make thy two eyes, like stars, start from their spheres, thy knotted and combined locks to part, and each particular hair to stand on end, like quills upon the fretful porcupine—' "

"You and your Goddamned Shakespeare!" Vaiden interrupted wrathfully. "Of all the fools I ever—!"

" 'What!' " Henley exclaimed in pretended amazement. " 'Drunk with choler? Beware of entrance to a quarrel—' "

Vaiden whirled angrily toward the doorway and lunged out to the street, muttering something that had to do with getting away from a certain damned fool, but not before he had caught the snickered quotation that followed him: " 'Stand not upon the order of your going, but go at once.' "

Henley turned laughingly back to the bar. A couple of other customers eyed him with some amusement. The bartender grunted, "That may be funny to you, Cass, but you got to admit that you druv off some trade with your crazy spoutings."

"Trade? Vaiden's trade? Cripes A'mighty! You should be tendering me a vote of thanks. 'Ingratitude! Thou marble-hearted fiend!' "

"Look, Cass," the barkeep said with some exasperation. "I'll buy you a free drink every time you come in here if you'll just leave Bill Shakespeare at the sheriff's office when you come."

The deputy considered the offer, perplexedly. " 'I do perceive here a divided duty.' " He shook his head, "Nope, Dan, I couldn't do it. 'The time is out of joint.' I'm not thirsty, now. Try me another time." He nodded to the other customers and sallied, grinning, from the saloon.

On Wednesday night Cass Henley was down at the T. N. & A. S. station when the eleven-eighteen train came through and deposited Murragh on the depot platform. "Successful trip?" Cass asked, as the two headed up Bowie Street.

"Found what I wanted," Murragh replied. "Had to plow through a lot of dusty records to locate it, though. I never realized before how many laws a group of legislators could pass. It's a good thing some of them are forgotten—particularly for us, or maybe not—"

"What in time are you talking about?"

Murragh smiled. "You wouldn't think that a pair like Vaiden and Welch, with a successful cow outfit, would descend to stage robbing, would you? I always did have a hunch they were after something bigger. I think now I know what it is."

"Are you talking now?"

"Sure. I'm asking what you did about that Twitchell business?"

"It worked out as we expected. Joe Phelan was glad to help. Ten minutes after Phelan talked to Twitchell, Twitchell was riding out of the Blue Star Livery on that paint horse Tony tried to hire to you one time. I'll bet Tony'll never see that paint again. Last I saw of Twitchell he was riding north like all the devils in hell were after him."

"Good." Murragh didn't say any more until they'd reached the hotel, then, "Wait while I take this satchel up to my room. I want to go over and see Linda. I'm counting on your help."

Ten minutes later Henley and Murragh were at the Gordon home. Linda and her father hadn't yet gone to bed. Before they could express much amazement over the late visit, Murragh got down to business: "It's this way, Linda—I have an order on your local bank here from the Silver Belle Mine. You know the banker. It's up to you to go with me, get him out of bed, if necessary, and accompany us to the bank—"

"An order on the bank?" Linda gasped. "But, but where—?"

"Got it last week when I was in Millman City. The Millman City Bank transfers certain funds to the Lanyard Bank. I have an order to collect. We'll need a couple of satchels, or valises, or something to put the money in—"

"You're taking the pay roll up to Sulphur Tanks tomorrow, instead of having it come down from Millman City Friday," Silvertop said, smiling.

"Correct," from Murragh. "I'll be riding the stage to Sulphur Tanks tomorrow morning. The money will be cached in the boot along with other baggage, if any. We won't use a strongbox. Won't bother sending a strongbox of rocks from Millman City again, either. Once the money's loaded on the stage—we'll do that tonight and, Linda, you'll have to accompany us to the stables and assure your night man we're not up to anything wrong—Cass and I will stay with the stage until it pulls out in the morning. We'll take turns sleeping in the coach. Tomorrow morning the regular guard will be along too, so I'm not expecting any trouble that can't be handled. This week's pay roll should go through without a break."

Linda's long-lashed eyes were shining. "You're going to make monkeys of those bandits again Friday."

"Maybe," Murragh stated, "there won't even be a holdup Friday, if a certain plan of mine works out. I'm just not taking chances, that's all. And, Linda—once more—keep your mouth shut."

At seven the following morning, when the stage pulled out on its northbound trip, Murragh was one of a half-dozen passengers riding in the coach. In one of the boots, along with his personal satchel and other baggage, were two grips which held the pay-roll cash for the Silver Belle miners.

19
A Weak Link

Around noon, at which time the stage arrived at Sulphur Tanks, Wyatt Holliday was on hand to meet Murragh, as were the paymaster and superintendent of the Silver Belle. The two grips of money were quickly carried to the back room of the stage station and counted, after which Murragh received a receipt. He helped the two company men carry the grips out to their waiting wagon and received their congratulations.

"We didn't learn until yesterday what you intended to do," the superintendent smiled. "I suppose you'll have still another trick for next week. How long do you think you can plan up such schemes?"

Murragh replied unsmiling, "So long as bandits continue holding up stages."

"That should be long enough," the paymaster grinned.

Murragh returned to the porch of the stage station, where Wyatt Holliday waited, and dropped into a chair by the marshal's side. Holliday said, "So you've put it through once more."

Murragh gave a sigh of relief. "I was certainly glad to get rid of that money. What's happened?"

"Got your letter Tuesday and took the Wednesday stage for here—now, wait, don't get impatient. Your man's here."

"I had the right hunch, then."

"He got in late Wednesday night, riding a paint horse that will probably never be any good again. He must have run the legs off'n that poor beast, and if it isn't a wind-broken example of what a horse killer can do, from now on, I miss my guess."

"Do you know where Twitchell is now?"

"Course I do. When he arrived he lit out for a shack over north of town. There's three others there. There's a low ridge, covered with brush, not far from the shack. I spied on 'em this morning. They're mighty furtive-acting, so I guess they're what you're after, Hoyt."

"Claude Balter one of 'em?"

"I couldn't say. I've never seen Balter that I know of. These fellers—and Twitchell—were sticking close to their place. I really didn't get a close-up look at any of 'em."

"If this comes out all right, I'd like to get those hombres away with as little fuss as possible."

"You're taking them to Millman City?"

"For the time being."

"That's the way I figured you'd want to do. I brought handcuffs along, and I've already arranged for horses at the livery."

"Cripes A'mighty, Wyatt," Murragh said appreciatively, "I don't know what I'd do without you."

"Forget it. If it wasn't me, it'd be somebody else glad to work with you—no, forget it, I say! Let's go find some dinner. My belly's commencing to think my throat's cut."

They left the stage station and strode along the main street of Sulphur Tanks, which proved to be a dirty-looking settlement, largely composed of saloons, honky-tonks, and miners' dwellings. There were a number of false-fronted buildings; the roadway was six inches deep with dust; the plank sidewalks were splintered and worn. A sooty haze overhung the town, giving the sun a brassy appearance. Smoke poured from the chimneys of the smelter farther out of town.

"How about the deputy sheriff here?" Murragh asked.

"I was talking to him this morning. He was plumb curious to learn what brought me here, but I figured you and I could handle this our own way. He won't interfere, and if we run into too much trouble I can count on him to help us. He's a good man in his way, but most of his law-enforcing has to do with arresting drunks and handling the miners on pay night, which same he does with a heavy hand and a gun barrel. His jail's full most of the time."

Holliday led the way up a side street and turned in at a small restaurant. "Had breakfast here this morning. It wasn't too bad."

"We could have eaten at the stage station, except—"

"Except that there's always too many people hanging around that section of Sulphur Tanks. The less people see you, the better it may be."

"That's what I had in mind." They entered the restaurant and ate dinner.

Just beyond the northern boundary of the town lay a low, rocky ridge covered with stunted mesquite and prickly pear. At the foot of the ridge ran a helterskelter arrangement of shabby frame houses. It was on the other side of the ridge that Holliday and Murragh drew their ponies to a halt about three o'clock that afternoon. Each man had led behind him two saddled horses. These extra horses were tethered to the lowflung limb of a cottonwood tree. As Holliday dismounted, a burlap sack hung from his saddlehorn gave off a clanking sound. They dropped reins over the ponies' heads and started up the side of the ridge on foot.

Finally, at the top, they lay side by side in the brush, peering down at the roofs of the houses beneath. Holliday said, "They're staying in that house with the bucket standing near the back door—see the one that I mean? There's a lot of empty tin cans scattered around. You'll note the other houses keep their cans in a neat pile."

"I see the place. I hope they're in there now."

"Me too. I've got a hunch they don't move out much, except at night."

"Anybody in the other houses likely to get curious?"

"I don't reckon. They're all miners' homes, I think. Probably nobody in 'em but women and kids. What's your plan, Hoyt?"

"You go back, get your horse, and ride up to the front

door. I'll slip down this slope and come in the back way. That sound all right?"

"Suits me, only if any of 'em recognize me coming, they may make a break for the back door. That would leave you facing four men."

"I'll make out all right," Murragh said quietly. "You just keep their attention at the front while I come in the rear. Let's get going, Wyatt."

Holliday backed down the hill. When below the top of the ridge he turned and scrambled down to his pony, got into the saddle, and started toward the end of the low hogback. Murragh waited until Holliday was well on his way, then started the short descent toward the rear of the house. There was considerable screening brush to shield his movements from below, except at the bottom where a stretch of about thirty yards, littered with rusty tin cans, lay before him. Once at the foot of the slope, Murragh rose from the brush and dashed toward the shack, approaching at a sharp angle so as not to be observed from the window located a few feet from the back door.

Reaching the back door, he paused and took his six-shooter from its holster. Almost at the same time he heard a horse stop in the roadway before the house, then Holliday's sudden knocking at the door. Voices sounded within, low and troubled. An argument was taking place as to whether or not the door should be opened. Murragh moved quickly to the grimy window and peered inside. Four men stood there, all facing the front of the house, their backs to Murragh. One of the men was Barney Twitchell. The other three were

221

unshaven, ugly-visaged individuals. All wore six-shooters at their right thighs. The house was shabbily furnished, with a couple of beds, a table, and a stove. Three or four empty boxes stood about, and there were some unwashed dishes on the table.

Again Holliday knocked. Murragh saw one of the men draw his six-shooter and back off a pace, his gaze fixed on the door. The man with the gun now gestured to Twitchell to open up, and backed another step, ready to shoot if the visitor wasn't to his liking.

Murragh figured it was time to act. He raised his gun barrel and smashed one pane from the window. Through the jangling of falling glass his words came, stern, uncompromising, "Raise 'em high, you hombres! Drop that gun, mister! You haven't a chance!"

The men in the room turned slack-jawed faces toward Murragh. Twitchell had paused in mid-stride on his way to the door. The man with the gun hesitated a moment, then dropped his weapon on the floor and raised his hands with the others. Murragh continued, "All right, Twitchell, go ahead, open that door. And don't any of you hombres make any sudden moves. I don't like sudden moves."

Twitchell opened the door. Holliday entered, his gun already in hand. Murragh went on, "Keep 'em covered, Wyatt. I'll be with you in a second."

He moved to the back door and found it locked. Raising one booted foot, he gave it a savage kick. There came the sound of splintering wood and the door swung inward. Murragh pushed it open and stepped into the room. He moved quickly across to the men, jerking guns out of their holsters and tossing them on the table.

"Now get back against the wall," he snapped. "Keep those hands high! Remember, I don't like trouble, so act accordingly."

Holliday said, "Nice work, Hoyt."

"Nice work yourself."

"Just hold 'em as they are. I'll be back pronto."

He turned and hurried out to his horse. The man who had first drawn his gun swore savagely at Twitchell: "Damn you, Barney, I knowed you shouldn't have come here. Now see—"

"You, what's your name," Murragh interrupted the tirade.

"Me? Milt Lynch."

"All right, Lynch, keep your mouth shut."

He questioned the other two men. Their names were Jode Proctor and Cal Osgood. They were a scurvy-looking trio in dirty range togs and battered sombreros, fit mates for Barney Twitchell, though unlike Twitchell they showed little fear. Twitchell was ashen; the hands above his head were trembling.

Holliday re-entered the house carrying the clanking burlap sack. He closed the door behind him. Murragh said, "Know any of these fellows, Wyatt?"

"They're all strangers to me—"

Lynch burst out at this point: "Is there only two of you hombres?" unbelievingly.

"For all the fight you put up, one of us could have handled this," Holliday said scornfully.

Lynch started cursing again. "We could have made a stand—"

"What's this all about?" Cal Osgood asked. "We ain't done nothing. We work in the mine—"

Laughter, cold and cynical, from Murragh and Holliday met this attempt. Jode Proctor was the coolest of the quartette. "All right," he said resignedly, "you've got badges. Maybe you've got authority to go with 'em. What I want to know, what are we being arrested for?"

"A fair question," Murragh nodded. "Stage robbery."

There was an instant's silence, then a chorus of denials, loudest among which was Barney Twitchell's: "I never robbed a stage in my life."

"Ever steal a horse?" Murragh inquired pleasantly.

Twitchell sagged visibly. Jode Proctor snarled, "Just keep still, fellers. These lawmen ain't got anything on us."

"Where's Claude Balter?" Murragh asked suddenly.

Proctor sneered defiantly. "Balter? Never heard of him. Any of you fellers ever hear of a Balter?"

"I never did," Milt Lynch denied.

"Not me," from Cal Osgood.

"I knew Claude in Lanyard," Twitchell commenced. "What do you want to know?"

"You, Barney," Milt Lynch rasped, "don't say anything you'll be sorry for." A hidden threat lay in the words. Twitchell gulped hard and didn't say anything more, despite Murragh's efforts to make him talk.

By this time Holliday had the rawhide thong about the top of the burlap sack untied, and he stepped forward with four pairs of handcuffs. "Step up and get your bracelets, boys," he invited.

Milt Lynch swore at him. "You ain't puttin' them

things on me, Mister Lawman—"

Murragh took one quick step forward, slammed the barrel of his forty-four against Lynch's jaw. Lynch emitted a yelp of pain. "It isn't any fun for me, either," Murragh said grimly, "but that's just a love tap to what you'll get if you don't get your mitts up plenty pronto!" For the first time a look of fear entered Lynch's eyes. He made no further objection but accepted meekly the cuffs that Holliday snapped about his wrists. The other three men offered no protest, and within a few minutes they were similarly fettered.

Holliday tossed the prisoners' guns into the burlap sack. Murragh said, "Wait until I give a look around, then we'll get started."

His search disclosed certain evidence. Hidden beneath the two beds, Murragh found eight rifles and several old sombreros. Two of the Winchesters were in good condition; the others were rusty and unserviceable. Murragh smiled grimly at the prisoners. "I don't imagine you boys will be arranging these things in the brush to intimidate passengers any more. I'm fairly certain you won't."

The prisoners didn't reply, beyond an exchange of furtive looks with one another. Except for Twitchell, they had fallen into a sullen silence. Twitchell kept repeating he had never robbed a stage in his life. The hats and rifles, with barrels sticking from the mouth of the burlap sack, were gathered up by Holliday. "Ready to leave?" he asked Murragh.

"Ready," Murragh nodded. He spoke to the prisoners, "Out the back way, you hombres. We've horses waiting for you beyond that ridge. Get moving."

It was the handcuffs that apparently proved to be the final straw in breaking the back of any further resistance on the part of the prisoners. They moved meekly before Murragh into the open and started to climb the ridge, while Holliday, mounted, came on behind. At the opposite side of the ridge the captives were put in saddles and started north, with Murragh and Holliday riding closely in their rear. Murragh said meaningly, "Just so you boys won't get any sudden ideas, I might as well warn you that those ponies you're straddling aren't any too fast. Not fast enough to run away from a lead slug, anyway."

Lynch, Osgood, and Proctor rode as closely together as possible, the chains of their handcuffs linked over saddle horns. They seemed to shun Twitchell, who rode, head down like a beaten man, off to one side.

It was nearly four o'clock the following morning when Murragh and Holliday, with their prisoners ahead, rode into the darkened streets of Millman City. Not long afterward the men were lodged in cells in the city jail. Holliday returned to his office at the front of the building while Murragh remained to talk with the prisoners for a time. An hour later he came out to the office looking weary but cheerful.

Holliday said, "The stage for Lanyard leaves in a couple of hours. You'd better drop down on my cot and catch a mite of shut-eye. I'll awaken you in time."

Murragh nodded. "Call me early enough so I can get some breakfast."

Holliday said, hesitatingly, "There's just one thing

bothering me, Hoyt: there's a limit to the time you can hold a man without giving him a hearing. Those fellows are material witnesses, of course, but—"

Murragh smiled. "I didn't forget that, Wyatt. Maybe they're going to be willing to be held until they're needed. In fact, I know they are."

"How'd you work it?"

"With Osgood, Lynch, and Proctor I gave 'em their choice of being charged with stage robbery or complicity in murder. There's a heap of difference in the sentences those two crimes draw. I simply told 'em that if they wanted the murder charge they could have a hearing at once. That was pure bluff, of course, but they decided they were willing to wait and take a chance on the robbery charge later. At the same time they're not admitting a thing. I think they've an idea Vaiden can get them out of this if they keep their mouths shut."

"How about Barney Twitchell?"

"Or Twitch Barnett, as he's known in Texas. He's the weak link in the chain. I had an idea I could make a deal with him. Trouble is, he doesn't know all the things I want to learn—unless he lied to me, and I don't think he did. I've already got plenty evidence, but I'll just have to think up a new way to play my cards. With Twitchell it was a question whether he wanted to play along with me and just face a charge of horse-thievery in Texas, or if he wanted to stay loyal to Vaiden and be charged as an accomplice to murder. That murder thing scares him, even if he doesn't know who committed it."

"And what happened?"

Murragh smiled wearily. "We made a deal."

20

Arrest

Cass Henley found Murragh eating supper in the JOE LOW Restaurant that night, shortly after the stage from Millman City had arrived. Henley crossed the floor to Murragh's table, grinning, and dropped on a chair across from him. Murragh looked up and said absent-mindedly, "Oh, hello, Cass . . ." His voice dwindled off to silence. Henley noticed that the food on his plate was scarcely touched, his coffee cup still full. There was a frown on Murragh's face as he gazed into abstract space.

Henley murmured, " 'So sweet is zealous contemplation . . .' "

"Quiet, you Avon-addled ape," Murragh smiled suddenly. "I was trying to think out something."

Henley started to rise. "Sorry, Hoyt. I'll get out—"

Murragh caught him by the sleeve. "Sit down, Cass. Talking to you should clear my mind. You see, I was just trying to work out a knotty problem, and I wasn't having any success."

"I saw Linda—she says you told her you got the pay roll to Sulphur Tanks without any trouble."

"As you and I expected. There wasn't any attempt to hold up the southbound stage today, either. Maybe no holdup was planned for this week. That rocks-in-the-strongbox idea may have made them wary of trying anything until they could think things over."

Henley said shrewdly, "Well, did Twitchell lead you to any other fish?"

"We caught four beauties—including Twitchell."

"Who were the other three suckers?"

Briefly Murragh related his and Holliday's activities of the previous day. When the story had been concluded, Henley asked, "What you aiming to do with those four prisoners?"

"Hold 'em as material witnesses for a trial."

"You mean you know who killed Uncle Jimmy Cochrane?" Henley looked excited.

"I think I've known that for quite a while, Cass. Dammit, I can't prove it, though. If I could only get someone to testify to what I know in my own mind—"

"Who killed him, Hoyt?"

"I'm not ready to say yet, until I get further proof. . . . What's been doing while I've been away?"

"Nothing much. Vaiden does a lot of trying to find out what's keeping you busy, but"—Henley smiled—"nobody seems able to tell him. Claude Balter's started coming to town again—follows Vaiden around like a little puppy dog—" Henley paused at Murragh's sudden exclamation and asked, "Does that mean anything in particular, Hoyt?"

"Maybe, just maybe," Murragh said slowly, his eyes narrowed in thought beneath the triangular slash of black hair across his forehead. "I've got an idea that might work . . ." Again his voice tapered off to silence.

Henley waited a while, then said, "The sheriff took his missus to El Paso to that doctor. Don't know when he'll be back. Mrs. Farley is going under the knife, you know."

"Good," Murragh said, musingly. He sipped his coffee.

"What?" Henley sounded surprised.

Murragh smiled sheepishly. "I meant it was good about something else. I was only half listening, Cass. I certainly hope everything will be all right with Jake's wife. . . . Any news on Isabel Fanchon?"

"She hasn't opened her shop all week. There's a lot of gossip running around town, of course, and I guess Isabel don't feel like facing any of the other ladies. 'Lonzo Vaiden's visiting Isabel tonight—"

"He's still in town, then?"

Henley nodded. "I've been snooping around. Claude Balter's staying at the Cowman's Rest tonight."

"He and Vaiden will probably be in town tomorrow, then."

"I think Vaiden plans to hang around until he can see if there's any news to be picked up on you. Now that he knows you're a deputy U. S. marshal he's getting plumb curious."

"Things are working out," Murragh said half aloud.

"What! What things are working out?"

"I'm just thinking out loud, Cass. Don't pay any attention. Certain things have to dovetail in my mind before I can answer your questions." Murragh ate moodily for a few minutes. Finally he went off on a new tack: "What about that gunsmith who has the shop on Main, in the next block? Does he know his business?"

"You mean Virgil Shattuck? Old Virg knows more about guns than anybody I ever talked to. Never yet saw the gun he couldn't repair, or make a part for, if necessary. One of your forty-fours in need of repairs?"

Murragh was again lost in his abstractions. "What? Huh? Oh—yes, I heard you. Virgil Shattuck, eh?" Murragh drained his coffee cup. "I'll give him a couple of guns to work on, maybe."

"He can take care of any sort of repair work necessary."

"Not repairs needed, exactly. Just a couple of minor adjustments."

"You must be expecting some action, Hoyt."

Murragh smiled wearily. "Lord knows, I hope so." Silence again followed. Finally Murragh rose from the table. "I'm going to the hotel and turn in. Didn't get any sleep to speak of last night. I'll see you in the morning, Cass. Meanwhile keep an eye on Vaiden and Balter for me."

"I'll do that."

Henley accompanied Murragh as far as the hotel, where they parted, then the deputy headed toward Pudge Ryan's Bar. Balter was standing drinking at the bar with a couple of Bench-H cowboys who apparently didn't enjoy his company but didn't know exactly how to get away without hurting Balter's feelings, Balter having the reputation of being a bad man to cross. There were a few other customers in the place. Henley had a bottle of beer, then strolled back to the sheriff's office, noticing on his way that a light still shone dimly in Isabel Fanchon's place.

At nine the following morning Murragh found Henley seated on the small porch that fronted the sheriff's office, chair tilted against the front wall of the building. There was another chair there. Murragh dropped into it. "Shady here," he commented cheerfully.

"Always is, this time of day. I'll have enough sunshine before the day's over." He added a trifle sarcastically, "Of course, you just walked here from the hotel to talk about the heat."

Murragh smiled. "All right, Cass, I'll come to the point. Usually, when a man's boss goes away, what does his assistant do?"

"I don't know what you mean. Nine times out of ten, though, the assistant starts putting some of his own ideas into effect, just to show his importance. Now look here, Hoyt, I'm not going to change anything that Jake Farley does. His way is all right for me."

Murragh looked surprised. "Who asked you to change anything? All I want you to do is enforce the law."

Henley looked relieved. "Well, Jake's always done that, so I'm in the clear."

"But, just for once, wouldn't you like to show your importance?"

"Dammit, Hoyt, what are you getting at?"

"Cass, I understand there's an ordinance against wearing guns in this town. Anyway, that's what the hotel clerk told me when I first arrived in Lanyard."

Henley snorted. "Nobody pays any attention to that old regulation any more. Jake just got that put through a number of years ago when it looked like Lanyard might go wild. But things settled down and, in time, we just let the gun-toting ordinance be forgotten. It's a nuisance for a feller to have to stop off and leave his gun someplace when he hits town and then pick it up again on his way out. There hasn't been any reason for enforcing that ordinance for a good many years now. Jake's kept a tight rein on things—"

"Nevertheless, a law is a law."

"I'm surprised you'd talk that way, Hoyt, about a little—"

"You know, Cass, I can make an order of this," Murragh smiled.

"Sure, if you insist, but it will look like I was—" Henley paused suddenly, eyes narrowing. "You're up to something," he accused.

"Are you with me?"

"Hell, yes! What do you want me to do?"

"I think it might be a good idea to demonstrate you're capable of enforcing the law when the sheriff's away. Lanyard could probably use any fines it collected, and it might be a sensible plan to make examples of a few fellows who ignore the ordinance on carrying guns— just to show them you're on the job, nothing more, you understand."

"And you think Vaiden and Balter might fit two of those examples?" Henley put forth shrewdly.

"Oh, I wouldn't want you to single out anybody in particular to vent your new-found energy on," Murragh smiled, "but of course, if Vaiden and Balter should happen to be in some bar when you make your—shall we call it a raid?—and you took their guns away from them, I shouldn't be displeased."

"Darn you, Hoyt," Henley grumbled, "I wish I could figure what you're up to."

"Me?" Murragh looked amazed. "I'm not going to have a thing to do with this. I expect to spend most of my day talking to Linda Gordon—and her father. As a deputy U. S. marshal I couldn't be expected to bother with these small-town ordinances." He paused. "Only, if you should happen to pick up Vaiden's and Balter's weapons, I'd appreciate—"

"Don't say anything more. I know what you mean," Henley growled.

"But there's nothing to it—"

" 'He jests at scars that never felt a wound,' " the deputy quoted in a solemn tone. "All right, I'll do it. First drink time for Vaiden isn't until around eleven o'clock. I reckon I'd better go talk to the justice of the peace and warn him he's going to have some fines to collect—" He suddenly remembered something. "I'll never get the J. P. to open court today. He always figures to do his serious drinking come Saturday. That means I'll be holding a bunch of guns until Monday morning."

"That's what I figured, too," Murragh replied.

Henley eyed him sharply. "You sure figure things ahead. Well, I'd better make a start toward becoming just about the most unpopular deputy Lanyard ever had. I'll lose every friend I have if I take all their guns."

"You don't need to bear down on your friends. Just pick up a few six-shooters to show people you mean business. That's all I meant."

"I hope I don't pick up the lead from the six-shooters," Henley said gloomily. "Oh well, 'Courage mounteth with occasion,' as the Bard says."

Murragh got to his feet. "I'll drop back and see you about two or three o'clock."

"Me or my dead body," Henley prophesied saturninely.

Murragh laughed lightly and headed up Main Street toward the Gordon stage office, where he invited Linda and her father to have dinner with him.

Shortly after eleven o'clock Henley entered Pudge Ryan's Bar, carrying a burlap sack already heavily weighted with several guns he'd confiscated. Vaiden, Balter, a Box-90 cowpuncher, and a couple of towns-people stood at the bar. The two citizens didn't wear guns; the other three did. Pudge Ryan stepped up to the bar. "What'll it be, Cass?"

"Nothing to drink. Three guns," Henley said shortly.

The men at the bar gazed at him, puzzled. Vaiden said, "What you got in that sack, Cass?"

"Guns. I'm taking yours now."

"What in hell are you talking about?"

"Look," Cass said testily, "you fellows know there's an ordinance against wearing your guns in town. All right, I'm taking them up. And I don't want any argument. I'm sick of arguing with you hombres who knowingly break a law—"

"That old law!" the Box-90 puncher exclaimed indignantly. "Hell's bells! Jake Farley let that slip long ago."

"I'm not Jake Farley," Henley snapped. "But while

he's gone I'm running the sheriff's job in this town. I'm tired of seeing that gun regulation ignored. It's time somebody was taught a lesson."

"Getting pretty big for your breeches, aren't you?" Vaiden sneered.

"Now I don't want any trouble with you, 'Lonzo," Henley said. "Just drop your gun in this here sack."

"The new broom's trying to sweep clean," Vaiden said sarcastically, "but all it will do is raise a lot of dust—"

Henley cut in, hard-voiced, "Maybe you'd like me to put you under arrest, 'Lonzo."

"By God!" Vaiden said. "This town is getting overrun with law, what with that deputy U. S. marshal coming in here, and now you're trying to show you're important too."

"I want your gun. Not talk," Henley flared. "Either I get that gun or I'm putting you under arrest. Lord knows I'm sick of arguing with all you gun toters, and I'd just as soon as not take some of you down to cells." He held the open mouth of the sack toward Vaiden. "What's it to be?"

Vaiden hesitated, then reluctantly drew his forty-five and dropped it carefully into the sack on top of the guns Henley already carried. The Box-90 puncher swore. "Never thought you'd get so uppity, Cass," he complained. Nevertheless his gun followed Vaiden's.

Henley turned on Claude Balter, who, so far, had done nothing but watch with his hard, agate eyes. "All right, Balter, follow suit."

Balter spoke for the first time. "You ain't taking my

gun." The tones were flat, unemotional, but there was a sort of violence about the man that couldn't be denied.

"Kick in," Henley persisted.

"You'll get my gun in a way you won't like," Balter said.

Henley put the sack on the floor. "This is known as resisting and threatening an officer of the law," he stated. "I think you'd better come down to the jail, Balter—"

"Ain't going to jail, neither."

"Maybe," Henley said, "you'd like Hoyt Murragh to come after your gun. He took it away from you last time—"

Balter swore, and his hand dropped to gun butt. Vaiden flung himself on the man and caught his arm. "Take it easy, Claude," he said sharply. "We don't want any trouble with the law. Hell, let this big-headed fool have your gun. All you'll have to do to get it back is pay a fine. I'll pay it for you when I get my gun back. Probably Henley and the J. P. are in cahoots to grab off some extra cash—but we'll just have to put up with it."

Still Balter resisted and argued. Henley said finally, "Balter, you're under arrest. You coming quiet?"

"Now wait a minute, Cass," Vaiden was suddenly placating. Before Balter could stop him, he jerked the gun from the man's holster and handed it to Henley. Henley, with a long sigh of relief, dropped it into the sack. Balter swore in a steady, unbroken monotone, whether at Henley or Vaiden, no one could decide.

Cass picked up the sack and started to leave. "Oh yes," he spoke over his shoulder, "court will open at ten

Monday morning. You can get your guns by paying whatever fine the J. P. imposes."

"Monday morning?" Vaiden snarled.

The Box-90 puncher wailed, "You mean we got to go the rest of today and tomorrow—?"

"Maybe I won't wait that long," Balter threatened.

Vaiden turned on the man to shut him up, and during the ensuing argument Henley made his escape. Outside, he tied the sack of guns to his saddle and climbed on his pony's back. At the next saloon he entered he took a fresh sack in with him, though the first wasn't yet filled. After a time he went back to his office, got two new sacks, and again started out. Now, however, the word had spread about what the deputy was doing, and there was a strange absence of guns wherever he appeared. Instead of guns he collected a varied assortment of jeers, abuse, and good-natured raillery. Finally, considerably disgusted, he went back to his office.

Murragh entered the office about a quarter to three. "Have a good day?" he queried cheerfully.

"No, and you damned well know it," Henley replied morosely. "What does this town think of me?"

"I've already heard a few remarks," Murragh chuckled.

"I've been called everything around the clock. Folks used to think I was a right hombre, but now—" Henley shook his head. "But you had to get me into this. What can I say? It's all your fault. I don't want people to think I'm just a swell-headed—"

"Ignore their attitude," Murragh advised gravely. "You know you're innocent of wrongdoing." His gray eyes twinkled as he quoted, "'What stronger breast-plate than a heart untainted?'"

Henley's face grew red. "Damn you, Hoyt Murragh," he growled, "you would hit below my guard." He laughed suddenly. "I just hope this is in a good cause."

"You can take my word for that," Murragh said soberly.

"All right. You'll find Vaiden's and Balter's guns in that lower drawer of the desk. Balter's has two notches cut in the butt."

"You're sure the other is Vaiden's? You didn't get them mixed?"

"Didn't put any more guns in that particular sack, after I got Vaiden's, Balter's and a cowpuncher's from the Box-90. The Box-90 boy's is a thirty-eight on a forty-five frame. Vaiden's and Balter's are the same model—forty-five, four-and-three-quarter-inch barrel. I checked what I had, before I went into Pudge Ryan's, then didn't waste too much time before I came back here and sorted out the guns. That's Vaiden's weapon, all right—number nine three seven six five."

"That's good work, Cass. I appreciate it."

"Go to hell," Henley said good-naturedly. "You got me into this. I might as well continue to make it look good." He seized an empty burlap sack and started toward the door. "I'll see if I can pick up a few more. Pull that door shut when you leave. I've got the key in my pocket."

Ten minutes later Murragh was entering the shop of Virgil Shattuck, Gunsmith. Shattuck was elderly, grizzled, with keen eyes shielded behind a pair of spectacles. Guns of various makes and sizes were scattered about his shop. At the moment Murragh entered, Shattuck was bent over his bench, on which a vise held the breechblock of an old Spencer repeating rifle on which he'd been working. He glanced up as the door closed behind Murragh and said, "Howdy."

"Mr. Shattuck," Murragh said, "Cass Henley tells me you're just the man to turn out a little job I want done."

Shattuck eyed the badge pinned to Murragh's shirt, wiped a smear of grease from his nose, and said genially, "Well, I always try to satisfy. You're Mr. Murragh, ain't you? Been hearing about you." Murragh nodded, and they shook hands. There was a moment's exchange of pleasantries, then Murragh drew from the waistband of his trousers the two six-shooters he carried there and handed them to the old man.

Shattuck took the guns in his gnarled hands, glanced carefully over them, then looked sharply at Murragh. "Same model. Must have been issued the same year or thereabouts."

"Maybe closer," Murragh smiled. "You'll notice one hammer is worn more than the other, due to having more usage. I want the hammers in those guns exchanged. Naturally, I'd like them to feel the same as they did before, if drawn back. There's probably some difference in tension—"

"The knurls on the spurs ain't wore the same, neither. Howsomever, a mite of acid and a file can work wonders sometimes. Sure I can switch these hammers so they won't feel no different than they did before in their own guns."

240

"That's exactly what I want."

Shattuck studied Murragh a moment. His eyes dropped to the badge, then came back to Murragh's face. "You know what you're doing?"

"I reckon I do. That's one reason I came to you."

Shattuck nodded, satisfied. "When do you want 'em? I got quite a bit of work ahead. Of course, just switchin' the hammers ain't no task, but—"

"The sooner I can get 'em, the better. Make it a rush job."

"How about tomorrow morning, say nine o'clock? I'll work on 'em tonight."

"That'll be fine. And thanks."

The following day Murragh dropped into the sheriff's office and talked to Henley for a time. It being Sunday, the streets looked deserted. Only a few of the stores were open. Virgil Shattuck had opened his shop for a short time, then closed it and returned home. Henley finally rose. "Be back in a few minutes," he said. "I've got to run across the street and get a sack of Durham."

When he had returned and was rolling a cigarette, Murragh said, "Oh yes, Cass, you might as well take Vaiden's and Balter's guns out of your desk and put 'em in the sacks with the other guns."

Henley eyed him steadily, then nodded and did as requested.

Murragh went on, "When do the men get their guns back?"

"Tomorrow morning at ten o'clock. There'll be quite a gang clamoring to get their guns. The justice of the peace will fine 'em probably five dollars each for violating a city ordinance, and that's all there'll be to it—except that I'll probably catch hell from Jake Farley when he gets back home."

"You'll be at the courthouse, of course."

"I wish I knew how I could get out of it. I'm going to have to stand a lot from those hombres—"

"Make sure that everybody gets his own gun back."

"There won't be any trouble about that. Everybody knows his own gun. . . . Now what's this leading up to?"

"Did I say it was leading up to anything? Wait a couple of hours after the gun-and-fining business is done with, then I want you to get a warrant and make an arrest."

"Yes?" Henley looked surprised. "Who do I arrest and what for?"

"Alonzo Vaiden. Charge him with the murder of Uncle Jimmy Cochrane."

"My God, Hoyt! Do you know what you're doing?"

"I'm gambling, Cass," Murragh said frankly, "but I think I can win. I don't figure you'll have any trouble with Vaiden, so long as you have a warrant for him. He'll argue and tell you you're crazy, but he can't argue against a warrant. He'll have to go with you peacefully. Bring him to the jail, book him, take his gun—"

"I know how to book a prisoner. Say, how come you don't make this arrest yourself?"

Murragh smiled. "You wouldn't want to put all the work on my shoulders, would you? Anyway, this is your county. The killing was perpetrated in Lanyard County. You see, Cass, as I'll be presiding at the trial as special prosecutor for this territory and pushing the proceedings against Vaiden, I'd rather you made the arrest."

Henley's eyes widened. "You! Going to be the prosecutor?" He sank weakly back in his chair, murmuring, " 'The storm is up, and all is on the hazard. . . .' "

21
The Motive

The news of Alonzo Vaiden's arrest for the murder of Uncle Jimmy Cochrane came as a distinct surprise to Lanyard, which immediately split into two camps, one of which, viewing Vaiden's reputation as a successful raiser of beef cattle in the county, could not conceive of any reason why he should have killed Jimmy Cochrane, and, consequently, jumped to the conclusion that a mistake had been made. The other camp, while liking Vaiden well enough, had always distrusted his follower, Claude Balter, and it was whispered about that perhaps Deputy Sheriff Henley had arrested the wrong man, though why Balter should have murdered Uncle Jimmy wasn't quite clear either. Neither camp believed for a moment that Vaiden would be found guilty of the crime. That Deputy U. S. Marshal Murragh should be scheduled to act as prosecuting attorney brought more surprise and considerable, speculation: was Murragh behind Henley's move and had Murragh committed a tremendous blunder?

Vaiden had been given a hearing by the justice of the

peace immediately after his arrest and pleaded "Not guilty." A date for the trial was set, and, in view of Vaiden's position in the county, he was released on relatively nominal bail, whereupon he once more appeared regularly on the streets of Lanyard, though minus his gun now, and proceeded to inform all and sundry of the extreme disappointment in store for Prosecutor Murragh, that Murragh and Henley both were "out of their heads," and that he welcomed the coming trial as an opportunity to prove, once and for all, that he was in no way implicated in Uncle Jimmy's death.

In the face of such conduct on Vaiden's part, more and more people commenced to believe in his innocence. Senator Max Welch, it was announced, would defend Vaiden; in fact, Welch had been called from the capital the day of the arrest and had been staying at the Rafter-AV ever since, preparing for the trial. Welch, too, fairly oozed confidence wherever he went, buying freely cigars and drinks in the hope of swaying popular opinion. He did a pretty good job, too. Even when prisoners Barney Twitchell, Milt Lynch, Cal Osgood, and Jode Proctor were brought by Gordon stage from Millman City and lodged in the city jail as material witnesses, the fact bothered Vaiden and Welch not at all, so far as could be discerned; if anything, their confidence seemed to increase, and Welch sneeringly speculated aloud as to the vast sum of money his client expected to gain when he sued for false arrest. The suit was to be instituted the instant the jury declared Vaiden "Not guilty."

Excitement grew increasingly day by day. Even when Sheriff Jake Farley arrived home (his wife's operation had been a success, but she'd remain in El Paso to recuperate), those who had been fined for toting guns forgot to make their complaints against Deputy Henley, much to Henley's relief, though it was noticed that men were again wearing their six-shooters, much as before. Privately, Murragh and Henley had conferred with Farley, who approved what they had done, though when one or two men remembered to ask the sheriff regarding the gun-toting ordinance, he had replied, " 'S'all right with me if you want to wear your hardware—just so you keep it holstered."

There was a matter of preparing the courthouse for the trial, too. A jury box had been knocked together; seats were arranged for spectators: a large crowd was expected to attend the daily sessions. Murragh was busier than the proverbial bee; there were documents to be drawn, letters had to be written, lists of witnesses to be made out, and notes regarding his procedure were formulated. Such periods of relaxation as he found, he spent with Henley, Silvertop, and Linda. Twice he and Linda went riding. Unconsciously Murragh and the girl were drawing closer together. Sometimes his friends were concerned at Murragh's long periods of silence when visiting with them.

As Linda said, one day, "Hoyt, you're worried." They were standing side by side before the short counter in the stage office. Silvertop had stepped out a short time previously.

Murragh's lips curved slightly. "Worried? Not

exactly, Linda. I'll be glad when this is over. I don't like waiting. I wish now the justice had set an earlier date for the trial."

"You know you're going to win, don't you?"

"As a matter of fact, I don't. I know certain things, but I have to have them confirmed before I can see Uncle Jimmy's murderer declared guilty. Some men in this state are putting a lot of faith in my ability. I don't want to disappoint them."

His hand was resting on the counter. Linda rested her own on it and said earnestly, "Don't you know, Hoyt Murragh, that you can't disappoint those men? They'll have faith in you—as we all will. You'll be doing your best; that's all anybody can ask."

He placed his other hand on hers, unconsciously tightened it. He said, "Thanks, Linda, but between the two of us, I'm taking a big gamble, hinging everything on one bit of testimony. Only don't tell anybody." He laughed softly. "Keep your mouth shut."

Linda smiled. "You've used those words a good many times to me, Hoyt."

"Someday," he replied, "I'll show you what I mean."

The girl met his gaze steadily. "I'll be waiting," she said. There was a few moments' silence while she removed her hand from beneath his palm. She went on, in a different voice, "Is the J. P. going to act as judge in this trial?"

"Wirt Stanton?" He chuckled. "Who told you that?"

"A lot of people in town think he is. They're—they're saying you're licked before you're started, that Senator Welch will have him so befuddled he won't

246

know whether he's coming or going."

"If Senator Welch has any idea of Stanton hearing this case, he's crazy. I can't believe he has. Wirt Stanton is a nice old fellow—though he does love his bottle—to act as J. P. and fine drunks and so on, but he's only a J. P.—he hasn't the knowledge of law—"

"That's a relief," Linda sighed. "I didn't know."

Murragh laughed. "Why, Linda Gordon, don't you know this is going to be quite a trial? The governor is sending down Judge Arnette from the capital, a clerk, bailiff, and so on—no, Welch won't pull any wool over Cyrus Arnette's eyes. By the way, Linda, I'll have to disrupt your stage service some. I plan to call Bert Echardt as a witness."

"Don't let it bother you. We have relief drivers. What witnesses do you suppose Welch will have?"

"I haven't the least idea. He'll probably figure to tear down my witnesses and bring in a few more of his own to say kind words for Vaiden . . ." The words drifted into silence as he fell into thought.

The day of the trial finally arrived. Lanyard's streets were streaming with people, and intense excitement prevailed. Wagons and horses crowded at the hitchracks. An hour before court opened, the courthouse was jammed with people. Two newspapers had sent reporters to cover the trial, but until after the jury was drawn these two worthy members of the press did their reporting in the hotel bar, gathering, so they claimed, the impressions of the common man as to whether Alonzo Vaiden was, or was not, guilty.

The drawing of the jury proved to be a tedious three-day affair, in which Senator Welch fought tooth and nail against any prospective juror of whom Murragh approved. On the second day, during the noon recess, Henley remarked, "How long does this go on? You don't like anybody Welch likes and vice versa. I thought you were going to be at each other's throats a couple of times. Neither one of you paid any attention to Vaiden. It was like you'd forgotten him."

"We have—until we get a jury suitable to both, or as near suitable as possible. Welch wants city men, and he knows what I'm after. I want cowmen—men who know horses and guns. I won't get all cowmen, of course, but if I can get a few strong-minded ones, they'll sway the others in the showdown—if it goes that far."

"What do you mean?"

"You'll see, if things work out as I'm gambling they will."

The morning of the fourth day, the trial proper opened on the lower floor of the courthouse, which was packed with perspiring humanity. Windows were opened on each side of the building, but such air as flowed through was quickly consumed in the sweltering heat. There was the usual cry of "Oyez! Oyez! Oyez!" accompanied by the rapping of the gavel. "Court is now open!"

The spectators rose as Judge Cyrus Arnette took his seat on the bench, then they quickly slumped down again. Arnette was a heavy-bodied man with rugged features, bushy eyebrows, and thick iron-gray hair. He was smoothly shaven and chewed tobacco continually. The twelve jurymen, dressed in Sunday best, were seated at the judge's left, their solemn expressions betraying the importance they felt at this sudden dignity that had been thrust upon them.

The witness stand was situated between the bench and the jury box. To the right of the judge was the clerk's desk, and on the desk was the bullet that had killed Uncle Jimmy Cochrane, and the deceased driver's shirts, showing bullet holes; these objects had been labeled Exhibits A and B. A short distance in front of the bench two tables were placed widely apart. At one sat Vaiden and Senator Welch. Though the law called for Vaiden to be handcuffed during the trial, Murragh hadn't insisted on this, and Arnette had approved Vaiden's appearance unfettered. Hoyt, on the other hand, uncertain of the Vaiden faction's reactions, had worn a gun to court each day, though the weapon was removed while court was actually in session. Seated with his back to the other table, Hoyt Murragh waited for the judge to signal him to commence. Murragh's coat was open, displaying a white shirt and black necktie; his belt and gun lay on the table behind him.

Judge Arnette produced a plug of tobacco, eyed it carefully, then bit off a sizable "chew." He masticated furiously a moment, glanced down to see that the customary cuspidor was at his feet, spat, contentedly shifted the cud to his right cheek and nodded to Murragh.

Murragh rose. "May it please the court, I'd like to make a suggestion. In view of the intense heat, I feel this court could dispense with coats without detracting from the dignity of this proceeding."

Several of the spectators applauded, though most of

them were in shirt sleeves. Arnette rapped sharply with his gavel and glared over the courtroom. "This is no play theayter," he stated sourly. "Anyone guilty of unseemly noise will be ejected." He turned back to Murragh. "The point is well taken. The court gives permission and takes advantage of its ruling." He removed his own coat, glared again at the spectators, and shifted his cud to the left cheek. The jury glanced appreciatively at Murragh. Murragh knew he had scored not only with the jury but with Judge Arnette as well.

Senator Welch scowled at Murragh even while removing his own coat to display an armpit-soaked shirt. He wished he'd thought of the idea. When the rustle had died down, Murragh faced the jury and read aloud the formal charge against Vaiden. Then, laying the paper aside, he dropped his formal tones and made a brief address:

"Gentlemen, you have heard the charge. Now I could take up your time and prolong this trial with a prolix flow of oratory stating what I intend to prove. However, I shall not do that, much as you may have been led to expect a protracted burst of eloquence from me. That kind of 'speechifying' I'd rather leave to someone who may wish to so indulge his own vanity at your expense." Here Murragh stole a quick glance toward Senator Welch. Welch crimsoned, made blustering sounds, and looked about to leap to his feet. Some of the spectators snickered. There was a quick pounding from the judge's gavel and a shifting of his cud to the right cheek as the courtroom quieted. Murragh continued:

"No, gentlemen, I have not the slightest desire to sway your decision with flowery words. After all, you were not chosen on this jury solely to hear me talk. You want facts!" He lowered his voice again, speaking calmly, confidently. "Well, you shall have facts—facts from the witnesses I shall bring before you. Forget me—let *their* words and their words alone formulate the verdict I am expecting you to return—that of guilty of felonious homicide—murder—in the first degree." Murragh's voice rose: "Gentlemen, I am demanding that Alonzo Vaiden be hanged! Don't allow that thought to leave your minds one instant while you are listening to the irrefutable testimony that will be placed before you." He waited just an instant in the sudden silence that followed his final word, then swung about and called his first witness.

While the witness was being sworn by the court clerk, Murragh glanced out over the courtroom. At the rear, seated at one end of a row of seats, was Claude Balter, his hard eyes, the color of bluish milk, fixed balefully on Murragh. Murragh turned back to the room. Vaiden and Welch, eyes fixed on the witness, were holding a whispered conference. The witness, a slim man with white hair, in citizen's clothing, took the stand.

Murragh said, "Your name, please."

"Jason W. Bainbridge."

"Address?"

"One nineteen Main Street, Millman City."

"Your occupation, if you please?"

"Attorney for the Kansas, Midland & Southwest Railroad."

"Thank you. Now, Mr. Bainbridge, your company has a contract with the Gordon Stage & Freighting Company, I believe."

"That is correct."

"Will you please tell us what this contract entails— no, it's not necessary to mention the amount of money involved, though I believe it's quite a tidy sum. Just give the facts briefly, please."

"My company receives from the U. S. Government a yearly subsidy for carrying the mail," Bainbridge explained. "Part of this subsidy we pass on to the Gordon company for delivering mail at various points beyond Millman City. The sum of money we pay the Gordon Stage and Freighting Company also calls for delivery of the Silver Belle Mine pay roll, of which mine the K. M. & S. Railroad is half owner."

There was a stir in the courtroom as this little-known fact became known. Murragh next asked, "Are you and your company entirely satisfied with the service rendered by the Gordon people?"

"Until relatively recently we have been."

"May I ask why your opinion has changed?"

"There has been a series of stage robberies, and the mine pay roll—"

There was a sudden interruption. Senator Welch had bounced to his feet. "I object! Such testimony is not only irrelevant but tends to connect the name of my client with stage robbery."

"Objection sustained," Judge Arnette ruled, and shifted his cud. "The clerk will expunge that last question and answer from the record."

Welch shot a look of triumph at Murragh. Imperturbably, Murragh went on, "Mr. Bainbridge, you have stated you are no longer satisfied with the Gordon company because of certain conditions I shall not name—"

"Object!" Welch bawled. "My client—"

"Objection overruled," Judge Arnette grunted, maintaining his reputation for irascibility. "Your client mustn't be too thin-skinned."

Welch sank back in his chair, red-faced. Murragh continued, "Mr. Bainbridge, it is true, is it not, that your company has considered suing in court to break the contract with the Gordon Stage and Freighting Company unless certain conditions are not shortly bettered?"

"That is true."

"Now, Mr. Bainbridge, I want to take up another subject. Am I correct in stating, though it is not generally known yet, that the K. M. & S. Railroad has now decided to go through with early plans and will, in the near future, extend the railroad down to Lanyard over the same route now used by the Gordon company?"

There was a sudden gasp of surprise from Linda Gordon, seated in the front row of spectators. A whispering started up through the room. Again Welch was on his feet protesting.

"On what grounds?" Arnette snapped.

"My client is on trial for murder. This testimony has nothing whatsoever to do with—"

"Your honor," Murragh interposed, "this testimony is important. Surely I'm to be allowed to bring out facts relative to the motive for the crime that has been committed."

"Objection overruled," Arnette nodded. "The witness may answer."

Bainbridge replied, "You are correct, Mr. Prosecutor. My company has decided to extend the road to Lanyard. That fact has been rumored for some time up around the capital, though it's not generally known through this territory, I believe."

"And are you aware," Murragh continued, "that years ago when Angus Gordon, first owner of the Gordon Stage & Freighting Company, was having trouble with competing companies, he succeeded in getting passed a law prohibiting more than one company at a time from engaging in transportation between Millman City and Lanyard?"

Bainbridge smiled. "My company only recently learned of that law."

"I can well understand that," Murragh said cheerfully. "I had quite a time digging it out myself. It had been practically forgotten—but it is still in force. However, in view of this law, how could your company plan to engage in transportation over the route now used by the Gordon company—even though Coyotero Pass is the only feasible point at which tracks could be laid?"

"The K. M. & S. Railroad stands ready to pay whatever amount is found satisfactory to buy that right of way."

"Then," Murragh continued, "whoever owns the stage route is in a position to make quite a comfortable profit on his holdings—?"

"Object!" Welch was on his feet, face red and perspiring, as he now realized what Murragh was doing. "I object—"

"I withdraw my question," Murragh said quickly, before the judge had an opportunity to make a ruling. "Your witness, Senator Welch." Murragh knew he had already impressed that final fact on the minds of the jurymen.

Welch whirled angrily on Bainbridge, hurling question after question at the man in the hope of shaking his testimony, but Bainbridge was too shrewd a man to become entangled by Welch's cross-examination. Finally Welch changed his tactics and asked, "Do you know of anything to lead you to believe Alonzo Vaiden is guilty of the murder of Uncle Jimmy Cochrane?"

"Not one thing," Bainbridge replied promptly. "I'm not fam—"

"That is all, Mr. Bainbridge," Welch interrupted. It had been a pretty feeble effort to salvage something from the testimony, but Welch shot a look at the jury and smiled confidently.

Murragh next called Silvertop Gordon to the stand and by deft questioning brought out the fact that Silvertop, in the event of Linda's death, would sell the stage company at once. This testimony was unsuccessfully protested by Welch, as were the references Murragh worked in relative to stage robberies, at one of which Silvertop had been present, as his bandaged arm attested. As to the law that Angus Gordon had succeeded in getting passed, prohibiting more than one transportation company operating over the

Gordon route, Silvertop vaguely remembered it now, though he had been in California at the time the law was passed. No, he testified, Linda was probably too young to have any recollection of such a law. Murragh nodded and turned Silvertop over to Welch for cross-examination.

Welch worked hard but was unsuccessful in getting Silvertop to change any of his testimony, so he switched to another tack, that of endeavoring to discredit the witness in the jury's eyes:

"Is it true you once made a living gambling?"

"True," Silvertop nodded.

"I understand your daughter traveled with you much of the time. Do you consider that a decent life for a young girl?"

Silvertop replied coldly, "Are you prepared to say anything against that girl's character?"

"That is not answering my question. What kind of father are you that would submit a young girl of tender years to the temptations of numerous gambling hells. Only a selfish, inconsiderate man—"

"Your honor," Murragh broke in, "I object to such heckling of the witness."

"I'm handling this witness," Welch flared.

"Mishandling is the word," Murragh snapped.

Judge Arnette pounded his gavel. It went unnoticed— presumably.

"Is the prosecutor attempting to teach me my business?" Welch snarled.

"Somebody should teach you!"

More pounding of the gavel. "This useless arguing

must cease," Arnette roared. "I'll cite both of you for contempt of court."

"Not me, please, your honor," Murragh said politely. "My contempt is confined to the defendant's attorney."

"The prosecutor—" Arnette commenced, but the words were lost in the laughter that swept through the room. The pounding of the gavel commenced again. By the time the room had quieted, Arnette didn't finish what he'd started to say and Welch was so angry that he dismissed the witness with no further questioning. Immediately afterward the court recessed for dinner.

At dinner Murragh sat with Linda and Silvertop in the hotel dining room. Linda was excited, full of questions regarding Bainbridge's testimony. "Don't you see," Murragh replied. "I'm trying to show the jury the motive for the murder? Vaiden wants your stage route. Whoever owns it can hold up the K. M. & S. for a nice profit when the railroad gets ready to build. Uncle Jimmy was killed, the stage was expected to be wrecked—and you with it. Then Silvertop would have sold out to Vaiden undoubtedly. Right, Silvertop?"

Silvertop nodded. "Funny thing about that law Angus got put through. I'd plumb forgotten that."

"But Welch, spending most of his time at the capital, would know about it. It was Linda that tipped me off. When she mentioned, one time, that Angus's competition had stopped suddenly, I felt sure a law must have been passed. That's why I made the trip to the capital. And you can bet that Welch had plenty of opportunity, too, to hear about the railroad's contemplated line to Lanyard—but let's eat. I've already done too much talking today."

22

A Point Scored

When court reconvened after dinner, Murragh noticed Isabel Fanchon among the spectators. In his mind he still played with the idea of subpoenaing her as a witness, but felt she knew little regarding the facts of Uncle Jimmy's death; besides, there was always the chance of her perjuring herself in Vaiden's favor. As his first witness of the afternoon Murragh called Zwing, the station man at Dry Bone.

Zwing was self-conscious and made a poor witness, though Murragh did succeed in placing before the jury an account of the manner in which Zwing and his wife had been kidnaped from Dry Bone Station the day of the murder. In the cross-examination Welch literally tore Zwing to pieces. Zwing stumbled nervously, stammered, wasn't actually sure how many of the masked men had appeared at his place by the time Welch had worked on him a while. Even Murragh's numerous protests failed to bolster up the witness.

"Your honor," Murragh said indignantly, "I object to this bullying on the part of the opposing counsel."

"Through with the witness," Welch flashed, before Judge Arnette had a chance to speak.

In view of the poor showing Zwing had made, Murragh decided not to call Mrs. Zwing. Of one thing he felt sure, however: three or four of the more calculating heads on the jury had had it firmly implanted in their minds that Zwing and his wife had been absent from Dry Bone Station all day on the date of the murder. Senator Welch had returned to Vaiden's side at the table, and the two were smiling and talking in whispers. Meanwhile Cass Henley and the sheriff had appeared at the back of the courtroom with Cal Osgood, Jode Proctor, and Milt Lynch in handcuffs. Murragh made a signal to Henley; Osgood and Lynch were taken away. Murragh called Proctor to the stand. Proctor was sworn and took his seat. By this time the smiles had vanished from Vaiden's and Welch's faces. Murragh started his questioning: "Your name?"

Proctor gave him a look. "Didn't you hear it a few moments ago?"

"I'll do the questioning. Your name, please?"

"Jode Proctor. I live in Sulphur Tanks and I'm a miner. I've been arrested for something I didn't do—"

"Not so fast, Proctor," Murragh said sharply. "Where were you on the day James Cochrane was murdered?"

"I don't remember."

"Perhaps I can refresh your memory. You were at Dry Bone Station most of the day."

"That's what you say."

Vaiden and Welch were smiling again. The judge was looking queerly at Murragh, expecting a request that Arnette order the witness to answer properly. Murragh looked a bit downcast. He said to Welch, "Your witness, Senator."

Welch rose. "I wish to waive cross-examination at this time, your honor, and request permission to recall

259

this witness later as a witness for the defense."

Arnette chewed tobacco vigorously for a minute. He glanced at Murragh. Murragh shrugged his shoulders. Inwardly he was smiling; the defense had fallen into the trap. He decided it wouldn't be worth while, now, putting Osgood and Lynch on the stand. . . .

"The court has considered the defense attorney's request," Arnette was replying to Welch, "and rules in the affirmative." The jury, puzzled, glanced from Welch to Murragh and wondered what the prosecutor would do next.

Murragh called Wyatt Holliday to the stand. After the preliminaries had been disposed with, Murragh said, "Mr. Holliday, will you relate, as briefly as possible, where you saw the defendant on the day James Cochrane met his death, and the circumstances regarding the defendant as you know them?"

Holliday shifted in his seat and talked to the jury rather than to Murragh: "Alonzo Vaiden was seated on top of the coach that morning, waiting for it to pull out for Lanyard. About that time I saw you, Mr. Murragh, and I greeted you by name. A minute later I glanced up, and Vaiden had descended from the coach and disappeared. You must have considered his actions strange, as you wrote and dropped a note to me just before the coach departed. The note asked me to check on Vaiden's actions. . . ."

A buzz of conversation swept through the courtroom. Vaiden and Welch looked startled. Welch started to his feet, then sat down again. The two men exchanged a whispered conversation. Judge Arnette was manipulating his gavel and demanding quiet. Holliday resumed:

"A minute or so after the stage had departed, Vaiden came rushing up. I didn't ask an explanation, but he started to tell me that his watch had stopped and that while he was having a last drink in the bar he lost track of the time—"

"Objection," Welch interposed hoarsely.

Arnette asked, "On what grounds?"

"The witness is insinuating there was something suspicious in my client's behavior. My client does not deny he missed the stage—"

"If the court please," Murragh interrupted, "may I point out there is no question of insinuation here? My witness is merely telling the facts, under oath, as he knows them. I request permission for him to continue."

"Objection overruled," Arnette grunted and shifted his cud. Welch glowered and sat down. Vaiden was watching Holliday closely. Holliday continued, "Vaiden next went to the Fortune Livery Stable in Millman City, where he hired two saddled horses and departed at once, leading one of the horses behind him."

"Do you mean," Murragh asked, "that he intended a companion to join him on his ride, or that he expected to make better time to his destination, by changing off when one horse grew tired?"

"I can't answer that, except to say that he told the attendant in the Fortune Livery that he was in a hurry to reach Lanyard and expected to get a fresh mount in Sulphur Tanks."

"In your opinion, could the defendant reach Dry Bone before the stage arrived—?"

"Objection!" Welch bawled.

Murragh said quickly, "I'll phrase my question differently. Mr. Holliday, wouldn't it be possible for the defendant to reach Dry Bone before the coach—?"

"I object!" Welch exclaimed, red-faced. "Your honor, the prosecuting attorney is leading the witness. As a matter of fact I shall prove that Alonzo Vaiden did not arrive at Dry Bone until long after the deceased had met his death and that of his own volition he reported the absence of the regular attendant from that station—"

"Your honor," Murragh cut in, "it has definitely been established that Alonzo Vaiden did leave the stage before it departed from Millman City. In view of the attempted wrecking of the stage below Dry Bone and that the murder had been committed in that vicinity—"

"Objection! Objection!" Welch shrieked, his face streaming with perspiration. He was jumping about like one demented. "Nothing in the testimony, to date, indicates that the murder was committed at Dry Bone. I request—"

"Objection sustained," Arnette growled. Murragh knew the words came too late; regardless of the judge's ruling, two thoughts had been instilled in the jurors' minds: one, that Vaiden had hurried to reach Dry Bone, after leaving Millman City; two, that failure to leave on the coach might indicate on Vaiden's part knowledge of a planned attempt to wreck the stage. The judge was still speaking, ". . . and the court suggests that the defense attorney display a little more dignity. This isn't a ballroom, and we can dispense with such frantic dancing about." Laughter burst from the spectators. Arnette pounded his gavel, chewed furiously and stated, "The prosecutor may continue."

"I've finished with Mr. Holliday for the time being, your honor, though I request permission to bring him back later, if necessary." Arnette granted the request, and Murragh said, "Your witness, Mr. Welch."

Try as he would, Welch failed to shake Holliday's testimony. He gave up after a few minutes, knowing that Holliday's fame as a law officer made a favorable impression on the jury and that it was better to get him off the stand as soon as possible.

Murragh next called Linda as a witness. Linda affirmed Holliday's testimony relative to Vaiden's missing the coach at Millman City; then Murragh requested the girl to tell in her own words what had taken place on the trip. This Linda did, bringing out the facts of a stranger being in Zwing's place at the Dry Bone Station, Uncle Jimmy's anger, and the other events leading up to the running away of the stage horses, after she and Murragh had heard the savage cracking of the driver's whip above. Here Murragh interposed a question:

"Wasn't it unusual, Miss Gordon, for Uncle Jimmy to employ his whip in such fashion?"

"It was. No good driver generally commits himself to such actions."

"Thank you. Proceed with your story, please."

Linda related how Murragh had discovered Uncle Jimmy's absence from the driver's seat, how he had climbed from the coach and retrieved the reins. Linda's eyes glowed in the telling. Her words praised Murragh's prowess. Judge Arnette chewed faster and faster in his interest. The jury was eying Murragh with open admiration. Welch could stand it no longer. He jumped to his feet, "Objection!"

"What grounds?" Arnette snapped. He had been enjoying the story.

"Your honor," Welch pleaded, "must this sort of thing go on? Is this court to lend itself to a burlesque of the law? If you please, a man's life is at stake here. Are we determining whether or not Alonzo Vaiden is guilty of the crime of which he is charged, or are we elevating the prosecuting attorney to the role of an unblemished hero for which—"

"Probably both," Arnette growled. "'Jection overruled. The witness may proceed." He ducked his head below the top of the bench, the brass cuspidor resounded under the impact, and he came up again, masticating energetically. Linda continued with her story of the trip until the coach reached Peyote Flat, where she had sent Bert Echardt back to search for Uncle Jimmy. At this point Murragh halted, saying, "I'm through. You may cross-examine, Mr. Defense Attorney."

"No questions," Welch half snarled. He realized the jury had reacted favorably to Linda Gordon's appearance and that it would resent any attempt at rough handling in order to break down her testimony. Besides, he considered, her testimony had added little that was actually detrimental to his client's interests.

Arnette nodded to Murragh. "Call your next witness."

Murragh brought Bert Echardt to the stand. Under questioning, Echardt related how he had found Uncle Jimmy's body on the stage road not far from Dry Bone and of his trip to that station to find it deserted, before bringing the dead man to Lanyard. Murragh said:

"Let's go back a little, Mr. Echardt. Your impression is that Uncle Jimmy fell from the coach after being shot?"

"That's right," Echardt replied.

"Please tell the jury in what position the body was discovered."

"When I found Uncle Jimmy, he was layin' face down between the wheel ruts—sort of across them."

"Right *between* the ruts?" Murragh asked skeptically. "Are you sure the body wasn't lying to one side or the other?"

"Yes, I'm sure," Echardt declared.

"Then I gather it is your idea that when he fell Uncle Jimmy pitched from the driver's seat, over the footboard of the coach, rather than on either side."

"That's the way I figure it."

"Thank you." Murragh turned away and said to Welch, "You may have Mr. Echardt now," before going back to his table.

Welch started in, "Mr. Echardt, you say you went to Dry Bone Station before returning to Lanyard. Are you absolutely sure no one was there?"

"Absolutely."

"Come, come! Surely you're not telling this intelligent jury that you searched all through the buildings."

"I went in the house and yelled for Zwing, struck a couple of matches and looked around. Then I went out to the stables and found some horses hadn't been taken care of. I worked around them for a spell."

"I understand. But for all your thorough search, you found not one indication of violence, did you?—I'm talking about Dry Bone Station, you understand. No signs of a struggle or anything of the kind?"

"No."

Welch directed a look of triumph at the jury and said, "You may leave the stand."

Echardt stepped down, and Murragh called Graves, the undertaker. Under questioning, Graves related how the body had been brought to his undertaking establishment. Murragh asked, "You removed Uncle Jimmy's clothing, didn't you?"

"Just the upper ones at first, when Doc Bradley came. Took the rest off afterward, of course."

"Were they quite dusty, as though he'd rolled in the road?"

Graves frowned. "No, now that you mention it, I can't say they were."

"Nor did I see any dust when I examined them at your establishment, Mr. Graves—"

"Objection!" Welch exclaimed.

"On what grounds?" Arnette asked.

"Is it necessary for the prosecutor to testify—?"

"Your honor," Murragh said, "I'm willing for my statement to be excluded from the record. I've finished with the witness." He nodded to Welch to take over.

"No questions," Welch snapped. "However, at this

time I wish to point out to our distinguished jurors that the prosecution has not, definitely and to date, offered one shred of evidence to indicate that my client is the murderer of James Cochrane. On the contrary—"

Murragh's taunting laugh rang through the room. "Are you so eager to hear such evidence, Mr. Defense Attorney? Don't be impatient. I'm—"

"Impatient is not the word!" Welch exclaimed, red-faced. "Indignation, rather, is what occupies me. There is a limit to how much I'll stand from your sly innuendoes, nasty insinuations, and underhanded hints—"

"Your honor,"—Murragh turned an injured expression to Judge Arnette—"is it with your permission that opposing counsel employs such slanderous, abusive language? Or is he suggesting that the bench has not given proper protection to his client? May I ask—?"

"You may not!" Arnette roared. He'd already started pounding his gavel. "This bickering must cease at once."

"If it please your honor," Murragh said humbly, "that is exactly the order I was about to request from the bench. I cannot pursue my duties in the face of—"

Laughter almost drowned out the banging of the gavel. The room finally settled down. Arnette's jaws worked furiously. He scowled at Murragh. "Call your next witness." The judge spat, shifted his cud; a ghost of a twinkle showed in his eyes.

Dr. John Bradley was called and sworn. Under examination he testified that the deceased James Cochrane had met his death approximately at four in the afternoon of the day the body was found. No exact time could be set, of course; that was impossible under the circumstances. He testified further as to the course the bullet had taken and of the procedure he'd followed as county coroner. Murragh said, "You examined the body thoroughly?"

"I did."

"What other wounds were found?"

"None at all except the single bullet wound made by a bullet from a forty-five six-shooter. Oh, there was a slight abrasion about the neck, such as might have been made by a tight collar."

"I noticed that myself. Did you ever know Uncle Jimmy to wear a collar?"

Bradley frowned. "No—no, I can't say I ever have."

"You're sure there were no other wounds on the body?"

"Absolutely sure."

Murragh nodded. "Now, Dr. Bradley, it has been testified that the body was found between the ruts of the stagecoach, leading the witness who gave that testimony to believe that Uncle Jimmy fell over the footboard, rather than to either side of the coach."

"That sounds very reasonable to me."

"Then will you explain to me, Dr. Bradley, why there were no other wounds on the body? Surely there must have been bruises, if not broken bones. And wasn't there just a chance that, in falling, a body would be struck by the hoofs of the wheel horses?"

"By God!" Bradley burst out. "I never thought of that. Why, of course there'd be bruises, cuts. I don't know what got into me that I didn't think—there'd simply have to be some marks on the body—I can't see— Mr. Murragh!" Bradley was overcome with excitement now. "Uncle Jimmy couldn't have fallen from that coach. He must have been kil—"

"That's enough, Dr. Bradley. Your witness, Senator Welch."

A hush had fallen over the courtroom. Murragh had scored a strong point, though only a few realized its import. Welch was on his feet, looking extremely perturbed. His mouth opened and shut before speech came. A trace of fear had crept into Vaiden's eyes, though otherwise he looked calm and collected. Welch finally found his voice:

"Dr. Bradley, isn't it possible you may have overlooked the bruises the prosecutor mentions? It has been testified that only the upper part of the body was stripped when you examined it."

"I examined the lower limbs through the clothing. The clothing was not torn—"

"Then you admit the legs may have been bruised?" Welch said quickly.

"Not at all. I consider it extremely unlikely." Bradley was thinking fast now. "You see, Senator, it would be pretty difficult for a body to fall feet first from the driver's seat, unless the driver jumped intentionally. That theory, I believe, is ruled out."

"But it could happen," Welch insisted.

"I doubt it. It is more likely the body would topple head first. The arms, head, or upper torso, would bear the brunt of the fall. If I found no bruises, cuts, or breaks in or on that part of the body, I doubt the lower parts would be injured. In fact, I'm commencing to believe Uncle Jimmy didn't fall from that coach—"

"You were not asked for that opinion," Welch snarled.

"I'm giving it all the same—"

"Your honor," Welch appealed to Arnette, "if the court please, may the witness be instructed to answer in a proper manner?"

"The witness," Arnette ruled, "will not make gratuitous remarks, but answer in a proper, respectable manner."

"Thank you, Judge Arnette," Welch said ingratiatingly. His manner changed as he turned back to Bradley. "You call yourself a doctor, I believe?"

"Whether you believe it or not, I've a diploma from a reputable medical college. I've practiced in Lanyard alone for the last twenty years." Bradley was growing angry.

"Never made a mistake during your years of practice, I suppose?"

"Every doctor makes mistakes at some time in his life."

"Your honor,"—Welch turned to the bench—"will you kindly instruct the witness again to answer with a plain yes or no?"

"The witness will answer as required, or at least in a reasonable manner," Arnette droned.

Welch said, "Have you ever made a mistake in your years of practice."

"Yes. Every doctor does at some time—"

"You admit it. Now about these bruises you claim you didn't see—or were they cuts—or broken bones?"

"I made no mistake in this particular case in my diagnosis."

From that point on, Welch became abusive, doing all possible to impugn Bradley's character, ability, and veracity, until Murragh leaped to his feet. "I object, your honor, to this browbeating of the witness."

"Objection sustained. The defense counsel will conduct his cross-examination in a more dignified manner."

"I'm through with the witness," Welch said shortly. He glanced at the jury and saw he'd made no headway in his attempt to shake Bradley's testimony in the minds of the men in the box.

At this point court was adjourned for the day.

It was nearly six o'clock by the time Murragh once more stepped out to the street. The sun was dropping swiftly toward the peaks of the San Xavier Range. The breeze that lifted across the sage and cactus and greasewood had become slightly cooler. He rolled a cigarette and walked on. At the corner of Main and Carson streets he encountered Cass Henley. "Rather rough day," Henley commented, as they came to a stop. "Jake and I were talking it over. What's this business about Jode Proctor? I can't see where he gave any support."

"About what I expected," Murragh explained. "I thought there might be a slight chance of him swinging to my side, but he and his pards, Osgood and Lynch, haven't changed a bit. When they consented to be held without a prompt hearing, when I first arrested them, I gave my word I'd bring no stronger charge than stage robbery against them. They know I won't break my word, and they're gambling that Vaiden will get them out of trouble in the long run."

"Will he, do you think?"

"Don't talk foolish, Cass. Unless I'm mightily mistaken. Vaiden and Welch figure to use Proctor and his pals to swear Vaiden wasn't in the vicinity of the spot where Cochrane met his death. Welch has requested permission to call Proctor as a defense witness, and I'm betting he'll ask for Lynch and Osgood too. They're pretty confident on that score, so confident that I managed to slip in a couple of bits of testimony that Welch would ordinarily have objected to. He's getting careless, which is what I want, because when I spring my surprise it'll hit Welch and Vaiden with just that much more force and, consequently, be more effective."

"There's something else I can't understand. Why did Doc—?"

"Don't ask me now, Cass. At this minute all I can think of is a couple of bottles of cold beer and a big platter of beefsteak. Until I've had those, I simply refuse to discuss the case any further."

Henley jerked one thumb over his shoulder toward the Saddle Horn Saloon which stood at their rear. "There's your beer, anyway." As he followed Murragh inside the saloon, the deputy quoted in a resigned murmur, " 'He was a man of an unbounded stomach. His own opinion was his law. . . . ' "

23

The Oak Tree

Murragh left the hotel and started the short walk to the courthouse, carrying in one hand a small valise. Bright morning sunlight flooded Main Street with warmth and light. Wagons, buggies, and saddled horses lined the hitchracks on either side, the horses switching tails at persistent, buzzing flies. Men spoke to Murragh as they passed; he replied absent-mindedly. He had planned carefully, set the trap. Would the opposition take the bait? If not . . . Murragh tried to push the thought from his mind. At the thought of failure a frown creased his forehead beneath the triangular patch of black hair.

But the gamble might fail, after all. In that case, whom would Welch bring to the stand to refute the prosecution's testimony? There were the Rafter-AV foreman and the cowhands. Would loyalty to the man who paid their wages urge any one of them to commit perjury and swear to an alibi on Vaiden's behalf? Might Isabel Fanchon be brought in to furnish an alibi? Murragh swore under his breath; he should have checked on her whereabouts the day Uncle Jimmy Cochrane was killed. What could Welch do with Lynch, Proctor, and Osgood?

Abruptly Murragh found Cass Henley confronting him. Henley laughed and said, "I spoke to you twice . . ." Murragh realized they were standing just a few doors from the courthouse, around the doorway of which a crowd had already collected. "My mind was miles away," Murragh confessed, "erecting barriers before I reached 'em. Fool thing to do, but I've got to look ahead. I only wish I could see inside Vaiden's mind for a few minutes." Murragh's face was sober.

"Cheer up, Hoyt. I think you've got him worried. Vaiden and Welch held a long conference in Vaiden's cell last night. I didn't hear what was said, of course, but once or twice their tones sounded like they were arguing."

"It may not mean a thing," Murragh replied, scowling. The two men exchanged a few more words, then Murragh said, "I'll see you later," and pushed through the crowd into the courthouse, the seats of which were already packed with people. Near the back of the room Claude Balter shot Murragh a glance from his pale agate eyes. Murragh could almost feel Balter's hard, unwinking gaze on his back as he passed on, and nodded to Silvertop and Linda, seated farther toward the front of the room.

Murragh moved slowly along the aisle to his table. Vaiden and Welch had already arrived and were conversing in low tones. The bailiff was going around opening windows to dispel the stale redolence that lingered from the previous day's burnt tobacco and perspiration. The jury was just filing into its box. In the far, right-hand corner, beyond the jury box, a small room had been partitioned off which had been given the flattering appellation of "Judge's Chambers." It was furnished with a small table, chairs, and a row of coat hooks.

Arriving at his table, Murragh dropped the valise beneath it. He removed his coat and Stetson, then took off his belt and holstered gun, placed them on the table, and tossed his coat over the weapon. He had nodded shortly in the direction of Welch's table when he came in, and called a cheerful, confident "Good morning" to Sheriff Farley, who stood across the room against one wall, with one eye on the spectators and the other on Alonzo Vaiden.

Murragh waited a few moments; then, as though impatient at Judge Arnette's non-appearance, he drew a folded packet of papers, tied with a length of hempen cord, from his pocket. He glanced through the papers, placed them restlessly on the table after a few moments, and commenced to trifle with the length of cord. Gradually his fingers fashioned the hempen length into a miniature hangman's noose. As though entirely unconscious that every eye in the jury box was on him, he idly manipulated the tiny noose, drawing the slip knot about one finger, loosening it again and repeating the performance. He thrust one finger into the loop and, taking hold of the other end, gave the cord a quick jerk.

He was abruptly conscious of Welch's angry voice at his shoulder. Welch's words were low, but charged with hate: "When Judge Arnette takes the bench I intend to, protest this intimidation of the defendant."

Murragh glanced up and around, as though startled. Vaiden's eyes, as though the man were hypnotized, were fastened on the miniature noose in Murragh's fingers. There wasn't much color in his face. The jury was still watching Murragh. Murragh laughed shortly and tossed the bit of cord on his table. He drawled, low-toned, "Do as you see fit, Welch, but I think you'd look rather foolish bringing up the subject of a hangman's noose yourself."

Welch swore and flung himself back to his table, just as the flimsy, yellow-pine door of the "Judge's Chambers" opened and Arnette appeared. The usual preliminaries were gone through, and then court was declared open. Murragh waited a moment while Arnette adjusted his cud of "eating tobacco" to the proper cheek, then rose.

"May it please your honor," Murragh commenced, "before calling my first witness this morning I wish to introduce into the evidence a material object to be known as Exhibit C." Upon receiving the judge's consent, Murragh motioned to Deputy Henley, standing not far from the bench. Henley came forward, handed Murragh a six-shooter, and again retired. Murragh tendered the gun to Welch. "Will you kindly have the defendant identify this gun?"

There was silence in the courtroom while Welch carried the six-shooter to Vaiden. The two held a whispered consultation; Vaiden looked carefully over the weapon. Finally Welch brought it back and asked the judge, "Does identification of this six-shooter by my client establish the fact that he has been placed upon the witness stand?" The judge looked at Murragh. Murragh shook his head. Arnette ruled, "It does not."

"Then may it please the court," Welch continued, "my client identifies this weapon as his own personal property, factory number nine three seven six five, which was taken from him by Deputy Sheriff Henley at the time of my client's arrest." He added sarcastically in lower tones for Murragh's ears alone, "Much good may this do you."

"I expect it will," Murragh replied pleasantly. "I could—"

Arnette rapped sharply once with his gavel. "The court does not wish to see today's proceedings opened with petty bickerings."

"Your honor," Murragh said, "I merely wished to have this gun properly identified now in order to speed the proceedings which have already been drawn out unduly—"

"True," Arnette interjected sourly. He chewed, spat at his feet, and shifted the tobacco cud to the right cheek.

"This gun," Murragh went on, "could have been identified by Deputy Henley, as he was the officer to whom the defendant surrendered it at the time of his arrest. However, it seemed more fitting for the defendant himself to identify his property. With the court's permission I wish the jury to inspect this weapon." The court graciously awarded its permission, and Murragh passed the gun to the foreman of the jury, a leathery-faced rancher from the northern part of the county.

The foreman checked the factory number, examined the cylinder and reported, "Colt six-shooter, forty-five caliber, four-and-three-quarter-inch bar'l; factory number nine three seven six five." He passed the gun to the next juror. Finally the weapon was returned to Murragh. The clerk attached to the trigger guard a small tag marked "C," and it was placed with the other exhibits.

If Vaiden and Welch were worried by the introduction of the gun into the proceedings, it didn't show in their faces, particularly as Murragh seemed to immediately forget the matter himself. The miniature hangman's noose on Murragh's table seemed to concern Vaiden more: he kept casting furtive glances at it from time to time, and some of the jurors had commenced to notice such actions. The clerk settled back in his chair, and Murragh called, as his first witness of the day, Deputy Sheriff Cass Henley. Henley was duly sworn and took the stand.

Led by Murragh's questioning, the deputy sheriff told of the ride to Dry Bone he and Murragh had made the morning after Uncle Jimmy Cochrane's body had been brought to the undertaker's. He touched on the story Zwing had told that morning, but devoted most of his recital to a description of that section of the road where the horses had run away with the stagecoach, dwelling on such points as the scars in the roadway showing where the coach wheels had skidded and so on.

Murragh said, "There was something in particular we noticed along that section of the road, wasn't there?"

"You mean that old oak tree?"

"That's what I mean. Will you please tell the jury exactly how that tree was formed, of the bough that overhung the road—?"

"Object!" Welch exclaimed.

"Grounds?" Arnette snapped.

"The prosecutor is putting words in the witness's mouth—"

"Objection sustained," Arnette ruled in bored tones. "The prosecutor must allow the witness to make descriptions in his own words."

Murragh turned back to Henley, "Kindly give us in your own words a description of that tree."

Henley related how the coach in passing along the roadway always rolled beneath the overhanging limb of the ancient oak tree. He described the size of the limb, told how he and Murragh had climbed the tree. Here Murragh interjected, "In your opinion, had anyone been in that tree before us?"

"Yes. There was sign to show that fact."

"I believe the jury understands what you mean by 'sign,' but for the sake of the record will you make that point clear?"

"Why, there were a couple of broken twigs where a man might have gripped—there was a fresh slash in the bark that might have been made by a spur—things like that."

"Thank you, that's all." Henley seemed surprised that the examination had ceased so suddenly. Murragh turned to Welch. "The witness is yours."

Welch asked a few unimportant questions, then shot at Henley, "Just why should anyone want to climb that tree before you did?"

"So he could shoot Uncle Jimmy when the coach came along by it."

A buzz of conversation droned through the court-room. Arnette rapped for quiet. Welch shot a quick glance at Vaiden, smiled, then asked sarcastically, "Now, Deputy Henley, are you trying to tell me that

Alonzo Vaiden goes around climbing trees and shooting people from ambush? You know him better than that—"

"Somebody did," Henley stated flatly.

"Ah,"—swiftly—"then you *don't* think it was Alonzo Vaiden who did the shooting—"

"Objection," Murragh flashed. "The defense attorney is trying to lead the witness."

"Objection sustained," Arnette nodded.

Welch tried another tack: "Are you prepared to state definitely it was the defendant that climbed that tree?"

Henley hesitated. Finally he voiced a reluctant "No."

Welch directed a triumphant look toward the jury box. He went on, "Now, Deputy Henley, you mentioned a spur mark on that tree as proof that someone had climbed it—"

"I said it might have been made by a spur."

"Now, Deputy Henley,"—Welch smiled as though very amused—"surely you know better than to try to make us believe anything so absurd. You're testifying before an intelligent jury. Even you should know that spurs are fastened at the rear of boot heels. Now, do you still insist someone climbed that tree backwards, as he might, say, walk up a flight of steps backwards—even if there existed a reason for so doing? All my experience tells me such a feat is impossible."

At this point Henley failed to resist one of his inevitable quotations; involuntarily, it popped out: "'There are more things in heaven and earth, Horatio, than are dreamt of in your philosophy.'"

Welch's jaw sagged; his eyes bulged. A gale of

laughter swayed the spectators. Most of the jurors, unfamiliar with Henley's ruling passion, looked blank, but decided after a moment to join in the general merriment, as did those spectators who were unacquainted with the deputy sheriff. The gale became contagious, swelled to a torrent that rocked the courtroom. The pounding of the gavel went unheeded. Tobacco juice dribbled from the corners of Arnette's mouth as he strove to keep a serious expression. He pounded more furiously.

Welch finally found his voice: "Your honor, this is no time for levity. A man's life is hanging in the balance—"

". . . or out of a tree," a spectator's voice came through a lull in the merriment. The laughter increased again. Arnette bawled, "Eject that man!" and the bailiff hurried to carry out the command.

Order was restored after a time. The judge eyed Henley severely. "You will reply to the defense attorney's questions in a sensible manner."

"Yes, sir," Henley said sheepishly. "Excuse me. What I meant to say was, that spur scratch was between the main trunk and the limb, where it curved, like as if a man standing on the limb had backed against the trunk."

"We will dispense with that tree as useless evidence," Welch said stiffly, "as it has not been proved my client was anywhere near it—"

"May it please the court," Murragh interrupted, "I should like the court to keep that tree in mind. It is very relevant."

"The court so rules," Arnette droned. "Go on, Mr. Defense Attorney."

But Welch found himself unable to continue the cross-examination. Tittering broke out sporadically in the courtroom, and the defense attorney was finally forced to excuse the witness from further questioning. Murragh rose to his feet. He stood, not speaking, while he waited for the courtroom to quiet. His demeanor was even more serious now than it had been before, and the spectators sensed important developments. "As my next witness," Murragh said, and his voice was grim, "I'm calling Barney Twitchell." Twitchell was sworn and came to settle his big muscular frame in the witness chair. Vaiden and Welch were looking anxious again, their heads close together, whispering. With the preliminary questioning disposed of, Murragh got down to business: "Mr. Twitchell, on the day Uncle Jimmy Cochrane met his death, you were at Dry Bone, were you not?"

"I was."

"Please tell this court what you were doing there?"

"I went there to carry out a job, that of driving the stagecoach when it left Dry Bone."

"How much were you paid for that job?"

"Twenty-five dollars."

"Who hired you for that job?"

"Alonzo Vaiden."

An excited buzz swept through the courtroom. Welch leaped to his feet with protests that were overruled. A banging of the gavel brought quiet again. Murragh went on, "Please state as clearly as possible exactly what took place while you were at Dry Bone that day."

"Well, I'd left the night before, and when I got there the others were waiting for me. Do you want me to name them?"

"I ask you expressly not to name them," Murragh said quickly. "Just state—"

"Objection!" Welch bounced to his feet. "May it please the court, I ask that the men referred to be named and those names placed in the record. The good name of my client—"

"Your honor," Murragh interrupted, "to name the men referred to at this time would jeopardize the interests of my case. Later, when I have presented all my evidence, I'll have no objection to their names being placed in the record, but now—"

"Objection overruled," Arnette interrupted. "Continue, Mr. Prosecutor." Welch retired, disgruntled, to his table.

Under Murragh's prompting, Twitchell went on, "When I got to Dry Bone, these men were waiting for me, and we hid out in the back stables, except one man who stayed in front of the station to wait for the stage when it came from Cottonwood Springs. When the stage rolled in, Uncle Jimmy was mad because the horses weren't ready, and he came back to get them himself. Proc—I mean one of the men was hidden in an empty stall, and when Uncle Jimmy went into the next stall to get a horse, this man grabbed Uncle Jimmy's whip which he had laid down while he got the horses—"

At this point it became necessary for Arnette to use

his gavel to quiet the increasing buzz of excited conversation. Twitchell continued, "Uncle Jimmy didn't notice that the whip was missing until the stage horses were harnessed. When he came back to the stables to get his whip, Os—I mean one of the men choked him from behind and a burlap sack was thrun over his head and he was tied up with rawhides. Then I took the whip and went out to the coach. I approached from a direction where Miss Gordon and you, Mr. Murragh, couldn't see who was going to do the driving. Then I got up on the seat and started out—"

"Alonzo Vaiden had told you exactly what to do?" Murragh asked.

Welch's protest at this point was overruled. Twitchell replied, "Yes, he had explained everything about the tree and—"

"What tree are you speaking of? Be definite, please."

"There's a big oak that grows at the side of the road a short distance from Dry Bone, with a limb that stretches out over the stage road. The coach has to pass right under it. Well, I whipped up the horses and then let them gradually lag as the coach got near the oak tree. When we was nearly there, Miss Gordon called up and asked if I was falling asleep or something, thinking I was Uncle Jimmy. With that I lashed out with the whip and the horses started to tear, but before they got really going I was under that oak tree limb. I flung the reins away, stood up and grabbed a-holt of that limb and hung on, while the coach kept going. Then I climbed into the tree, waited a few minutes before I clumb down and started back to Dry Bone. I was met with a horse and told to go back to Lanyard and keep my mouth shut. But I never knew Uncle Jimmy would be killed. They said he wouldn't be hurt a-tall—"

Hisses sounded through the courtroom. There were excited exclamations. Arnette pounded the gavel for quiet. The jurors were directing looks of extreme dislike toward Vaiden, who was ashen. Murragh waited a moment, then said, "That's all, Twitchell. Take the witness, Mr. Defense Attorney."

Welch attacked savagely. "Twitchell," he commenced, "this is all a cock-and-bull story, as you well know. No intelligent jury will put any faith in it. Now tell me once more the names of the men you say were at Dry Bone."

Caught off guard, Twitchell was about to reply, when Murragh leaped in with a protest, adding, "Your honor has already ruled on that point."

"Objection sustained," Arnette said sharply. "The defendant's attorney will watch his tongue. This court does not care for chicanery in any form, especially when designed to overthrow a ruling of this court."

"May it please your honor, I offer apologies," Welch said, though inwardly seething. He whirled back on Twitchell: "You say your name is Barney Twitchell. Weren't you also known as Twitchell Barnett, or Twitch, in Texas a few years ago?" Twitchell admitted the fact. "And isn't it true that Texas still has out for you a warrant, charging you with a crime, and that you escaped from jail before you could be tried?"

"That's true," Twitchell replied frankly.

Welch fixed him with a withering look. "A jailbird,"

he sneered. "Your testimony, even under oath, isn't worth that . . ." He snapped his fingers in the air. "Just what sort of a deal have you made with the prosecutor to come here—"

"Objection!" Murragh was on his feet. "The defense attorney not only is endeavoring to detract from my witness's testimony, but he impugns my character—"

"The witness admits the charges, and I don't think you have to bother about your character," Arnette droned. "Objection overruled."

Welch shot an exultant look at the jury and continued, "No, I don't believe anyone will put any trust in the word of a jailbird."

"Mr. Vaiden didn't seem to mind when I told him about what had happened in Texas." Twitchell was showing a little spirit under Welch's goading. The jury glanced at Vaiden, who was mopping at his white forehead with a handkerchief. From that point on, Welch made little progress, though by this time both he and the witness were drenched in perspiration. Eventually Arnette interfered and pointed out that the defense attorney seemed to be getting nowhere and that, unless he had fresh questions to ask, it might be better to delay matters no longer. Welch finally conceded he could do no more by excusing the witness from the stand, and the sheriff again took Twitchell in charge.

Murragh promptly rose to his feet. "May it please the court, the next step I wish to take may appear a trifle irregular, but with your honor's permission I will take the oath as a witness and continue with some pertinent evidence—"

Welch leaped to his feet, spouting protests. Arnette considered the matter, then handed down his ruling: "The court feels the prosecutor might have incorporated such evidence as he may have in his talk made at the beginning of this trial, or in the summing up when he rests his case. This being so, permission is given, as requested. Should this court judge any testimony the prosecutor offers as irrelevant, inapplicable, or illegal, it shall be stricken from the record. Proceed, Mr. Prosecutor."

Red-faced, Welch started renewed protests, but Arnette cut him short with an icy, "The court has made its ruling."

Murragh went to the clerk and took the oath. He returned and, standing before his table, commenced to speak: "Deputy Sheriff Henley has testified that he and I rode to Dry Bone Station the morning following the murder. While there, I made a search of a small lean-to shed beyond the stables and discovered certain objects which, I believe, should be labeled D, E, and F Exhibits. I now produce them."

He stooped for his valise, opened it on the table, and drew out an old burlap sack and several lengths of rawhide. Next he took from one pocket the exploded forty-five cartridge case which he had picked up following his discovery of the burlap sack that morning at Dry Bone. He had already scratched an identifying mark on the empty shell.

"Gentlemen," Murragh continued, "you've heard how Uncle Jimmy Cochrane was first throttled, then a burlap sack was thrown over his head to further stifle any cries he might make. In addition, he was bound with these rawhide thongs. And while in that helpless condition, he was shot to death with a bullet from this empty shell—Uncle Jimmy Cochrane, an old man well past sixty years, an elderly man who had never harmed anyone in his life, a man who loved horses and treated them with the utmost consideration. And that is the old man whose frail, stiffening body was carried out and deposited—carelessly, I point out—across the wheel ruts of the coach he'd driven so many years—"

"Objection!" Welch snarled.

"Grounds?" from Arnette.

"The prosecutor is endeavoring to play on the sympathies of the jury, and thus sway—"

"Objection overruled," the judge snapped.

Welch slunk back to his seat.

Murragh went on, "Those who knew Uncle Jimmy remember well his long gray whiskers." Here Murragh carefully turned the burlap sack inside out. "You can still see hairs from Uncle Jimmy's beard clinging to this burlap sacking. I'd like you to examine closely these objects I place before you."

He carried the various objects to the jury box. Welch hurried across to see them too, but when he attempted to belittle such evidence he received only angry glances and hard-eyed scrutinies that were directed as well at Alonzo Vaiden. Vaiden tried to meet the jurors' eyes with cool indifference, but the effort was futile. An icy fear had commenced to grip his being.

When the jury had finished its examination, Murragh carried the sack and rawhide strips to the judge's desk in an intense silence that was broken by Welch's sneering words, "May it please the court, I wish to impress on the jury that while the prosecutor has produced an empty forty-five shell that *may* have killed James Cochrane—I do not know as to that, though I'll go so far as to admit the possibility—I defy the prosecutor to prove that that shell was fired in Alonzo Vaiden's six-shooter. He cannot do it!"

Murragh smiled thinly. This was what he'd been waiting for, building up to. He reached to the clerk's desk for Exhibit C—Alonzo Vaiden's gun. He said quietly, "With your honor's permission," and then deliberately, dramatically, cocked the weapon, pulled the trigger and sent a bullet crashing into the pine planks at the foot of the bench. Black powder smoke welled in the air. There were startled cries from a few women in the audience. Conversation buzzed. The judge banged with his gavel, and the room quieted.

"I do not remember," Arnette commenced sternly, "giving my permission for any such display of firearms—"

"My apologies, but it was necessary," Murragh said swiftly. Turning, he strode quickly to the foreman of the jury and handed him the gun. "Please extract the shell I have just fired and then compare it with this shell that was responsible for Uncle Jimmy's death. You know guns, you've had many years of experience with guns, most of you—and so you are well aware of the fact that the firing pin on every gun hammer leaves its own distinctive mark on the cartridge primer, unlike that made by any other gun hammer. In this particular case the mark—or dent or impression, whatever you may call it—is a mere shade off center and leaves a tiny circle in the bottom of the depression, due to the firing pin being somewhat blunted through use. I ask you gentlemen to compare these two shells and then state whether or not they were exploded by the same gun hammer."

A hush had crept through the courtroom. Vaiden stared with expanded, fascinated eyes, and a trace of bewilderment in his face, while the foreman of the jury plugged out the empty cartridge case and compared it carefully with the first shell Murragh had given him for examination.

An expression of fury came into the foreman's leathery features; he shot a quick glance of hate in Vaiden's direction, then in a voice trembling with rage he gave his verdict: "Both shells fired by the same hammer, by God!"

Vaiden slumped back in his chair without waiting for opinions from the other jurors. Somehow, Murragh had produced an inescapable fact that no amount of rebuttal testimony would change in the jury's collective minds. Vaiden knew he was lost, that now a verdict of guilty was as certain as death. His eyes slipped toward the tiny hangman's noose still lying on Murragh's table, and a shudder ran through Vaiden's frame. Anything, anything was better than death. There was one slim chance . . .

Welch was on his feet, protesting, arguing with the judge. Vaiden reached out and caught Welch by the sleeve, drew him back. The two men conversed in undertones. Welch kept shaking his head, but finally surrendered angrily to what Vaiden was proposing. He slowly rose to his feet and reluctantly addressed Judge Arnette:

"Your honor,"—Welch's voice was none too steady—"may I request an adjournment at this time? Also, a consultation with you and the prosecuting attorney, at once?"

And in that moment Murragh knew he'd won his gamble. He scarcely heard the foreman of the jury as the man came forward, laid Vaiden's six-shooter and the two shells up on the judge's desk and said, "We all agreed on that hammer."

Arnette banged his gavel. "Court's adjourned! Bailiff, clear the courtroom!"

24

Conclusion

Judge Arnette had descended from behind his bench. The courtroom had been cleared. Beyond the rows of empty chairs Murragh saw Sheriff Farley and the bailiff standing at the open doorway. The clerk of the court, a dapper individual in a bow tie, was engaged at the bench, checking off the various exhibits against a written list.

"Perhaps," Arnette suggested, "you'd better come into what they call my chambers—though God knows why—for this consultation Senator Welch requests."

"If you don't mind, Judge Arnette," Murragh said, "I'd like to have your clerk attend this consultation."

"I'm not sure I want—" Welch commenced, putting on his coat.

Vaiden interrupted: "Let's have the clerk if Murragh wants a record of what's to be said." Welch shrugged his shoulders, but it was plain he didn't like the idea.

"Bring your things, Sam," Arnette spoke to the clerk. The clerk laid aside what he'd been doing and prepared to follow the judge and his companions into the "Chambers." There was an open window, opening on a sort of alley, at the rear of the room, through which, a short distance beyond, Murragh could see the T. N. & A. S. railroad tracks. Arnette closed the flimsy pine door, indicated chairs to his guests, then sat down, beside the clerk, at the table. He said to Welch, "Senator, do you expect Mr. Murragh to enter *nolle pros* at this stage of the trial? I suppose that's why you ask for a conference."

"For once, you're mistaken, Judge Arnette," Welch said nervously. "What Vaiden intends, I do not know. He and I cannot agree on the way his defense should be conducted. That being so, I'm forced to withdraw from the case. He'll have to employ new counsel. That's all I have to say. . . . Good day, gentlemen."

Murragh was out of his chair and caught Welch as the man's hand touched the doorknob. Seizing him by the coat collar, Murragh whirled Welch around and sent him spinning across the room to fall into a chair by the window. Welch went white, then red with indignation. "I object to such treatment—" he commenced.

Arnette growled, "Objection overruled. I've heard

292

Murragh's a bad man to buck, Senator. You'd better decide to stay here."

Murragh stationed himself between Welch and Vaiden. "He'll stay," Murragh promised shortly.

Vaiden said, "Thanks, Murragh. The yellow-bellied crook would have run out on me." Vaiden had recovered much of his composure by this time and was cool again, almost defiant. "After all, it was Welch's scheme: we'd get the stage company and then hold up the railroad—"

"That's a lie!" Welch burst out.

Murragh struck Welch a back-handed slap across the lips. "Don't interrupt," he snapped; then, to Vaiden, "Now what do you want?"

"I want to make a deal with you," Vaiden stated brazenly. "Murragh, I can't figure out just what's happened. The bustard who killed Uncle Jimmy must have got hold of my gun someway. But I know when I'm in a tight. If this case goes to the jury, that jury will hang me, sure as hell. I don't want to hang; anything but that. I'll stand trial for stage robbery, or whatever you see fit, but not for murder. You call off this murder charge against me and I'll tell you who really killed Uncle Jimmy. And the same man killed Kennard, too."

"Keep talking." Murragh's face was expressionless.

"Murragh, you figured out pretty smart just about the way things went, unless you got your information from Twitchell—"

"I had my suspicions. I just needed Twitchell's confirmation to back them up, Vaiden. Things worked out as I'd figured them—"

Vaiden cut in eagerly, "Then you know I wasn't at Dry Bone when Uncle Jimmy was killed?"

"Keep talking, I said," Murragh replied coldly.

"I admit I hired those horses at Millman City, but I didn't get to Dry Bone until—until everything was done. That fellow who took Zwing's place was a hoodlum I hired in Sulphur Tanks—I hired a couple of his friends to take care of Zwing and his wife that day, too. Those three have left the country by this time. But you don't care about them. Balter, Proctor, Osgood, and Lynch are the ones you want. They're the stage robbers. Sure, I'll spill what I know about 'em. I'm saving my own skin now. We never intended to hurt Linda Gordon with that runaway-stage business—just wanted to scare her into selling out."

Murragh said, "I think you're a liar. It'd have been the same if the coach had been full of people. The minute Miss Gordon told me that Uncle Jimmy used his whip very sparingly when driving stage, I knew he couldn't have been driving the stage when it left Dry Bone. I saw that oak tree and made a good guess on what happened. I knew it would require a tall, muscular man for that job. Twitchell fitted in—especially when I saw him talking to you, Vaiden. Now what about Kennard?"

"He lost his head over Isabel Fanchon shortly after he came here. Isabel worked on him, at my request. He told her what he was doing here. One thing led to another, and pretty soon he was sharing in holdup profits. After you came here, he got scared and made a nuisance of himself. We had to get rid of him. He stole your gun; I told him that a certain man wanted to kill you with your own gun. He fell for the idea. You could have been killed that night at the same time. If it hadn't been for me, you would have been. Remember that, will you?"

"I'll remember," Murragh said coldly, "that you didn't want me killed because it might kick up too much fuss. You thought you could frame me into jail, though."

Vaiden was silent. Murragh waited. Vaiden said finally, "Well, do we make a deal?"

"You haven't told me who killed Uncle Jimmy yet."

"Claude Balter. You can prove that by Osgood, Lynch, and Proctor. It wasn't intended that Uncle Jimmy be shot. He was to be hit over the head to make it look like he killed himself in a fall from the stage. But Uncle Jimmy recognized Balter's voice, even with that sack on his head, and lacked the sense to keep his mouth shut. He called Balter by name; Balter lost his temper, jerked his gun and killed Uncle Jimmy—say, don't you believe I'm telling the truth? It was Balter—"

"I know it was Balter," Murragh admitted with a thin smile. "I've known it for quite a time. But I needed somebody else who knew to admit the fact, before I could act against him. It was Balter who killed Kennard too, wasn't it?"

"Why, yes, it was, but—"

"That much I guessed. You're too smart to commit murder, Vaiden, when you can hire someone else for the job. Balter was the logical man, in my mind."

"But how did you know about Uncle Jimmy?"

"I've known it ever since I took Balter's gun away from him. I kept the empty shell his hammer rested on and compared it to the shell I found at the lean-to where Uncle Jimmy was killed. I brought you to trial to charge you with murder so I could scare you into admitting who it was killed Jimmy Cochrane—"

"Harr-r-umph!" Judge Arnette cleared his throat. "Highly irregular, Murragh." He was chewing furiously.

"Nothing's irregular that will bring a crook to justice," Murragh said grimly. "Yes, Vaiden, I'll withdraw that murder charge against you, but you and Welch are both accessories before the fact, you're actually more guilty than Balter. You may not hang, but, by God, I'll see to it that your sentence is as stiff as the law allows. I may take action against Isabel Fanchon; I'll decide later."

Welch commenced a craven whimpering. Murragh told him to shut up. Now that he'd escaped hanging, Vaiden's mind was concentrating on something else. Arnette's cheeks were puffed out; he looked for some place to expectorate. Not finding a cuspidor beneath the table, he rose and stepped near the open window and sent a brown stream of saliva spurting through it.

Murragh stiffened slightly, then moved easily over to the window and looked out. There, a few yards away, he saw Claude Balter sneaking off in a crouching position. Murragh didn't say anything, but turned back into the room, preparing to leave.

Meanwhile Vaiden had been concentrating on his own problems. If it weren't for Murragh, there'd be a chance of his going scot free in another trial. Next time he'd get a reliable defense lawyer. And there was something queer about those shells, too. "Look here, Murragh," he said. "You say the shell from Balter's gun proved he did the killing. Then how do you explain that a shell from my six-shooter showed the same primer mark as one from Balter's?"

Murragh laughed shortly. "Remember the day Cass Henley took your gun and Balter's gun away from you both on a charge of violating that ordinance? I took your guns to Virgil Shattuck and had the hammers switched. Your hammer is in Balter's gun right now; that's Balter's hammer in your gun. I could have changed the walnut grips on the butts, but after all, a man's hand is pretty sensitive to the feel of his gun, and when I framed you, Vaiden, I had to frame you right."

Vaiden's eyes widened. "You tricked me, you dirty son—You tricked me," he half whispered, staring at Murragh. Arnette grunted something unintelligible. Vaiden's face went crimson; then the pure white of rage, unreasoning, uncontrollable, crept up his cheeks. "By God, you tricked me. Why, damn you, Murragh—" He started to rise.

Murragh slapped him back into his chair. "You had it coming, you bustard," he said, hard-voiced. "Now behave yourself while I go after Claude Balter."

He flung open the door and stepped outside. The sheriff and the bailiff were still talking in the front doorway. "Here's your prisoner, Jake," Murragh called down the length of the courtroom to Farley. "Take

Welch, too. I'll explain, later. I'm going to pick up Claude Balter."

The sheriff replied with something Murragh didn't catch, and turned back into the long room, moving leisurely. Murragh went to his table, where he'd left his coat and gun. He started to strap on his cartridge belt. The sounds of a commotion came from the "Judge's Chambers," and a warning cry was heard from Judge Arnette. Alonzo Vaiden came plunging through the doorway, features contorted with insane rage.

Murragh finished buckling his belt. "What's up with you, Vaiden?" he demanded sharply.

But Vaiden was beyond answering, reasoning, now. Caution had been flung to the winds; his sole, obsessive thought now was to even the score with Murragh. Murragh watched him curiously, wondering what the man was intending to do. Vaiden had swerved to the judge's bench and seized his own gun—Exhibit C—which everyone else had forgotten momentarily. That gun still contained four cartridges.

For a second Murragh didn't realize what the man was after. The next instant he saw Vaiden whirl and caught the hate-crazed features above the leveled gun barrel. "You'll never trick another man," Vaiden announced hoarsely, "you son of a—"

A leaden slug splintered the edge of the table at Murragh's side. Murragh fired two shots, close together. He released a third bullet from his six-shooter as Vaiden's knees started to sag. Through the drifting black powder smoke he saw Vaiden crash to the floor, saw the gun slip from the stricken man's fingers and go spinning across the pine planks.

"My God," Jake Farley gasped at Murragh's shoulder, "that was fast! I couldn't even get my own gun out." The bailiff came running to join them. Arnette, the court clerk, and Welch came crowding out of the partitioned-off room. Welch looked very sick. Methodically Murragh plugged the empty shells from his forty-four and slipped fresh cartridges into the cylinder of the gun. The sheriff crossed and knelt by Vaiden's side. Then he got to his feet, shaking his head.

Arnette said, "Vaiden seemed to go crazy all of a sudden—"

"I've got to go get Balter," Murragh cut in. "Last time I saw him he was sneaking toward the back entrance of the Blue Star Livery. Probably doesn't want to appear on the street until he can get a horse for a getaway."

He turned and hurried from the courtroom, pushing through the crowd that had collected in front, attracted by the sound of shooting. Murragh ignored questions and kept going. The noonday sun felt hot on his bare head. There were quite a number of people standing along the sidewalks. One man was just passing the livery when a rearing, plunging pony, eyes wild and mane flying, came tearing from the wide-arched entrance, already in full flight, with Claude Balter, spurring madly, on its back. The passer-by was struck by the pony's shoulder and sent crashing into the dusty road. Other pedestrians scattered for safety.

Murragh cried, "Stop, Balter!"

Balter savagely swerved the pony to straighten it out, nearly sweeping the animal from its hoofs with his vicious reining. He was passing in front of Murragh now. There came a burst of fire from his right hand as he shifted in the saddle. A bullet ripped into the front wall of the courthouse. Murragh lifted his own gun, triggering one swift shot. Balter seemed raised, propelled, by some invisible force that hurled him forward on top of the pony's head. The beast stumbled and went crashing down, hoofs thrashing wildly in the dust.

Through the haze that rose from the roadway, Murragh saw Balter strike on one shoulder, roll over and over and then come erect, catlike, on both feet. The man's left arm dangled limply at his side, but flame and smoke spurted from Balter's right hand. He wasn't running away; he was coming toward Murragh, the leashed violence of the man released at last. He came plunging through the yellow dust-fog, while Murragh moved to meet him.

For just an instant before Murragh thumbed his next shot, he had a brief glimpse of that same expressionless face, the color of a fish's belly, and the same immutable milky-agate eyes. Dust puffed abruptly from the left side of Balter's vest, and Murragh fired once more. A sort of blurred smear passed across, obliterated, the dead-white features, and Balter went to his knees, though some persistent reflex action forced him to continue firing.

Something jerked at Murragh's left sleeve, and he knew a bullet had passed through the cloth. He closed in another pace and released a fourth shot, the impact of the heavy slug knocking Balter sprawling in the roadway, where he lay without further movement.

In an instant the street was swarming with men. Everyone was talking at once as the crowd converged on Balter's lifeless form. Tony, from the Blue Star Livery, was tugging excitedly at Murragh's left arm. "I tried to stop Balter from taking that horse, Mr. Murragh. It wasn't his—"

"There was a man knocked down back there," Murragh cut in.

"He's all right; I saw him get up. I gotta go see 'bout my horse."

Murragh reloaded and pushed through the crowd gathered about Balter's body. Then he saw Cass Henley coming toward him. Henley said anxiously, "You hurt any?"

"Not a scratch."

"That's good news. I just heard somebody say you'd shot Vaiden, just before you got Balter."

Murragh nodded moodily. "He lost his head—got hold of his gun. I couldn't do anything else."

Henley whistled softly. " 'The cannons spit forth their iron indignation—' " He broke off. "Say, that was a real clincher you produced at the trial. I still don't understand how you figured—"

Murragh drew him away from the crowd and explained briefly how he'd tricked Vaiden into naming Balter. "My God," Henley breathed softly, "and you knew it was Balter all the time."

"I'll give you more about it later, Cass. I want to see Linda—"

"I passed her on the way here, after taking Twitchell back to the jail when court adjourned. Linda heard the shooting. She's worried about you. When I called her 'the fiery-eyed maid of smoky war,' she didn't even smile. You go ahead, I'll take care of things here."

Murragh found Silvertop and Linda at the edge of the crowd. His heart leaped at the relief he saw in the girl's eyes. Silvertop said, "I hear you did some right smart shooting, Hoyt."

Murragh said soberly, "But I don't like it. I hate killing."

"All of us do. Sometimes it's necessary."

"But you're all right, you're not hurt?" Linda said anxiously. She was clutching his arm hard, and now several people were standing around, looking at Murragh. Murragh said wearily, "I'm all right. I just want to get away from this crowd." He looked at the girl. His voice was more unsteady than she'd ever heard it.

Linda said, "We'll go down to the stage station and close the door. Nobody will bother us there. I want to know about the trial and what happened after court adjourned."

Murragh looked at her, smiling at the seriousness and fond concern that showed in the girl's dark eyes. Unconsciously he brushed at the triangular slash of black hair against his forehead. He said softly, "There's a great deal, a very great deal to tell you, Linda. . . ."

Both had completely forgotten Silvertop as they started toward the stage office, the girl clinging tightly to the arm of the tall man at her side . . .

Cass Henley left the crowd in the roadway and approached Silvertop, who was still standing on the sidewalk where they'd left him. He was smiling after

Linda and Hoyt as they hurried along Main Street. Henley asked, "Where're Hoyt and Linda going in such a rush?"

Silvertop chuckled, "I reckon Linda figured the time was ripe for Hoyt to demonstrate how to keep her mouth shut. They're heading for the stage office."

Henley's eyes lighted up. "Stages have meant a lot to that pair. But then, 'All the world's a stage and all the men and women merely players: They have their exits and their entrances; and one man in his time plays many parts. . . .' "

Center Point Publishing
600 Brooks Road ● PO Box 1
Thorndike ME 04986-0001 USA

(207) 568-3717

US & Canada:
1 800 929-9108